Praise for the Accidental Alchemist Mysteries

The Elusive Elixir

"Pandian's imaginative third Accidental Alchemist mystery... will please those who like their cozies filled with magic."

—*Publishers Weekly*

"Pandian writes fun, light-hearted mysteries and is an expert at developing sympathetic characters, both major and minor."

—*Bustle*

"A quirky, incredible series... The characters are immensely unique and the writing is A+, so you won't want to miss a word."

—*Suspense Magazine*

"The unbelievable premise is no problem given the inventive powers of Pandian."

—*Kirkus Reviews*

The Masquerading Magician

"People who enjoy character driven stories with mystery, magic, supernatural creatures, and historical intrigue will greatly enjoy this inventive, well-written tale."

—*Portland Book Review*

"A fine, whimsical, paranormal book... this plot certainly holds your attention."

—*Suspense Magazine*

"[*The Masquerading Magician*] is enjoyable and holds together quite nicely."

—*Reviewing the Evidence*

THE
ALCHEMIST'S
ILLUSION

Gigi Pandian

MIDNIGHT INK
WOODBURY, MINNESOTA

FIRST EDITION
First Printing, 2019

Cover design by Kevin R. Brown
Cover illustration by Hugh D'Andrade/Jennifer Vaughn Artist Agent

Midnight Ink, an imprint of Llewellyn Worldwide Ltd.

Library of Congress Cataloging-in-Publication Data
Names: Pandian, Gigi, author.
Title: The Alchemist's illusion / Gigi Pandian.
Description: First Edition. | Woodbury, Minnesota : Midnight Ink, [2019] |
    Series: An Accidental Alchemist mystery ; #4.
Identifiers: LCCN 2018036981 (print) | LCCN 2018039695 (ebook) | ISBN
    9780738755229 () | ISBN 9780738753010 (alk. paper)
Subjects: | GSAFD: Mystery fiction. | Fantasy fiction.
Classification: LCC PS3616.A367 (ebook) | LCC PS3616.A367 A77 2019 (print) |
    DDC 813/.6—dc23
LC record available at https://lccn.loc.gov/2018036981

Midnight Ink
Llewellyn Worldwide Ltd.
2143 Wooddale Drive
Woodbury, MN 55125-2989
www.midnightinkbooks.com

Printed in the United States of America

For Joni.

ONE

THE LAST RAYS OF daylight were descending over the Willamette River when I looked into the eyes of a man who'd been buried six hundred years ago.

I grasped the chain I wore around my neck, now bearing both my gold locket and the pewter carving of a phoenix that my friend Dorian had given me as a good luck charm. The commingling metals were cool against my chest.

"Are you okay?" A young man with flecks of dried red and orange paint on his hands startled me as he touched my elbow. "You look like you've seen a ghost."

He wasn't wrong. Not exactly.

"I'm all right," I said.

He looked unconvinced as his gaze fell to my tightly clenched fist, but he nodded politely and pulled open the glass door leading into the art gallery. The narrow space along the river was wedged in between larger warehouses. I hadn't noticed it on my last waterfront walk the day before. Which wasn't surprising. The Portland art scene was thriving, with new spaces popping up all the time. But that didn't explain the painting visible through the glass front window.

The man who'd shaken me to the core wasn't flesh and blood. But his presence shone as resolutely in pigments as it had in life. Nicolas had never let a living soul capture his image. It was impossible for this painting to exist. Yet here it was.

How had an artist painted such an accurate likeness of my mentor, Nicolas Flamel?

I hadn't seen Nicolas in over three hundred years, and he'd officially been dead for many more. The Paris grave in which he'd supposedly been buried in 1418 was discovered to be empty when it was exhumed years later. The graves of both Nicolas and his wife, Perenelle, had been a ruse so that no curious Parisians would believe they were alive and look for them. They hadn't wanted to risk being burned as witches. Which was fair enough, considering they weren't. But if people knew the truth—that they practiced alchemy—they would have been condemned for practicing witchcraft anyway, just as I had been. So they'd fled and reinvented themselves.

I stepped closer to the portrait. The deep charcoal blacks in the background were at first glance merely shadows, but within those shadows were lush reds and indigos that hinted at the materials in a workshop that lay beyond the subject. With rows of oddly shaped glass jars filled with indistinguishable contents, this could have been an apothecary's home. Normally I would have been more interested in those ingredients hidden in the shadows, but I couldn't take my eyes off the man in the center of the painting.

Many artists had come up with their own imaginings of Nicolas Flamel, once he'd become famous a century after his supposed death. Those sketches looked nothing like the man. Yet in front of me was the real Nicolas, with his sunken cheeks and wild hair the color of sulfurous ashes tossed in a haystack. The painter had even captured the haunted look in his piercing silver-blue eyes.

Nicolas had never agreed to sit for a portrait. *Never.* Just as I never let myself be photographed. If I did, people would see that I'd been twenty-eight years old for much longer than they believed natural.

I'm Zoe Faust. At least that's what I've called myself for over three hundred years. Aside from every hair on my body having turned white, I stopped aging the year I turned twenty-eight, in 1704. I was born with the name Zoe, but I christened myself Faust because I felt like I'd made a deal with the devil when I accidentally discovered the Elixir of Life. If only I'd listened to Nicolas ... But that was a long time ago.

I touched my hand to the glass between me and the painting. The artwork bore no signature, nor was there an explanatory placard nearby. The eyes in the portrait were unnerving. Whoever painted it must have known Nicolas personally. I was certain of it.

I shifted my position as a gust of cool wind blew my hair into my eyes. From a new angle, I noticed a strange detail in the painting. The walking stick resting against the cabinet of glass jars took on a different appearance. The ornate carvings now looked like calligraphic letters. I moved closer. The walking stick was also a book. *Alchemia.*

I smiled. The painting was using anamorphosis perspective—meaning it altered the viewer's perception when observed at different angles. Together with the rich colors applied with thick dabs of paint that stood out on the canvas and gave it its personality, it reminded me of the work of the famous Renaissance artist Philippe Hayden. Nicolas and Perenelle had appreciated the alchemical subject matter of Hayden's paintings. They'd owned several of his works of art. Unlike me, the Flamels were good at turning lead into gold.

3

My silver raincoat blew in the wind as I stepped backwards, away from the window, looking for the name of the new gallery. My breath caught when I saw the distressed wooden plank hanging above the entrance. Two chains squeaked as the sign swung gently in the wind. Painted script as thick and black as tar spelled out the purpose of the place: *Logan Magnus Memorial Gallery*.

Logan Magnus. A man who had killed himself two weeks prior in a most distressing way—poisoning himself by swallowing container after container of the toxic paints and binders he used in his artwork. Had he discovered an unknown work of art by Hayden? Or could Logan Magnus have been the one to paint this portrait? I would never be able to ask the artist how he had possessed the only true likeness I'd ever seen of the man I was desperately trying to find.

TWO

I met Nicolas Flamel in the year 1700. He was the only person who would work with me in spite of the fact I was a woman. He recognized my aptitude for alchemy, and saw that my brother and I were in a desperate situation. Perenelle was less convinced, but she went along with Nicolas's wishes.

My brother and I had fled Salem Village as teenagers, when my aptitude with plants had convinced the townspeople I was a witch. After leaving Massachusetts and making our way across the Atlantic, we nearly starved to death in London until I began selling my healing plant tinctures, which caught the attention of an alchemist who thought my brother was the apothecary.

I knew nothing of alchemy at the time, until Nicolas took me on as his pupil. He explained that alchemy was about transformation, whether transforming homegrown plants into healing elixirs, impure metals into pure gold, or a crushed spirit into a happy one.

I had always excelled at one of those three types of transformation: plant transformations. In alchemy, plant-based herbal medicines are created through spagyric transformations, using the same steps used in making gold, including fermentation, distillation, and extracting elements from the ashes. I never got the hang of making gold, but I understood plants. And here in Portland I was working hard on the third type of alchemy: finding happiness. For a long time, I hadn't thought I deserved it.

In my windy spot in front of the painting that reminded me so much of a time long ago, I lifted the chain I wore around my neck to look at my locket and phoenix pendant. The locket served as a reminder to honor the past. It held a miniature portrait of my brother Thomas and a photograph of my love Ambrose. Until recently, I had always felt responsible for both of their deaths. But now the new phoenix charm served as a symbol of hope for the future.

After spending most of my life on the move so that nobody would notice I didn't outwardly age, I'd put down roots in Portland nearly a year ago. I was tired of running. Tired of hiding. My cozy Craftsman house in the Hawthorne District no longer contained a hole in the roof, my backyard vegetable garden sprawled into the front yard, and I had a unique roommate who was my best friend. I could walk out my front door and down the street to the farmers' market and Blue Sky Teas, the teashop where I could always find a group of friends—and I'd fallen in love with one of them. Max and so many others I'd met over the past year made me hope I could stay here in Portland for at least a little while longer. As for what would come next... I yearned for the day Max would be ready to learn the truth about me.

The art gallery's sign above me squawked more loudly in the increasing wind. Summer was coming to a close and the autumn equinox was approaching. Thunder rumbled in the distance, and I cinched my silver coat more tightly around me, but I remained outside on the threshold of the gallery.

Oregonian artist Logan Magnus was a local celebrity in my adopted hometown. He was known as an experimental modern painter, which was ironic because he mixed his own pigments and used organic materials rather than modern synthetic ones, so he was more old-fashioned than I was. Lead, mercury, and turpentine were reported to have been the main poisons he'd swallowed. I knew the substances well. They overlapped with materials I used in alchemy.

Could Logan Magnus have been an alchemist who'd known Nicolas centuries ago? It would certainly explain his use of pigments... No, I knew that was impossible. Not because Logan was dead. Alchemists can die just like anyone else. But one thing you can't do is grow up in the public eye, which Logan Magnus had done. His father had been a famous artist as well, so there were plenty of photos of Logan growing up in the 1960s and 1970s. Besides, this painting looked like a Philippe Hayden. Was Logan Magnus experimenting with a new style?

The sun dipped below the horizon. Max would be expecting me soon, but I needed to get a better look at the painting first.

All I had left of Nicolas was a note I'd discovered when I returned to Paris earlier that summer. The blue ink had faded over the years so I hadn't been able to read it beyond the two lines written in old French. *Dearest Zoe, If you find this one day ...* and an even more important one: *I hope you can help.* I didn't know what I could help him with, or even if he was still alive. That uncertainty left me feeling like a fraudulent painting, with my inner reality different from my outward appearance—but if you peeled away the slightest bit of paint, you'd see the truth.

The door of the art gallery was within reach. Poised between stepping inside to chase my past or walking on to embrace my future, I hesitated. Taking a deep breath, I took a step forward, only to stumble backward as the door flung open.

A beautiful woman in elegant all-black clothes stepped outside. In shiny black heels, she stood several inches taller than me. Bright streaks of silver-white cut through her long black hair like impossibly thin bolts of lightning slicing through the night sky. Instead of pushing past me, she stopped inches away. She clasped a strong hand around my wrist.

"You," she said. Her voice was calm but filled with a smoldering rage. "It was you. You killed him."

THREE

NORMALLY THE PEOPLE OF Portland were a friendly lot. I could occasionally upset someone when they thought I was proselytizing about my plant-based diet, but strangers didn't frequently accuse me of killing people. Though admittedly it had been known to happen more than I would have liked. Alchemy comes with a lot of baggage.

But it wasn't supposed to happen here in Portland, my fresh start.

"You have the wrong—"

"It was you," the stunning dark-haired woman said again, tightening her grip until it was sure to leave a bruise. "You have his—" Her voice broke off as I twisted free. "Stop her!" she cried.

A group of joggers turned their heads in our direction, but I didn't stop to see if they acted beyond craning their necks. If there's one thing I've learned in over three hundred years of staying alive in war and peace, it's that it's best to get away from people trying to harm you.

But as I ran down the waterfront path, not pausing to look back, I wondered … who did she think I had killed?

My heart beat as furiously as it had during the Red Phase of an alchemical transformation, but for less pure reasons. It was the fear of being exposed. I've stayed alive by helping people while living a quiet life. It's an existence that requires moving frequently, which is why I'd lived out of my 1950s Airstream trailer for years. I'm fearless when it comes to many things, but I'm terrified of being thrust into the spotlight.

In her high heels, there was no way she'd be able to keep up with me. I hoped nobody else tried, but I wasn't taking chances. My rust-colored boots splashed through a puddle from the previous day's storm. I kept running until I could no longer catch my breath. I slowed to a walk, hoping nobody had followed. My entire body was shaking.

I was in no shape to see Max. Dorian expected me to bring home groceries after visiting him, so I'd reverse the order and pick up groceries for Dorian before heading to Max's house. I couldn't lie to Max. I hadn't yet told him the whole truth about myself, but lie to his face? That, I couldn't do.

———————

Twenty minutes later, as I walked up the sloping driveway to my house, I was no longer as apprehensive, but I couldn't stop thinking about both the strange accusation and Logan Magnus's painting of Nicolas. With a brown paper bag blocking most of my view, I unlocked the front door of my house. As soon as I'd closed it, I felt fingers wrap themselves around my wrist.

Again.

I dropped the bag and spun around, my heart racing. So much for not being on edge. There was nobody at eye level, but the grip on my wrist was very real. It came from someone two feet shorter.

"*Je suis désolé* for startling you," Dorian said, his black eyes innocent as he looked up at me. "I am so pleased to see you. I was getting very hungry."

He let go of my wrist and jumped up and down impatiently, his bare feet thumping on the hardwood floor, then scooped up the slightly squished bag of produce and scampered toward the kitchen.

Dorian isn't my child. He isn't even *a* child. Dorian Robert-Houdin is a nearly-150-year-old gargoyle. Who's also a chef. It's a long story.

The key facts are that Dorian was once stone but was accidentally brought to life through a dangerous form of alchemy. I met him when he snuck into a crate I'd shipped to Portland from Paris. Dorian wanted my help deciphering the ancient alchemy book that had brought him to life as a living gargoyle in the first place, but its alchemy was unraveling and causing him to die a slow, unnatural death that would keep him awake but trapped in stone forever. Through our efforts this past year, he'd recently discovered the true Elixir of Life for himself. The once-perilous book had been stolen before we could destroy it, but it was no longer a danger. I hoped.

Dorian could hold still and pretend to be stone if anyone not in our inner circle were to see him. Though it was a perfect way to hide, he rarely did it these days. He was still traumatized from having been taken into police custody in stone form before.

Now he flapped his wings with glee as he removed the stalk of brussels sprouts sticking out of the bag. "*Très bon.* We have caraway seeds, garlic-infused olive oil …"

I forgot to mention what is perhaps the most important thing about Dorian. He's French.

I could see the wheels spinning in his mind as he thought about transforming the raw ingredients into sumptuous meals. He'd apprenticed for a blind chef before going to work as a personal chef for blind people, all of whom believed his lie that he was a disfigured man uncomfortable being seen. Until Dorian met me, he'd lived a lonely and secretive life.

Setting the bag and stalk of brussels sprouts on the kitchen counter, Dorian retrieved the stepping stool. The three-and-a-half-foot-tall gargoyle had originally been carved for the gallery of gargoyles at Notre Dame Cathedral in Paris, as part of the 1850s renovation by Eugène Viollet-le-Duc. The architect then realized that Dorian was too small to be seen from the ground, so the gargoyle was cast aside for the larger chimeras that now adorn the cathedral. It meant Dorian was also too short for the height of an average kitchen counter.

The sight of a gargoyle cooking in my kitchen had taken a bit of getting used to. Dorian resembles the famous Thinker gargoyle now atop Notre Dame, with similar horns and snout. His horns now wriggled more freely, and his wings were soft, like the feathers of a phoenix risen from the ashes. Though unlike a bird, he couldn't fly.

"Superb," he said, sniffing the pears. His snout crinkled in ecstasy. "I am beginning to think the Elixir reinvigorated my senses. Not taste, but smell. The olfactory senses are the strongest. You experience them both when you smell the aroma before taking a bite, and also right before you swallow. It is as if I have been rescued from a desert island where I lived only on coconuts and the water I captured by condensation . . . before being rescued by a prince who is secretly my father."

"Have you been watching daytime television soap operas again?"

Dorian crossed his arms. "If a certain alchemist would get me the books I requested from the library, I would not have to."

"My library account was suspended for defacing library books."

Dorian gasped. "What have you done, Zoe?"

I scowled at the gargoyle. "It's your doing. It's all the cookbooks you've written in."

"But I am fixing them! How can one properly capture the complex flavors of a stew without deglazing a pan? Or use garlic without letting it rest? Or—"

"I know, Dorian, but you can't write in library books."

"But—"

"For *any* reason."

He looked at me thoughtfully for a few moments. "What if a recipe would poison someone?"

"You found a poisonous recipe?"

"No. Not as of yet. But this would be an exception, no?"

I sighed. "If you find poison, you can fix it. But that's it. All right?"

He relaxed his arms and studied my face. "What is wrong, my friend?"

"I've had the strangest evening."

"You have broken Max's heart?"

"What? No! Why would you say that?"

Dorian shrugged. "You are home earlier than expected. I understood you were having dinner with Max."

"I didn't want to see him while I was upset, because I didn't want to lie to him."

"Nor to see him when your hair looks like you have run through a field of brambles."

I ran a hand through my hair. It's cut at an angle and falls well above my shoulders. Since it's naturally bright white, I keep it cut stylishly to make it look as if I dye it to be trendy.

"What has upset you?" Dorian asked, blinking up at me.

"I saw a painting that looks like Nicolas Flamel. Before I could look more closely, I had to run away—because a woman accused me of killing someone."

Dorian's clawed hand flew to his mouth. "*C'est terrible!* For an alchemist, you are not very good at hiding."

"I got out of there, didn't I?"

"True."

Dorian pushed open the swinging door and disappeared into the living room. I followed in time to see him peeking carefully through the curtains we always kept drawn.

"*Les flics* have not descended," he declared. "I see no police cars. I believe you are safe. Why do you attract such inopportune people? And I understand why you *believe* you saw Nicolas in a painting. It is because of the letter he left you. But it is no use, Zoe. You cannot decipher it. Even after you used heat to recover more of the ink, it revealed nothing more."

Over the past several months, I'd tried everything I could think of to raise the ink beyond the few visible words. *Dearest Zoe, If you find this one day ... I hope you can help.* All my efforts had achieved was showing darker versions of doodles in the margins. But now ...

I swore. It seemed so obvious now.

"Dorian, it really is a painting of Nicolas. And I was wrong about the methods I've been using to raise the ink. That portrait tonight showed me how I can decipher his note."

FOUR

THE ARTIST SQUINTED AT the painting, arm outstretched with the brush in hand, then frowned. The shadows ...

"Your methods are fascinating, Philippe," a voice from behind said.

Coarse bristles slipped across the flax canvas, transforming the deep blue of the sky into a sickly puce.

"I have never seen paint like yours," the interloper added.

Philippe Hayden glared with fury at the man who'd entered the studio. It had taken the painter a full week to transform the green malachite crystals into Egyptian Blue. And this painting had been turning out so well, a true representation of alchemy.

No matter. When you knew how to transform minerals into pigments as well as Philippe, you could create more precious Egyptian Blue. It wouldn't do to offend the visitor, Edward Kelley.

Edward was an enigma to Philippe. The man's ears had been sliced as a message he was not to be trusted—his crime was some form of fraud, Philippe had heard—yet he still charmed his way into courts. Edward was the only alchemist in Rudolf II's court who'd ever had a kind word to say about Philippe. The others dismissed the painter as an uncivilized barbarian or an eccentric at best. An eccentric! In the court of Bohemia, of all places, where the "Mad Alchemist" king's mood swings were infamous, peacocks roamed the castle grounds, and alchemists' workshops lined a prominent street within the walls of Prague Castle. Yet it was Philippe Hayden who was considered eccentric.

"You were supposed to bring me Dragon's Blood," Edward said. He didn't look or act his forty years. Only a few flecks of gray threaded the thick brown hair that fell to below his shoulders.

Philippe frowned. There wasn't much cinnabar left to create the dark orangey-red paint that could transform dull sunsets into dramatic ones. Cinnabar, fancifully known as Dragon's Blood, was precious to both artists and alchemists. Philippe set the paint brushes in a solution of vinegar and handed the thumb-sized chunk of cinnabar to Edward. "I lost track of time."

"What are you painting?"

"Before it was ruined?" Philippe stopped speaking before saying something even more regrettable.

"Surely you can fix the sky. I did not wish to startle you, but it was as if you were in a trance."

It's called concentration, the painter wished to tell the dilettante. "This is an alchemist's workshop at sunset."

"A creative interpretation," Edward murmured. He looked over the painting, then took his leave.

Philippe bolted the heavy wooden door. It wouldn't do to have people able to enter without warning. Nicolas Flamel had been right. Secrecy was essential for both of them. The painter smeared more dirt-colored paint under bright blue eyes and cinnabar-colored hair, wishing they were duller and less apt to draw attention, then checked the lock again.

Philippe turned back to the canvas and its hidden alchemical messages. These teachings were not the obscure codes that required an insider's knowledge to be deciphered; they needed only an observer's interest and intelligence. That way, anyone worthy—not just hand-selected men—could discover alchemy's secrets.

Sharing this arcane knowledge through art was what had ostensibly brought Philippe to Prague Castle. Yet there was a deeper, secret reason why Philippe was there. One the artist had not admitted even to Nicolas Flamel.

FIVE

"THE NOTE FROM NICOLAS doesn't use physical alchemy," I continued as Dorian stared at me, becoming more animated as I spoke. "It uses the *concepts* of alchemy, not the science. I've been using physical chemistry and alchemy to try and raise faded ink. But what if this wasn't a straightforward letter that faded? I think the message was disguised all along."

Dorian narrowed his eyes.

"You're skeptical, I know. But this—"

"*Non*. You are right. It is a sound theory. I was simply contemplating what to cook with this new bounty."

I laughed and wrapped my arms around Dorian. I hadn't felt this hopeful since finding the note. "Go ahead and cook. You can keep me company here in the kitchen. I can do my experiment right here. I'll be right back."

Dorian hopped up on his stool, deftly lifted a chef's knife, and began dicing turnips. Next to my old wooden cutting board was a glass bowl of acidulated water. That's the fancy name for water mixed with a little bit of acid, such as lemon juice, to keep certain fruits and vegetables from turning brown before the cook is ready to use them. The bowl was filled with sliced apples. I looked forward to sampling whatever creation he was making.

Dorian had taught me just how similar alchemical transformations are to culinary transformations. Both involve organic matter reacting to what's put into it. And as with cooking, the personal intent one adds to alchemy makes all the difference.

Filled with anticipation, I left the kitchen and headed for my basement alchemy lab.

When most people think of alchemy, they think of medieval men hunched in a dark workshop turning lead into gold. I never got the hang of that, perhaps because I didn't care enough. My strength was extracting a plant's essence to create a purer version of its healing powers.

Since alchemy was a precursor to modern chemistry, alchemical tools share a lot in common with what you'd find in chemistry labs. My basement lab was where I'd tried everything I could think of to raise the faded ink in Nicolas's note. I'd increased the temperature of the ink and paper with different heat sources, bathed and starved the ink of light, and changed the alkaline balance of the paper. Yet each of those experiments was about *chemical* transformation. As I now realized, I'd been approaching it all wrong. It was an *artistic* transformation I needed.

I retrieved the note from where I'd left it locked inside a cabinet drawer and hurried back up the stairs. I pushed through the kitchen's swinging door, held the faded paper flat in my hand, and raised it to eye level.

"What are you doing?" Dorian asked. He'd moved on to mincing onions.

"Anamorphosis," I said, squinting at the paper. Nothing. I rotated it 90 degrees.

"What is that, Greek? I wish you would speak Latin like a civilized person."

Since the strange alchemy book that had originally brought Dorian to life had been written in Latin, it was his first language.

"It's an art term," I said. "The most famous example is the sixteenth-century painting *The Ambassadors* by Hans Holbein the Younger, where he painted a skull that you can only see if you view the painting at a sharp angle. Philippe Hayden's paintings used the same technique."

I held the note parallel to the floor but at eye-level. The paper was slightly lumpy from the experiments I'd done on it, so I kept shifting it, looking for a way to make the lines turn into something more. I'd assumed the faint sketches behind the writing were simply old unfinished doodles from Nicolas's quirky mind; paper was a lot harder to come by in those days. But perhaps, just as Hayden's artwork contained hidden layers of meaning that were revealed with shifting perspectives, so too did this note.

"Hold this." I handed Dorian the paper and ran to the attic, taking the stairs two at a time.

Hayden wasn't as famous as Michelangelo or other Renaissance painters, but I knew his work well because of the Flamels' interest. The artist had painted alchemical subjects more accurately than any painter of the time. That had raised controversy amongst alchemists because they felt such paintings released the arcane knowledge of their secret art into the world more freely than was wise. Nicolas and Perenelle liked Hayden's work because they understood that telling the truth about alchemy, through artwork, was the right thing to do. Unlike most alchemists, they believed that sharing this level of true knowledge *wasn't* opening the floodgates. Representing true alchemy in art was not directly handing people the Philosopher's Stone and the Elixir of Life. People still had to work to achieve those goals through personal transformation. Hayden's work included enough clues to lead interested, worthy individuals to the books that would reveal more.

I reached the attic and flung open the steamer trunk that sat beyond the organized shelves. The room held the inventory for my online business, Elixir, where I sold items I'd accumulated over the years in order to keep myself going financially. I'd only ever managed to transmute stone minerals into a few ounces of gold, so I'd tried various things over the years to make enough money to live in the ever-changing world. I was an apothecary for many years, but I tended to give away more medicines than I sold because I've never been good at turning away someone in need. That's when I began saving the simple items that took on more value over time. During the decades I traveled around the United States in my Airstream, I sold small items at flea markets, but after buying my fixer-upper in Portland, I'd sent for the larger items I'd been keeping in storage in Paris. And that, of course, was how Dorian found his way to me.

I cast aside my Victorian Vampire-hunting kit and an unruly stack of World War II trading cards. A glint of light in the far corner of the trunk caught my eye. The cylindrical mirror would do the trick. I tucked it into my pocket and hurried back down the stairs.

"There." I held the curved mirror to the paper, revealing the sketches to be letters. "Dorian, listen to this."

The words came in and out of focus as I held the paper and mirror in unsteady hands. I read the words in the old French they were written in.

"I might not survive, but if I do, I will be imprisoned ... I am not afraid to die. But I fear for the world if I do not complete this important task. I must prevent ... You must ... stop them ... You will find ... "

Dorian's horns drew together, the equivalent of scrunching his brow in confusion. "Your mentor spoke like Yoda?"

"It's missing some words. Some of the ink really has faded too much to read. And the wrinkles in the paper aren't helping."

"Read it one more time, *s'il vous plait*," Dorian said.

As I complied, he wrote the words on the notepad he used for shopping lists. "*Maintenant*, I have an idea."

He tossed onion skins into the compost bin, dried his hands on a kitchen towel, and hopped off his stool. He opened a drawer and removed a rolling pin and motioned for me to hand him the note. With the paper in one hand and the rolling pin in the other, the gargoyle marched over to the dining table, where he began to roll the fragile paper with the wooden pin.

If it had been anyone besides Dorian, I would have objected. But he used cooking tools with a softer touch than I used to think possible.

"We make a good team, you and I," he said, handing the flattened paper back to me with pride. "Try again with the mirror."

"*I might not survive,*" I began reading again, "*but if I do, I will be imprisoned ... I am not afraid to die. But I fear for the world if I do not complete this important task. I must prevent ... You must ... stop them ... You will find ... *" I broke off and gasped. "There's another line! *In the Philippe Hayden painting.*"

I'd been right about the portrait. It was by Philippe Hayden. And it contained a clue to the whereabouts of Nicolas Flamel.

SIX

Dorian kissed the rolling pin. "I have always told you my high-end cooking supplies were worth it. I have enabled your first break-through. I am glad you have a clue to find Monsieur Flamel."

How had the painting ended up in Portland four hundred years after its creation? Dare I hope Nicolas was still alive?

"What was the dangerous task he mentions, and how did his portrait come to be here?" Dorian asked, echoing my own thoughts.

"All this time," I murmured, feeling my throat constricting. "All these years when I never heard from him, it wasn't because he'd abandoned me and lost his humanity—it was because he was either dead or imprisoned."

Who was he asking me to stop? What information had Philippe Hayden hidden in the painting? And what had become of Perenelle? Nicolas hadn't mentioned her in the legible portion of the note I could read.

"Do not look so forlorn, *mon amie*," Dorian said. "You are the person who taught me to have hope, and it is why I am alive today.

You will find Monsieur Flamel, and I will find my stolen alchemy book. Alas, I have not seen any signs of it yet." Dorian pointed his rolling pin at the pile of European newspapers sticking out of the recycle bin. "But I have hope."

Backward alchemy was a dark alchemy that used unnatural shortcuts and had claimed many lives. We'd put an end to it, but Dorian felt responsible that we couldn't entirely close that chapter of our lives while the book still existed.

"The book is harmless now," I said as I grabbed my silver raincoat.

Dorian frowned. "You are leaving to be with Max now?"

"I'm going to see the painting again first, but yes, then I'm going to see Max."

Dorian clicked his tongue. "I have read enough novels to know what it is to be in love. Max is in love with you. It is clear you mean the world to him. Yet you can never tell him the truth about yourself. It is impossible. Mark my words. If there is one thing you must fear, it is that the man who loves you will be your downfall."

"Now I'm definitely convinced you've been watching too many soap operas. *The man I love will be my downfall*? Really?" Dorian was certainly a dramatic little gargoyle.

He blinked at me. "This was said in a Gothic novel, not a television program. A young governess with a heart-shaped face visited a gypsy fortune-teller—"

"I get the picture," I said. "But that's fiction. This is real life."

"This means you are going to tell Max about alchemy? And about me?"

"I need to figure out the best way. But yes. I'll tell him, at least about me."

Dorian's gray jaw fell, revealing gray stone teeth. "Temperamental alchemists," he grumbled.

"He's a good man, Dorian."

"If you need me," he said, shaking his head, "you know where to find me. I will be here in my kitchen."

Though I'd bought the house, this was certainly his kitchen. I'd lived out of my trailer for more than half a century, so I didn't need much in terms of a kitchen. One copper pot on a single burner to cook legumes and hearty root vegetables, and a blender to make vegetable soups and smoothies. The kitchen in the Craftsman house hadn't been updated since the 1950s, but that hadn't bothered me. I loved the porcelain gas stove and pink fridge. Both were tiny compared to modern standards, but they seemed huge to me. Dorian had other ideas.

"Cilantro—*bof*!" Dorian muttered from beyond the kitchen's swinging door. He must have spotted the fresh cilantro I'd picked and placed in a jar of water on the counter. "It is not even supposed to be in season! Sometimes I wish the alchemist was not so good with plants."

Dorian had been horrified to learn I ate a plant-based vegan diet. We'd found common ground when we'd discovered that we both agreed the most important thing was the quality of the ingredients themselves. He'd learned how to cook French delicacies with only plant-based ingredients. He was more surprised than anyone that it had worked. And I was surprised by how it no longer felt strange to have a gargoyle as my best friend and roommate.

———

At Max Liu's door, I rapped with the shiny brass lion-head knocker. I had arrived sooner than I'd expected to, since the Logan Magnus memorial art gallery was closed when I drove by, a black curtain drawn across the windows. Seeing the Nicolas painting would have to wait until the next day.

Max opened his crimson-colored front door. His normally perfect black hair was askew, and his deep brown eyes reflected tenderness and passion back at me.

Simply being with Max gave me a euphoria I couldn't remember ever having felt before I met him. We could talk about everything and nothing, and enjoyed both chatting for hours and sitting in contemplative silence. And those dark eyes, and the black hair that drove him crazy when it wasn't perfectly in place…

"Sorry I'm so late," I said.

I expected him to smile and pull me into a kiss. Instead, he frowned and sneezed. I noticed, then, that his nose was nearly as red as his front door.

"You didn't get my texts telling you not to come?"

I still hadn't gotten used to cell phones. I looked at mine and saw I'd missed two texts and a voicemail message.

"I'm glad I missed them," I said. "This way I can take care of you." And he could take care of me.

"I don't want to get you sick, Zoe."

"I won't get sick. But I wouldn't care if I did. Now, let's see what you've got in the kitchen. I'll bring you some of my own home remedies tomorrow."

I led the way to the kitchen, and Max leaned against the kitchen doorway while I assessed the contents of the cabinets. I could feel him watching me, but I didn't expect the words that followed.

"Zoe," he said, "you lied to me."

SEVEN

Max's voice was calm rather than accusing, but I was afraid to look up at him.

Instinctively, my hand went to the locket at my neck. Instead, my fingers found the phoenix charm. Before I could speak, Max waved a newsprint magazine in the air and broke into a grin. "You told me you didn't like being photographed."

He tossed me the free weekly Portland newspaper that had come out that day. He'd folded it open to the restaurant section. A quarter of the page was filled with a large photograph taken inside Blue Sky Teas, the neighborhood gathering spot located down the street from my house. Normally I would have been happy for the shop's owner, Blue, especially after the hardship she'd faced to carve out a life she loved. But this wasn't the right type of publicity. Blue wasn't the one in the center of the photograph—I was.

I nearly choked. Not having my image captured was how I'd survived so long. But here I was, prominently featured in the paper nearly every Portlander read. The caption inaccurately read, *Pastry chef Zoe Faust cooks up tantalizingly tasty treats at Blue Sky Teas. The Hawthorne District's favorite cozy teashop serves unexpected flavor combinations in both its teas and pastries.*

This couldn't be happening. *Breathe, Zoe.*

"Even though you're not looking at the camera and the photographer caught you mid-blink, you're every bit as beautiful as you really are. I'd better be careful I don't attract a rival. Good thing I have a gun." Max's smile faltered. "I was joking, Zoe. Cop humor. What's wrong?"

"I didn't know this was taken." Was the photo how the woman at the gallery had recognized me?

Despite always being so careful not to be photographed, I'd let my guard down in Portland. I knew I could never have a normal life, but I'd fooled myself into thinking I could. Because I wanted it so much. I squeezed my eyes shut, hoping against all reason that it wasn't time to move on. Dorian and I could pack our belongings into my Airstream trailer and hit the road. Perhaps we could visit my friend Tobias, the only other true alchemist I knew. It was nearly time for him to move on as well. He'd stayed far too long in Detroit already.

Max stepped across the kitchen and took my hands in his. "It's okay," he whispered.

His gentle touch and words made the most acute fear melt away. But he only held my hands for a moment, then backed away into a coughing fit.

"Sit," I said, leading him to the breakfast nook before I returned to the cabinets. I could worry about myself later. For now, Max needed me. I found sparsely stocked cabinets of teas, herbs, and spices; lemongrass, shallots, and garlic in an earthenware bowl on the counter; and an empty fridge.

"Really?" I said, stepping back so he could see the barren shelves.

Max's lips curved into a smile. "Can you honestly tell me you're surprised?"

"No." I smiled back.

I sautéed the garlic and shallots in olive oil in a small saucepan, then added two cups of water and cayenne, black pepper, turmeric, and a dash of salt.

"Are the wild nettles still growing in your backyard?" I asked.

"You're lucky I've been too busy to pull them out."

I donned gardening gloves and picked the prickly greens, carefully rinsed them in cold water, then added them to the simmering soup.

"You're trying to maim me?" He sneezed.

"The heat gets rid of most of the prickliness. And this"—I held up the immersion blender I'd found in a drawer—"gets rid of the rest."

My style of cooking is to think in terms of principles rather than an ingredient list, which provides a necessary flexibility. I only follow recipes for making herbal remedies, and even then I listen to the plants. Both activities start with high quality ingredients that are on hand, and the simple soup I was making for Max would be perfect not in spite of foregoing a recipe, but because of it. I'd lived through times of rationing and famine. People appreciate what they have so much more than in times of bounty. Nicolas had agreed.

Damn. Why couldn't I have been content living in the present? Why had I kept grasping at the past, finding the note from Nicolas and working on it until I solved its riddle? The selfish part of me wanted only to look forward. I'd fallen in love with Max and built a life this past year. But now that I knew Nicolas was imprisoned, I couldn't let him down.

The question was, could I still save Nicolas while preserving the normal life I wanted more than anything here in Portland—at least for a few years?

The breakfast nook in Max's kitchen looked out over the main living room. The juxtapositions in his house mirrored the two sides of him: the modern rationalist and the old-fashioned traditionalist. The house was sparsely furnished, the living room containing only a white couch and coffee table that rested on the hardwood floors, with nearly floor-to-ceiling artwork covering the two main walls. The canvas prints were scenes of beautiful forests that made it feel almost as if we were outdoors

The only knickknacks in Max's house were antiques from his grandmother, like her cast-iron teapot. In someone else's hands, the modern furnishings could have been cold and sterile, but the living room in Max's home felt like the middle of a serene forest.

Now that I'd done all I could for Max and his illness, my eyes fell to the newsprint weekly and my thoughts turned back to fear. Max must have seen the change come over me.

"So," he said, "are you going to tell me why you hate being photographed?"

Was I?

EIGHT

I LOOKED AT THE creases around Max's eyes as he smiled, and I thought again of the time we'd spent together this year, as well as the dear friends I'd made, including my best friend, who shared the big old house I'd fixed up over the summer. I didn't want to flee. I wanted to stay and fight for the life I'd built. I also wanted to find out what had happened to my old mentor. Why couldn't I have it all? I had to tell Max the full extent of my secret.

"I think I know the reason you hate having your picture taken," Max continued.

"You do?" I croaked.

I'd discussed the principles of alchemy with him before, but it hadn't gone well. Max's paternal grandparents had been apothecaries in China before coming to the US, and Max had told me about the things he'd seen his grandmother do when he was a child. He was brilliant at growing and transforming his own tea blends, but beyond that he'd consciously rejected anything he didn't fully understand. Wanting a rational life was one of the reasons Max had joined the police force. He could help people in a way that made sense. What was he going to tell me now?

"Of course I do," Max said. "You're self-conscious that all your hair is white even though you're so young. And although the photographer didn't see the parts of your body with scars, I think maybe you're self-conscious about them too. But you have no reason to be."

I smiled and kissed his forehead. Max had seen me up close enough to realize my hair was naturally white. I didn't lie to him about it, and told him it was the result of life. He assumed I meant a trauma, and he wasn't exactly wrong.

"You should get some sleep," I said. "I'll bring you some home-made remedies for your cold tomorrow."

"Let me walk you to your car."

"You're too sick to be chivalrous. I'm only parked a block away."

Max frowned. "A whole block? It's late, and there's not usually—" He broke off.

"What?" My eyes narrowed. "What am I missing?

"Logan Magnus."

"The artist who killed himself?" I didn't like the sound of Max's voice. He wasn't usually so worried.

Max cleared his throat. "There are similarities between his death and other unsolved cases. It's a far-fetched theory. Probably nothing. But it's enough to make Detective Vega concerned that it might be murder, not suicide. A copy-cat murder. Those are never good."

"You believe the theory?"

"I don't know what to think."

"But your gut—"

"Not mine. Vega's. I trust her. I'll reserve judgment until she has all the facts. We're getting strange tips all over the place. Par for the course, and most of them are probably fake, but ... Until this is solved, I want the people I care about to stay safe."

When I reached home, it was after ten o'clock. Visiting Max had achieved the opposite effect of what I'd desired. I was about as far from relaxed as I could imagine. I hadn't thought the evening could get more intense. But on top of being accused of murder and deciphering Nicolas's note, my photo had appeared in the paper and I'd learned that Logan Magnus might not have taken his own life. What I had hoped would be a fun date night had turned into a train wreck.

My body is attuned to nature and planetary cycles, so in spite of the tornado spinning my life out of control, I was ready to sleep. Which I would do as soon as I talked to Dorian, walked through my backyard garden, and locked up the house.

The first task proved impossible. Dorian had already gone out for the night.

Gargoyles don't need to sleep. At night, Dorian kept busy by working as the pastry chef at Blue Sky Teas, with me as his cover. Since only a few of us knew of Dorian's existence, it was safest to use me as his front. For my own home cooking I used the same ingredients as the gargoyle chef, but in a much simpler way. Dorian was the one who truly transformed the flavors of ingredients into something new.

When not in my kitchen or Blue's, his favorite indoor space was my attic. Though initially intended to store my inventory for Elixir, Dorian had taken over the space as his room, because the spacious attic with its sloping ceilings contained the gargoyle's best escape route. What had originally been a hole in the ceiling was now a proper skylight window that he could easily crack open to leave and enter the house. The skylight was located underneath a Pacific yew tree that shielded the back of the roof from prying eyes.

In addition to baking during the night, Dorian liked to explore the city under cover of darkness. To avoid security cameras, he'd taken to wearing a cloak. Anyone who happened to look at a camera's grainy three a.m. footage would only see a child who'd snuck out of their house and was running around playing superhero. I was secretly relieved he wasn't able to fly. Who knew what mischief he'd get up to then.

It was probably for the best that I'd missed him. I wasn't coherent that late, and I didn't want to worry Dorian more than was necessary about my photograph appearing in the paper. Instead, I stepped into one of my sanctuaries: the backyard garden.

Looking at the sprawling tendrils of mint, the bushy green tops of carrots and turnips poking through the soil, and the thyme ground cover, I thought about what might be most helpful for Max's cold. I could make another fresh soup with the ingredients from the yard, and I'd look through the cabinet of tinctures I kept in the house for stronger herbal remedies. Nicolas had always encouraged my aptitude with plants. Unlike Perenelle, he'd wanted me to follow my own interests and aptitudes, not stick to a strict alchemical regimen.

I never felt more alive and at peace than when surrounded by nature, especially plants I'd helped nurture myself. I was teaching my neighbor Brixton, the teenager Dorian called my "unofficial nephew," how to garden. There's nothing quite like seeing an angry fourteen-year-old discover pursuits they excel at. *Fifteen*, I reminded myself. He was growing up so quickly.

I had been barely older than Brixton when I'd found myself fleeing home and becoming Nicolas's apprentice. In the early eighteenth century it wasn't easy to find people who ran away, especially those who frequently changed their names to avoid trouble. And more importantly, I'd been running from my past after the tragedy. I hadn't been looking for anyone. And I hadn't wanted to be found.

I needed to know what had happened to Nicolas. Was it too late to save him as he'd once saved me?

The orange sky of sunset had long since transformed to the indigo of night, but I left the porch light off. I wasn't so old-fashioned that I didn't use electricity, but I enjoyed watching how the colors of the sky and greenery changed with the movements of the sun and moon.

I was filling my copper watering can with water when my phone rang.

"She's dead," the deep voice said.

NINE

THE VOICE ON THE phone was one I knew well. Alchemist and former slave Tobias Freeman.

"Is it Rosa?" I asked him.

"She's at peace now. I was with her when she passed. She was ready to go. Still ... "

"I'm so sorry. I know how much you loved her. How much you two loved each other for decades."

"More than half a century." His voice broke.

"Put me to work. I can help with any—"

"I knew you'd offer. That's why I took care of it before calling. Don't feel hurt. I know I could have called on you. But this feeling in my chest. I'd forgotten how much the body can hurt. I knew I'd fall apart. I couldn't handle sympathy. I wouldn't have made it through."

Water spilled over the edge of my watering can and lapped onto my boots. I'd forgotten about the running hose. I shut it off and sat down on the steps of the porch, looking out over the dark garden.

The plants were already folding in on themselves in anticipation of the night. It was a subtle movement, but I noticed it.

"I'm glad you're calling now," I said. Although I hadn't found Tobias again until a year ago, I'd come across him in the late 1950s without realizing it. A song called "Accidental Life," by an artist who called himself the Philosopher, had shot up the charts. That song always made me feel like home, wherever I was. I'd carefully preserved the 8-track for decades. I hadn't realized it was written by my old friend Tobias, whom I'd known as Toby. We'd met back in the nineteenth century while I was doing my small part to help with the Underground Railroad. Toby had been watching the methods I used to create herbal remedies more carefully than I'd realized, and after I left he discovered the Elixir of Life.

"I'm a free man," he said. "The first time I said those words, it was the most magnificent feeling in the world. But this time … I don't know that I've ever felt such a void."

"Will you stay in Detroit?"

"Nah. It's time for me to move on. It's been too long already. I only stayed and risked it for Rosa."

"Come to Portland," I said without thinking. Was I really going to stay? "It'll be good for you. And you know I have extra room. Even with Dorian, this house feels almost too big after living out of the trailer for so long."

"I don't want to impose—"

"You'd be doing me a favor." To say it would be good for him would make it sound like a burden, when it wouldn't be at all. "I have my first solid lead on what happened to Nicolas."

"Flamel?"

"He's imprisoned and he needs my help. And I could use yours."

———

I awoke with the sun, as I always did. Since it was shortly before the autumn equinox, that meant it was shortly before seven o'clock. Blue Sky Teas would be opening soon. I could get tea and breakfast there, and hopefully the art gallery would be open by mid-morning.

I drank a large glass of water with a squeeze of lemon, and after a quick shower walked to the teashop. I felt apprehensive from seeing the article, knowing that all of Portland now believed I was the one baking the great breakfast pastries. But it was also comforting that my oldest friend would be coming to visit. He would be going through a tough time for a while, and I was glad I could help. I also felt hopeful because I loved this time of year, when day and night were in balance and the last of summer crops were being harvested before fall arrived. Summer fruits always tasted the sweetest right before they were about to disappear for another full cycle of the year.

When I reached Hawthorne, a line spilled out onto the sidewalk. A good crowd could always be expected at Blue Sky Teas on a Saturday morning, but nothing like this. I saw through the front windows that the long line snaked around the live weeping fig tree that stood in the center of the cozy space. Blue had created a welcoming gathering spot in both appearance and sustenance. Even before Dorian had begun cooking pastries for the teashop, Blue's heavenly homemade teas beckoned to people from across Portland.

The setting was as comforting as the teas. A plaque above the orange door read, "There is no trouble so great or grave that cannot be diminished by a nice cup of tea—Bernard-Paul Heroux." Around the weeping fig tree, the eight tables had circular tree-ring tops. To celebrate the approach of autumn, the weeping fig tree was decorated with strands of red, orange, and yellow lights. Beyond the central tree, a series of alchemy-inspired paintings lined one wall. The subject of this set of paintings was plants in lush forests at various stages of growth. Eyes peeked out from the background darkness, and the older trees dipped their leaves into flowers that looked like glass vials, leading to a final transformation that suggested they were about to step out of the forest.

The amateur artist who'd created the paintings that complemented Blue Sky Teas so beautifully was Heather Taylor, the mother of my young friend Brixton. She'd made this series of paintings reminiscent of alchemy after seeing the alchemical items I sold at Elixir. Heather didn't know alchemy was real, but Brixton was one of the few people who knew my secret—and Dorian's. It was an accident that he'd seen the gargoyle, but after a shaky start he'd become one of our most trusted friends in Portland.

I spotted Brixton behind the counter. Since he'd turned fifteen that summer, Heather thought it would be good for him to get his first part-time job, where she and "Aunt Blue" could look out for him. His dark curls could use a haircut, and each time I saw him I could have sworn he'd grown another inch.

The eight tables were full, and a handful of people stood with their tea and pastries around a high table near the picture window. One woman stood apart, neither in line nor around a table. At the sight of her, my whole body froze. It was the woman from the art gallery. *She must have seen the paper.* That's how she knew to find me here. It was exactly what I'd been afraid of.

Before I could regain my composure, Blue walked over from behind the counter. "Zoe!"

Brixton stayed at the cash register to deal with the long line.

"Did you see the paper?" Blue said with a grin. In her enthusiasm, her silver curls bounced on her shoulders. "Your food is a hit. Are you up for increasing the volume and variety?"

Before I could reply, the woman cut across the shop.

"Let me see it," she said, pointing a finger in my face. "The necklace," she continued before I could speak, and now that she was close to me it was clear her voice was shaking. "Let me see it."

Breathe, Zoe. My hand instinctively moved to cover my locket, even though it was safely underneath my blouse. That must have been why she'd accused me of murder at the gallery. I'd been holding my locket and pendant in my hand, pulled out from under my sweater. But if that's all it was, then surely it was a mistake.

"I recognized it when I saw you at the gallery," she said. She stepped so close I could see the faint scar from an old nose ring on her thin nose. She towered over me, her long black wrap dress hanging loosely over a gaunt frame. The woman unnerved me, but I didn't sense violence from her.

"Is there a problem?" Blue asked. I was struck by the contrast between the two women. Both had naturally beautiful silver-streaked hair, but Blue let her curls run wild and dressed her round body in baggy jeans and soft wool sweaters. The woman from the art gallery had sleek hair and impossibly high heels.

The woman's thin shoulders fell, the first sign of vulnerability I'd seen in her. "Please … I'll leave just as soon as you show me your necklace. I just … Please."

"It's okay," I said to Blue. I pulled the chain up, revealing the gold locket and the pewter pendant. If I gave her a closer look, she would see that it wasn't whatever she thought it was.

But instead of being disappointed, she gasped and nodded. "Where did you get it?" She reached out her hand for the phoenix pendant but Blue pulled me away.

"You need to leave," Blue said. She spoke more powerfully than I'd ever heard before. It wasn't volume. It was command. I remembered that the Blue Sky who stood beside me with her shoulders squared used to be a trial lawyer before running away from her old life and opening the teashop in Portland.

The woman from the gallery had spoken quietly, not wanting to raise a scene, but at the sound of Blue's voice, several customers paused and turned our way.

"If you don't leave right now," Blue continued, "I'm calling the police."

"Please do," the woman said. "You'll save me the effort."

Blue hesitated. She caught my eye for guidance. Why did the strange woman want the police involved? I shook my head. Blue lowered the phone she was holding.

The woman picked up her own phone and began dialing.

"You're wearing the pendant I made for my husband, Logan Magnus," she said. "He was wearing it the night he was murdered."

TEN

The night moon was rising over Prague castle as Philippe Hayden crushed the ochre that would serve well as the yellow and vermillion of a sunset.

The artist continued to be amazed by the fact that intent was unnecessary to transform colors. Patience, yes, but painters did not need the purity of intent that was necessary in alchemy. Tyrian Purple came out the same whether or not you chose to focus your intent on the rotten shellfish and urine needed to create the color. It was probably better not to focus too much on the unappealing methods needed to create many pigments. An alchemical transformation would only work if alchemists put their energy—their very essence—into the process as well.

Leaving the paint to set in its tempera binder, Philippe pulled a black cloak over thin shoulders and flipped the hood over short auburn hair, then locked the door before walking up Golden Lane. Along with the moon, a few strong stars had pushed their way through the gray night sky. Thankfully, it was enough light that one didn't need a lantern. The alchemist did not wish to be detected.

Golden Lane was located inside the outer walls of Prague Castle, but beneath an open sky. Smooth stones lined the narrow alleyway. It couldn't be said that Rudolf II spared any expense on his castle. Rudolf was not only the Holy Roman Emperor, but also King of Bohemia, King of Hungary and Croatia, and Archduke of Austria.

Repairs had already begun on the house Philippe was looking for: the house of the alchemist who had disappeared the previous day. If the court gossip was to be believed, the devil himself had come for the alchemist and pulled him straight through the roof, leaving brimstone soot behind. How else could a person have disappeared without a trace? Of course, as Philippe and the other alchemists knew, the intense heat required for alchemical experiments often resulted in unexpected explosions. Black ash smelling of sulfur would be left behind. And if you destroyed the dwelling in which you'd been living for free … well, it was best to leave secretly.

What Philippe wished to know was whether the unfortunate man who'd caused the explosion had discovered true alchemy. If so, Philippe wished to save any notes he had left behind. It was late enough in the night that nobody would detect an unlawful entry into the man's rooms.

The workmen who'd begun fixing the roof the previous afternoon had not bothered to lock the door. As Philippe stepped across the threshold, it was evident why. The contents of the rooms had been reduced to a charred heap of scraps. Glass vessels had shattered, wooden tables had splintered into unsalvageable shards, and the air smelled of brimstone even now. In the dim moonlight and hellish surroundings, it was easy to imagine the devil appearing.

Pushing aside irrational thoughts, Philippe looked methodically through the ashes. A cut from a broken jar of mercury was worth it.

Underneath the shards of glass were two bound books. Their outer bindings had been damaged, but the inner pages revealed the truth about the missing man. He was a doctor seeking medicines. Not an alchemist. The painter smiled and tucked the books under the cloak, in hopes of returning them one day. It was a shame so much deception was necessary in Rudolf's court.

Philippe stepped silently out the door, but stopped almost immediately, aware of not being alone.

One of the castle's peacocks strutted across the stone walkway, his colorful feathers tucked away. Castle residents gave Rudolf's strange creatures wide berth, not wishing to anger the inscrutable man who ruled the kingdom.

Philippe chuckled, amused that the animal had caused the fright, and could not help but step closer to the majestic creature. In the moonlight, the colors of its feathers looked almost translucent, like the swirling colors mixing together during an alchemical process.

The peacock heard the sound before Philippe did. The creature cocked its head and scuttled away. Philippe turned toward the sound—a loose stone?—in time to see the edge of a dark cape flutter around the corner.

Had someone been following Philippe Hayden?

ELEVEN

DORIAN HAD STUMBLED UPON the phoenix charm washed up on the edge of the Willamette River on one of his nighttime walks a couple of weeks ago. The beautiful design was evocative of alchemy—a rough lightning bolt behind a phoenix rising from flames, symbolizing rebirth. Viewed head-on, the lightning bolt and flames seemed to be consuming the bird; but from above, she was winning, fighting her way past the elements that fit so perfectly around her. A loop was hidden behind the top of the lightning bolt, which was what enabled the tiny sculpture to be worn as a pendant necklace.

At least, that was the story Dorian told about where he got it. He wouldn't have stolen it, and he definitely wouldn't have killed anyone. The question was, would he have lied to me about where he found it? If I trusted what he told me, he must have found it where Logan Magnus's killer had tossed it, perhaps trying to get rid of evidence in the river

The woman accusing me had attempted to shield her face from the cameras after her husband's untimely death, but now I knew who she was. She was an artist in her own right. Welder Isabella Magnus.

Underneath the weeping fig tree at Blue Sky Teas, the implications sank in that I was wearing the charm of a dead man. A police officer stepped into the teashop.

"It would be easiest to talk down at the station, ma'am," he said. "If you'll come this way with me."

I tried not to look as panicked as I felt. I wouldn't have a chance to consult Dorian about where along the waterfront he'd found the pendant.

"Hey," Brixton called, rushing out from behind the counter. "Where are you taking Zoe?"

"It's okay, Brix," I said, as Blue held on to his shoulders. He was impetuous, and I could tell his Converse-clad feet were itching to rush forward.

"She'll be back soon, honey," Blue said.

————

I hated being at the police station without the security of Max at my side. But Logan Magnus's questionable death wasn't assigned to him. Max was friends with many of his fellow detectives, but I'd learned detectives didn't like it when you stuck your nose into another cop's case.

The phoenix pendant was taken from me, and I was ushered into a room with a noisy vent overhead. It looked to be a cross between an interrogation and a meeting room. A plainclothes officer introduced herself as Detective Vega—the detective Max had mentioned was working the Logan Magnus case. She was about Max's age, around forty, and wore her long chestnut hair pulled into a pony tail.

While her hair was casual, she was dressed formally and stylishly in a sage-green tailored suit.

She sat down across from me and smiled. "Tell me about where you found the pendant."

"I'm sorry I don't remember more than that it was along the edge of the river," I said. It wasn't helping that in addition to not knowing exactly where along the waterfront Dorian had found the phoenix charm, I was light-headed because I hadn't yet eaten breakfast.

"How can you not remember where you found the pendant? It's quite memorable." Her demeanor remained friendly, but her face registered surprise.

"I walk all over the city. It's been a couple of weeks since I found it, and I've gone on a lot of walks since then."

"We could go on a walk." She leaned across the table. "You can take me on your route. That should trigger your memory."

"I really don't remember—"

"All right. Then let's talk about your online business. Elixir, is it?"

I felt the skin on my forearms prickle and glanced up at the clanking vent. "Why are you asking me about Elixir?"

"Just making conversation to try to spark your memory. You sell antiques. You must come across works of art like that pendant, and paintings by artists like Logan Magnus—perhaps some of them have turned out to be forgeries?"

"Forgeries? Why are you asking me about—"

A curt rap sounded on the interior window. A flash of annoyance crossed Detective Vega's face, but she stood and opened the door. A young officer stood in the doorway.

"I'm in the middle of talking to a witness," Detective Vega said.

"I wouldn't interrupt if it wasn't important," the officer said. "There's been a disturbance at Ms. Faust's house. Someone was trying to break in."

Detective Vega swore, covering my own gasp.

"Don't worry," the officer said. "We caught him."

My heart thudded, but I remained silent. There was no good answer I could give. My secret alchemy lab was in the basement. I'd taken steps to protect it, but people who meant me ill had broken in before. I didn't think the men I'd recently defeated would come back to Portland. I also didn't think they'd arrested a gargoyle; the officer's face was too calm for that. That left . . .

"Oh God," I said. "Please tell me it's not Tobias."

The officer's neck and cheeks slowly transformed from a light tan to beet red. He cleared his throat. "You know him?"

"He's a close friend," I said. "Not a burglar." I hadn't thought Tobias would take a red-eye and arrive so quickly, so I hadn't told Dorian to expect him, nor waited at home myself to let him in. "Didn't he tell you he knew me?"

"Well, yes. But a neighbor reported a suspicious character looking in your windows, so we brought him in. I saw you in the paper, so I know you're like a local celebrity, so lots of people would know your name . . . "

"We'll get this straightened out," Detective Vega said, seeing the anger fuming on my face.

As horrible as the situation was, it could also be my out.

"I'll take you to the general area where I think I found the phoenix pendant," I said, "*after* I make sure Tobias is all right. I'm sure you're right that I'll remember more once I'm there. But right now I need to get my friend situated. At home."

Detective Vega gave a sharp glance at the young officer but nodded. They'd screwed up, and they needed my help. I was led to a waiting area and told Tobias would be brought out.

Someone must have alerted Max to the fact that I was there. After I'd been sitting in a lumpy waiting room chair for ten minutes he appeared, looking physically better but still with tired, guarded eyes. "The nettle soup helped," he said with a hesitant smile. "I'm sorry for the screw-up with your friend."

"His wife just died, Max. That's why he came for a visit."

Max swore, but his second apology was cut short by the appearance of Tobias himself.

Broad-shouldered and muscular, Tobias Freeman had physically transformed himself since I first met him. I hadn't been a full-fledged conductor on the Underground Railroad, but I'd helped treat men and women who were injured or ill. Tobias had been both, a scrawny young man nearly starved to death with the skin on his back so torn up I didn't know if he'd survive. When I'd found my friend again this past year, I had barely recognized him—except for his hazel eyes that had always reminded me of gold. Today those eyes were weary.

"You don't need to burden the detectives with my problems," he said.

Oh no. Tobias hadn't been telling people Rosa was his wife. Even people I trusted, like Max.

"I'm sorry for your loss," Max said. "And for this mix-up. I'm Max." He extended his hand. "We met briefly last year."

"I remember," Tobias said, accepting the hand. "On my last visit to see Zoe."

"On behalf of the department," Max said, "please accept my apologies."

"It's not like it's the first time," Tobias said, "and I doubt it'll be the last."

A uniformed officer approached Max. "Liu, you got a sec?"

Max nodded and excused himself.

"This wasn't how I envisioned seeing you again," I said to Tobias.

"You're older than me. You should know better than to think you can predict how life'll go." Tobias pulled me into a hug.

"I'm sorry I mentioned Rosa," I whispered. "But you had good ID?" We had to update our identification cards every decade so our outward appearances would match the information.

"I've got a good guy," he whispered back. "Besides, they didn't process me, just ran the number on my license."

I should never have revealed that the elderly Rosa was Tobias's wife. Around Max, I let my guard down. Maybe Dorian was right that Max would be my downfall. Or worse, the downfall of someone I cared about.

TWELVE

I WAS GOING TO strangle the gargoyle.

I had to stay calm long enough to find out where Dorian had discovered the pendant, so I could take Detective Vega there. Then I'd return to the gallery to see the painting of Nicolas.

Tobias and I took a taxi back to my house. I hated that we couldn't talk openly, but we'd be home soon enough. The taxi dropped us on the street, and we hurried up the sloping driveway to my Craftsman.

"You going to show me this note from Nick you deciphered?"

"If he's still alive and we're able to rescue him, you'd better not call him that to his face. But before we can help him, there's something more urgent we need to discuss. Once we're inside."

"I still can't get over how your 1942 Chevy still runs," Tobias said as we strode past the truck I'd bought new.

"Damn right. And it still pulls the Airstream."

Tobias paused in front of the silver trailer in the long, sloping driveway. "Doesn't this thing have too many memories to keep?"

I shook my head. "The opposite. Why else would I keep such a recognizable truck and trailer? The risk is worth it."

"I sold my old car right after Rosa died. That's why I flew here, even though I still hate damn airplanes." He paused and looked from me to my truck. "I sold the car because it was *our* car. Mine and Rosa's. Didn't feel the same without her."

"I'm so sorry you had to go through that today. Especially so soon after Rosa passed away."

Tobias shrugged and resumed walking up the driveway. "It's been over a month now."

"A month?" I stood in silent shock for a moment, and had to run to catch up to him as he reached the porch steps.

"I told you if I'd called you earlier, it would be too difficult. And since our friends in Detroit thought she was my mom, I didn't want things getting tangled. My friends there helped me take care of everything. Helped me grieve properly. The first stage. It was a beautiful service. Now I'm ready to spend time with someone who knows the truth."

I followed Tobias up the steps. He picked up a camouflage print rucksack from underneath the bench.

"I was wondering what had become of your bag," I said.

"Good thing I'd already left the bag on your porch before the squad car showed up. They must have assumed it was yours."

I reached for the doorknob with the nickel silver key in my hand, but before I could insert it, the door swung open, revealing an empty living room.

"*Je suis désolé*," Dorian said from behind the door. His voice was agitated.

We slipped inside and closed the door.

"You have my humble regrets," Dorian continued. "I was unable to do anything when I saw the police. I saw you from the window and was coming downstairs to open the door for you. *Mon Dieu! Les flics* have beaten you? Your face—"

"Rosa passed away," I said, locking the door and making sure the front curtains were securely drawn.

Dorian's black eyes filled with sadness. "My sympathies, Monsieur Freeman."

"Dorian," I said, "we need to talk about—" But the gargoyle scampered away to the kitchen before I could finish my sentence.

"He looks different," Tobias said as he set down his rucksack inside the door.

"After he found the Elixir, his body transformed. But you can tell he's the same little gray gargoyle. He's still the food snob that he always was, although his senses have come more alive. Now he's even more set on becoming a famous chef. Physically, the transformation affected his wings most of all. They turned from stone to something softer. Not quite like any feathers I've ever seen—"

"Wait, he can *fly* now?"

I shook my head. When I'd first seen Dorian's true wings after he found the Elixir of Life, my first thought was that they were like the wings of an angel—neither the feathers of a bird nor the wings of a bat, but as if they were an otherworldly element I'd never before seen. Which made sense, since alchemy in its purest form reveals our true selves, and gargoyles carved for cathedrals were creatures in between mortal and heavenly beings. Unearthly souls meant to keep us mortals in check. But attempting to use his wings to fly had been a failure.

"That's good." Tobias let out a long breath. "I don't even want to know what kinds of trouble he could get into then."

"Agreed. It's because of him that I was already at the police station."

"Damn, I didn't even think about how quickly you got to the station to get me. You were *already* there?"

"Dorian found an abandoned pewter charm that he gave me because he thought I'd like it. A phoenix with an alchemical feel to it. I loved it. I added it to my necklace chain. But it turns out it belonged to a local artist…" I looked around. "Where did Dorian run off to?"

Before we reached the kitchen, Dorian came through the swinging door with a steaming mug in his hands. He reached up and handed it to Tobias.

"Drink," Dorian said.

Tobias sniffed the mug and smiled. "Irish coffee?"

"Do not worry. I am aware alchemists cannot drink much caffeine without it affecting them strongly. This affliction descended upon me when I discovered the Elixir." Dorian shuddered. "I have found the perfect blend of caffeine and alcohol. It will relax you, but you will still sleep well this evening."

He was a thoughtful little gargoyle.

"Zoe does not get any," Dorian added, ruining the effect. "She cannot handle her caffeine."

I pinched the bridge of my nose and took two deep breaths. "The three of us need to talk. I don't know where to begin, so I'll begin with this." I tossed the crumpled weekly paper I'd taken from Max's house onto the dining table.

Dorian took the newsprint in his claws and read the caption of the photo: *Pastry chef Zoe Faust cooks up tantalizingly tasty treats at Blue Sky Teas. The Hawthorne District's favorite cozy teashop serves unexpected flavor combinations in both its teas and pastries.*

Tobias shook his head.

"*Mon Dieu!*" Dorian cried. "*C'est terrible!*"

"I know."

"*Terrible*," Dorian muttered again. "I did not bake enough pastries."

"What?" I stared at him.

"This newspaper came out yesterday, no? Blue Sky Teas will be flooded with discerning patrons this morning." He flung his hands into the air. "What shall we do?"

"You're worried about Blue running out of pastries?"

"*Oui*. It is a bigger travesty that this short-sighted reviewer narrowly construes me as only a pastry chef, not the versatile chef I truly am. But we cannot worry about that now. As an alchemist, there is time for me to craft the perfect creation to be awarded a Michelin star. Yet I must think of how to rise to the challenge, as it is not generally awarded to dishes unless they are served immediately from the oven. Yet as you know, it is impossible for me to cook in public, for—"

"Dorian," I snapped. "You're missing the point. I've been exposed."

Dorian blinked at me. "You are already exposed, *mon amie*. You bought a house. You have an *amour*. You are a *tante*—an unofficial auntie to Brixton. This?" He flicked a claw at the newspaper article. "Inconsequential."

"Why do I get the feeling," Tobias said softly, "that Zoe is keeping something from us."

"The fallout is already beginning," I said. "Because of this photograph, Isabella Magnus knew exactly where to find me after I ran away from her at the gallery."

"She was not gracious when you returned it?" Dorian asked. "This is hardly—"

"The pendant," I growled, "was designed by Isabella Magnus, and belonged to her husband—Logan Magnus. The artist who owned the portrait of Nicolas and died earlier this month, and who the police suspect was murdered."

Dorian's clawed hands flew to his cheeks.

"And I'm due back at the station," I continued. "I was only able to get away because they felt bad about the mix-up with Tobias. The detective on the case needs me back there to show her where 'I' found the phoenix pendant. Dorian, I need you to tell me exactly where you found it, so I can show her."

Dorian's wings and shoulders slumped, but he didn't speak.

"Dorian?" I asked hesitantly. It wasn't like him to be silent.

"It is my fault you are implicated," he said.

"Who said she's implicated?" Tobias asked. "She's going to show the detective where you found it, and we'll be done with our involvement."

Dorian bit his gray lip. "I found it near the river," he murmured.

"Near?" I said. "You mean right next to it, right? You said it had been submerged in the water and had washed up on the shore."

"I believed it had been," Dorian insisted. "At least at one point in time. It was on a riverside path and covered in rust."

Tobias and I exchanged glances. "Blood?" he said.

I shook my head. "Logan Magnus poisoned himself. Or was forcefully poisoned. But we're getting off track. Dorian, can you draw me a picture of where you found it?"

"*Oui*. But it is clear what we must do to save you, Zoe." Dorian raised his clawed pointer fingers into a steeple under his chin.

"I definitely don't like the sound of that," Tobias said. "Why does she need saving?"

Dorian cleared his throat. "I may have found the charm on a path not *directly* next to the waterfront ... Now that I think more carefully, it was not physically possible for the pendant to have washed up from the river."

56

"Why would you—" I began.

"Because it was shiny and beautiful! And it seemed to have been abandoned."

"I told the police it was along the water. How am I supposed to explain—"

"You could lie," Dorian suggested. "Show them a different place."

Tobias put his head in his hands.

"I see why it is a dangerous proposition to lie to the police," Dorian said. "One lie leads to another..."

"And we want them to solve their case," I said.

"Without any of us being implicated," Tobias added.

"*Alors*," Dorian said, "I now understand what must be done. I will investigate and solve the mystery of who killed Logan Magnus."

"No," Tobias and I said at the same time.

Dorian thought of himself as a modern Poirot. He was gray, after all, so he literally had the "little gray cells" the fictional Belgian detective spoke of. The trouble was, he got into far more trouble than Agatha Christie's character ever did. Unfortunately, he'd read each of Christie's novels, as well as most of the canon of the Golden Age of detective fiction.

"What harm could I do?" Dorian asked, shrugging his stone shoulders.

"Is he always this cocky?" Tobias asked me.

"You have no idea."

THIRTEEN

DORIAN HANDED ME A pencil sketch of where he'd found the pendant. The location wasn't directly next to the water, but at least it was on a path that did at some points come close to the water.

"Monsieur Freeman is staying with us?" Dorian asked, eyeing Tobias's duffle bag.

"For a little while," Tobias said. "I needed a change of scene."

"Tobias is going to help me find Nicolas," I added. "As soon as I get this situation with the police settled."

Dorian blinked at me. "Am I not the great detective Dorian Robert-Houdin?"

"You are," I said. "But Toby can go places with me where you can't be seen. I want him to come to the gallery with me. Here." I handed Dorian the note from Nicolas. "While I'm out, you can show Tobias how to read the note. See if you two see anything else in it."

"*Bon*," Dorian said. "And you owe me a rematch of gin rummy, Monsieur Freeman. Do you also play chess? I now have a superb chess set."

"Until it sells," I reminded him.

To make the attic a cozy living space where he could cohabitate with the alchemical artifacts sold through Elixir, Dorian had hung much of the art on the walls, put his favorite objects on display shelves, and used an antique table and chairs for the hand-carved wooden chess set. He was teaching Brixton to play.

"I need to go," I said. "Unless you two need anything else, I'm going to grab a handful of dried fruits and nuts for breakfast and be off." If I didn't take care of myself first, at least basic care such as eating, I'd be no good to anyone.

Dorian gaped at me. "You have not eaten *le petit déjeuner?* But it is nearly time for lunch."

"I was planning to have tea and breakfast at the teashop, but then—"

Dorian clicked his gray tongue. "This will not do. One moment."

He disappeared into the kitchen and returned with a plate of misshapen scones, rolls, and muffins in one hand, and a glass mason jar of mixed berry compote in the other. As a Frenchman, he believed that presentation was an important part of enjoying food, so he only left perfectly shaped food to be sold at Blue Sky Teas. The rest he brought to our house.

"I have used the last of the cardamom for this recent batch of fruit preserves," he said as I spread the sweet and faintly spicy mixture of blackberries and strawberries over a nutty muffin. "I wished to use the last crop of berries of the season. I have made enough to fill many of our mason jars. We will need more for the apples that are now in season."

"You've got some flour on your wing," I said.

He unfurled his wings, which spanned a good six feet, and shook the flour onto the floor. Tobias gave a low whistle, transfixed by the sight. I understood the feeling.

"*Très* embarrassing," Dorian mumbled as he tucked his wings into their resting location along his back.

"You've always told me that was the mark of a true chef," I said.

"Not the flour. My wings." Dorian spoke softly and his gaze fell to the floor. "They look as though I should be able to fly, and yet..."

"How do we know you're supposed to fly?" Tobias asked. "Gargoyles are attached to cathedrals."

Dorian looked up at Tobias and his cheeks flushed dark gray. "Am I 'supposed to be' one of the greatest chefs of the ages? Perhaps not as was fated in the stars, yet I have done this for myself. I learned from my father how long it takes to perfect an act. Was it fate that brought him the books on magic when he had ordered clock-making manuals? Perhaps it was an accident. Perhaps it was fate. But he achieved what no other Frenchman had done before."

"I concede," Tobias said. "How can one argue with that?"

"I really should go." I bit into a ginger scone topped with blackberry compote. "Detective Vega will send a car to the house if I don't show up soon."

"Though I do not approve of eating as an afterthought while walking," Dorian said, "a police escort would not be desirable."

"You'll be okay on your own?" Tobias asked.

"I will. Let's not get you too close to the police again. Especially after I screwed up—"

"Let's hope Max was too concerned about you to pay attention to what you said."

"*Allo*," Dorian said, waving clawed hands in front of our faces. "I am another living soul in your presence. Yet you speak of things I do not know. Would you please enlighten me?"

"I told Max that Rosa was Tobias's wife. But Tobias had been telling people he was her caregiver or her son, because she grew old, but he's still only fifty."

"Hey, I'm only forty-nine," Tobias quipped. "That's how old my body was when I found the Elixir."

"I told you, Zoe Faust," Dorian said, "that you are too comfortable in front of Max Liu for your own good."

"It's all right," Tobias said. "But Zoe is right that I should stay away from the police."

"Chess?" I heard Dorian asking Tobias as I slipped out.

Tobias laughed. The rich, deep sound made me smile. It had come so infrequently when I'd first met him. "So that was why you plied me with that Irish coffee."

"*Moi*? I am but an innocent gargoyle."

I scoffed at the thought. If only.

FOURTEEN

I LED DETECTIVE VEGA along the waterfront path that would take us to the spot where Dorian had found the pendant. It was far from the Logan Magnus art gallery, but on the same eastern side of the winding Willamette River.

"You came here at night?" she asked. "I know you're new here, so I should tell you this isn't a part of town to come to at night. There are several homeless encampments by the warehouses. Most of the people are just down on their luck, but it attracts some people you don't want to mess with."

I'd decided it would be best to stick to as much of the truth as possible, both for myself and for the case. I was going to show her both when and where Dorian found the pendant.

"It's peaceful at night," I said.

"And a bit macabre in this industrial part of town, with all of these abandoned warehouses..."

"I like walking in cemeteries too, Detective."

She snorted.

It was the truth. I came to terms with death a long time ago. I would have lost my mind if I hadn't. It didn't make it easy, but I was now at peace with the fact that I hadn't been able to save my brother from the plague, and with what had happened to my love Ambrose. But I felt wretched that Nicolas might still be alive but imprisoned somewhere, similar to the anxiety I'd felt when Dorian had been dying an unnatural death, doomed to be awake but trapped in stone forever. I hoped that if Nicolas was imprisoned as his note suggested, that at least he was with Perenelle. Even though she'd always baffled me, Nicolas loved her dearly.

"Did Logan Magnus like to walk here too?" I asked, looking for one of the indentifying markers Dorian had mentioned.

"That's not how this works," she said.

"Having a civilized conversation?"

"You were asking about the case. But if you call asking about things that aren't your business civilized conversation, how about telling me about how you got Max out of his shell."

"I wasn't aware he was in one."

"Seriously?"

I thought back to the first time I'd met Max, as he stood on the porch of my new home the day I moved in, in search of a trespassing kid. He'd been a study in contrasts from the moment I saw him: wanting to uphold the law but also defend Brixton from breaking-and-entering; open to the possibilities of the world but also holding back; so close to letting his guard down but resisting with every breath. I knew from our first fleeting encounter that he was caught between two worlds, like I was, which was one of the things that drew me to him. But in a shell? That was a new idea.

"You know about his wife, of course," Detective Vega said. She looked at me expectantly.

If she was hoping to get a rise out of me, she failed. "Chadna," I said. "A tragedy that she died so young."

Detective Vega nodded. "That was before I knew him. But we've been friends a long time, and he's never dated in the years since. Not seriously. Not until you."

Max had told me that when we'd first started dating, but somehow it felt different coming from one of his friends who'd seen it from the outside.

"That's some family of his," Detective Vega said. "Mina in particular."

Unlike her question about Max's wife, I didn't think this question was meant to shake me. But it did. I'd known Max for three quarters of a year but I had no idea who Mina was. He'd spoken about his grandparents, but I knew his grandfather had gone back to China after his grandmother had died.

"Mina?"

"You haven't met Mina and Mary yet?" she asked. "His sister and mom are forces of nature."

I shook my head. Why hadn't he introduced me to his family if even fellow detectives had met them?

We arrived at the spot where Dorian's drawing indicated he'd found the pendant, in front of an empty warehouse that was rather creepy even by day.

"Here," I said. "This is the spot. Somewhere right around here."

"You didn't think to turn it in to a Lost and Found?"

"What Lost and Found? It was so dirty that I was certain it had been here for years. I would never have kept it if I thought someone was missing it. And the metal isn't worth more than a few dollars."

"It was dirty?" Detective Vega repeated. "You didn't mention that at the station."

"We only had a few minutes to talk before you arrested my friend."

A hint of embarrassment flashed in her eyes, but she quickly covered it. "Were you planning on selling it through Elixir?"

"I don't know why that matters, but no. I liked it and was wearing it myself, as you know."

"You didn't think to have it authenticated to see if it was worth anything? If it was real?"

"Real?"

"You know, real as opposed to fake."

"No, I don't know." What was she getting at? I worked with enough metals to know pewter when I saw it. "You mentioned forgery earlier ... What are you really asking?"

The detective sighed. "The papers got ahold of this, so there's no use keeping it from you. There's an art forgery ring here in Portland. We closed in on one of them, a guy who calls himself Neo, who'd been creating high quality forgeries of old paintings."

"Portland PD has an art crimes team?"

"I wish. It would make my life a lot easier. We got a tip. It turned out to be legitimate. We got a warrant for the studio and seized the fraudulent artwork, but the forger fled before we could collar him and find out about his associates."

"And this has to do with me or the Logan Magnus case because ... "

"It's not like TV where we solve a case within an hour. I'm putting together pieces of a puzzle. Logan Magnus was a local artist who was involved in the art community here. It was rumored he knew what was going on. It's a possible piece of the puzzle."

"And I've given you another piece. This is where I found the pendant. Now I have to be somewhere."

———

When I stepped through the front door, my house was eerily silent.

"Tobias? Dorian?"

Silence.

I pushed open the swinging door to the kitchen. The scents of sourdough bread and ginger cookies lingered in the air, but the room was empty. "This isn't funny, guys."

The sound of tapping on the hardwood floors was a welcome one. A moment later, Dorian appeared in the kitchen.

"Why are you home?" he asked.

"I'm picking up Tobias to go to the art gallery."

Dorian rolled his eyes. "Alchemist, you have many talents, but adapting to technology is not one of them. Look at the small metal device you keep in your purse."

I pulled my phone from my bag. Sure enough, Tobias had sent me a text message saying that he'd gone to Blue Sky Teas.

"Why did he go to the teashop?" I asked Dorian.

"He wished to see Heather's paintings."

"He doesn't know her. Why did he want to see her artwork?"

"I may have mentioned they were inspired by alchemy, inspired by the items in Elixir. Why are you looking at me like that? I cannot have a conversation with our friend?"

———

I found Tobias sitting at a table under the weeping fig tree. He wasn't alone. He was sitting with Max.

Blue came out from behind the counter and gave me a hug. "Is everything okay?" she asked.

I nodded. "I just had to show the police where I found the new charm on my necklace. What's the deal with—"

"They've been inseparable for the last hour." She grinned. "I don't think they even noticed when I came over to take their plates and refresh their tea. That's always a good sign, when friends and lovers get along."

I found myself feeling a mix of worry and happiness, and I wondered which would win out. I was keenly aware of the silly grin on my face as I watched Max and Tobias, who were both completely oblivious to my presence. They looked like long-lost friends.

Tobias was the first to notice me. He waved me over to the table.

"Three times a day," he said to Max as he stood. "That'll kick the last of your cold."

"Your cayenne tea recipe?" I asked.

"Good guess," Max said.

"He thinks cayenne can cure anything."

Tobias laughed. "Because it can. I gave Blue the recipe, so she's making a cup for Max before he heads back to work. You ready to go to the gallery?"

"He's a great guy," Tobias said once we were outside.

"I still shouldn't have let it slip about Rosa. I wasn't thinking. I tend to let my guard down around Max."

"Turned out for the best. That's what we bonded over. Being widowers. I didn't expect how cathartic it would be talking to him about it. It was good for me to talk with him, Zoe. As long as he doesn't go poking too deep into the past, it'll be okay."

I hoped he was right.

"I've been thinking," Tobias said as we got into my truck. "Are you sure it's wise to go back to the gallery right now?"

"The portrait has to be the painting Nicolas talked about in his note. It's our only clue—"

"That's not what I meant. It's where Logan Magnus's widow accused you of murder."

"I already gave the police the pendant and showed them where Dorian found it. Even if she's at the gallery, what can she to do me?"

Tobias gave me a wary look. "I don't know if it's endearing or frustrating that you've retained a degree of innocence after all these years."

"Endearing," I said. "Definitely endearing."

But when we reached the waterfront art gallery, we found an even bigger problem than whatever havoc Isabella Magnus might wreak.

The painting of Nicolas Flamel was gone.

FIFTEEN

"They must have moved it," I said to Tobias. But as I walked through the gallery, I didn't see the painting. The space was dark. It was difficult to find things. The portrait had to be here somewhere...

The gallery was lit only with natural light and candles in open-topped glass cases. No electricity. I thought at first the owners were making do as best they could with the converted warehouse space, until I saw a cell phone being charged in an electrical outlet. The lighting was intentional. The shape of the space affected the light as well. The front doors and window were made of glass, but the rest of the long, narrow space contained no windows.

I understood why the curators had made their decision. The whole set-up made the paintings feel magical. In the flickering candlelight, the colors of the paint jumped as if the people and objects inside the frames were moving. Gold leaf danced, carbon black shadows sheltered hidden secrets, and whites glowed as if they couldn't be contained by the canvas.

This was how art had been viewed in churches in Medieval Europe. Before my time, but not by much, so I was familiar with the concept. Long before movies could be imagined, *this* was what made representations of people come alive. The effect was similar to magic lanterns, but using color rather than shadows.

"Look at that," Tobias whispered. He came to a stop in front of *The River of Flames,* one of Logan Magnus's most famous paintings, a conceptual work of art that depicted a raging, twisting river leading to a rusty faucet. The colors he'd used in the river were vast, ranging from bright lead white and true silver that made the river appear clean and crisp to earthy ochre reds that appeared to be flames. At the end of the river, depending on the way the light caught the painting, the water coming from the faucet either flowed up from the drain like the flickering flame of a candle or down from the spout like water tainted with modern chemicals. It was a trick of the light, but one that was realized to full effect in the dark gallery.

"He used the real materials," I whispered back. Even though the paintings were dry, I could smell the faint scents of the minerals used to make the colors. The tinny odor of lead white, the bitter scent of ultramarine, I even caught a sulfurous swirl of cinnabar in the air.

Before the Renaissance, artists had mixed their own paints. But a combination of modern inventions, such as stable binding materials, made it possible for artists to concentrate on painting and leave to others the painstaking work of transforming minerals into pigments and pigments into paint. The profession of "colormen" was born. These tradesmen would sell their paints directly to artists. It was a boon to artistic productivity, but a shame that the knowledge was lost to so many artists themselves. Painters became separated from their raw materials.

I knew the basics of pigments and paint creation because many painters had bought their raw materials from me. The raw materials that create paint were also used as medicines, which meant they were sold by apothecaries. Apothecary shops were the first art stores.

There was, of course, a dark side to this knowledge. Books like *The Craftsman's Handbook*, written in the early 1400s, revealed to modern artists exactly which pigments they could use to mimic old paintings and how to faux-age their creations. The knowledge could be used for innocent purposes, like Logan Magnus's artwork. But it had also been used by forgers. Which Detective Vega said Logan knew something about.

"I've seen pictures of his art," Tobias said, "but it doesn't capture this. Not at all. Do you smell that? I bet he even mixed his own paints. You don't think he's ... "

"No." I shook my head. "He wasn't an alchemist. At least not the way you mean. Logan Magnus didn't grind and bind his own paints starting when it was necessary to do so."

"How do you—"

"He grew up and aged in the public eye. Don't you remember his father, artist Lawrence Magnus?"

"The guy who did those psychedelic paintings in the '60s?"

Before I could answer, the candlelit paintings seemed to come alive around us. A group of people had entered the gallery, and the gust of wind that followed them inside caused the candles to flicker violently.

The Underwater Underground had a similar theme to *The River of Flames*, showing modern junk under water, with ghostly men and women dressed in medieval clothing using the appliances. As the flickering candlelight shone upon them, the people appeared to come alive and move.

The works of art had a hypnotic effect that made it difficult to move quickly. I shook myself. We weren't here to appreciate art. I pushed Tobias along, but no matter how many paintings we passed, I didn't see the one I was after. I left Tobias back at *The River of Flames* as I sought out the office. As I glanced over my shoulder, his gold-flecked hazel eyes remained transfixed on the twisting river in the haunting painting.

At the far end of the narrow warehouse, a four-foot-square self-portrait of Logan Magnus had been hung next to an equally large photograph of the painter at work. The photograph was one I'd seen in the paper after his death. He was dressed all in white, as was his famous style, his slacks and dress shirt covered in paint flecks from all the colors of the rainbow. A few strands of his messy brown hair were coated in red paint. In the large size of the original photograph, fine lines were visible on his face, which was set in concentration as he worked on a painting.

Along the back wall of the gallery near the photograph and self-portrait, a woman sat behind a desk. "Excuse me," I said. "Where did the painting go that was in the window yesterday? The one of the man with haunting eyes."

She reddened. "That was a mistake."

I guessed the woman was in her late twenties, but the tone of her frustrated words made her sound like one of Brixton's high school classmates. Her eyes were lined with kohl and gave a smoky, ethereal look to her pale face. Her hair was cut in a similar style as mine, at a sharp angle and not quite reaching her shoulders. But hers was as black as mine was white. And there was something else about her ... She'd been crying.

"The painting was put up by mistake?" I repeated.

"It's not a Logan Magnus."

"Then how—"

"Archer didn't send you, did he?" Her eyes narrowed and she scrutinized my white hair and silver raincoat. "You look like his type."

"Archer?" Her gaze unnerved me.

Her face relaxed. "I'm sorry. Never mind. Like I was saying, it was a painting Logan owned, not one he painted. It's back in storage where it belongs. The swap was a practical joke in very poor taste. That's why I'm here myself to oversee things now."

"I'd still love to see—" I began.

"The gallery turned out beautifully," cut in a man with an English accent, speaking to the woman I was talking with. "I'm glad you used this space. Much better than those other properties. It's a truly worthy memorial for Logan."

In the dim light, I hadn't seen him approaching us. His deep voice startled me. In his three-piece suit, he was dressed more formally than anyone else in the art gallery. More formally than anyone I knew personally in Portland, but he had long hair that balanced out the formality, deep brown with hints of gray that fell to his shoulders.

The two hugged like people who knew each other intimately before the man turned to me with a charming but sad smile. "Please forgive me for interrupting," he said—but I was hardly listening. My attention was forced elsewhere by a voice I'd hoped I wouldn't hear again.

"Mr. Freeman?" The commanding voice echoed loudly above the hushed tones spoken in the gallery.

I turned to see Detective Vega approaching Tobias. I hurried over and reached his side as the detective did.

"I'm going to need you to come with me," she said.

"Is there a problem?" Tobias asked in a calm but wary voice that told me he'd uttered the words more times than he cared to count.

73

"Were you following us?" I asked. My voice carried, and several heads turned our way.

"Why don't we go outside?" Detective Vega said.

"She didn't have to follow me," Tobias said, putting his hand on mine. "We told Max we'd be here. And Detective, you can say anything to me in front of Zoe."

Max...

Detective Vega shot me an annoyed glance before nodding. She spoke more softly now, but her voice left no doubt about its authority. "I need to ask you about your whereabouts when Mr. Magnus was killed, Mr. Freeman—and also about your fraudulent identification."

I watched her inquisitive eyes study Tobias's reaction. She thought he was involved in the murder of Logan Magnus. Something in his convoluted past must have raised her suspicions, but it was my fault for bringing Tobias here.

Not only was my mentor being held captive, with my only clue to his whereabouts having vanished, but now my oldest friend was under suspicion for the murder of the man who'd owned the painting that could tell me where to find Nicolas.

Pressing my hand to the smooth, cool glass of the gallery's front window, I watched helplessly as Tobias went with the detective.

SIXTEEN

1597, PRAGUE, BOHEMIA

HIS FACE PRESSED TO the rough, cold stone, Edward Kelley could barely believe his eyes. It was his ears that had been sliced for fraud, and his hands broken for disloyalty, but there was nothing wrong with his vision. And he wasn't intoxicated. Was he? He thought back. No, he was certain he wasn't intoxicated.

Edward knew the castle grounds better than most. He'd found many of its hidden secrets, including the purposefully loose stones that enabled him to secretly look into many alchemists' rooms. This was one of the ways in which he was able to ensure favor with patrons: by gaining a breadth of knowledge about alchemy, which he'd always believed was a fraud—until today.

Through the narrow opening, Edward watched as Philippe lifted a glass vial from a flame and twirled the container in a rhythmic, clockwise motion. The liquid bubbled, and changed from a dull gray to bright yellow.

Philippe tilted the liquid vial over the table, but instead of the wet mess Edward expected to see splash across the wooden surface, *flakes of gold appeared.*

Edward gasped, then quickly covered his mouth. His heart beat furiously. He'd never been discovered while spying before. He needn't have worried. Philippe was far too focused on his work to pay any attention to the faint sounds of the man spying on him. Edward had suspected the painter was hiding a big secret. But this? He had not expected this.

Philippe Hayden wasn't only an artist who painted alchemical scenes. The man was a true alchemist. *Alchemy was real.*

———————

Philippe grinned as the flakes of gold appeared. With art and alchemy comingling so easily now, each process became more natural. Other artists at Prague Castle painted only what they imagined alchemy to look like, not alchemy as it truly was.

To be fair, the challenge for artists was not only their ignorance of alchemical processes, but also their dependence on patrons. And those patrons had specific ideas about what they wanted hanging on their walls.

Whatever negative opinions could be formed about Rudolf II's birthright or his moods, it was indisputably true that he was a great patron of science and the arts. He brought natural philosophers to his court to practice astronomy, alchemists to make gold for his kingdom, and artists to celebrate his reign. His curated *Kunstkammer* collection was one of the greatest libraries in the world.

As much as Philippe wished to return home to France, there was an important task to complete under Rudolf's roof. And it was so close…

SEVENTEEN

I THINK OF MYSELF as a realistic optimist. It's how I've survived for over 340 years in relatively good physical and mental health. It was why I hadn't truly believed Tobias would be arrested. But at the police station, I wasn't allowed to see him and nobody could tell me how long he would be held.

My palms sweating, I knew where I had to go. I drove to Blue Sky Teas. Given that she used to be an attorney, Blue would be the best person to go to for help. She'd reinvented herself here in Portland after escaping a life that had been abusive in multiple ways. But she'd had to break the law to escape. Her old name was Brenda Skyler, and she'd changed it to that of the woman we knew and loved, Blue Sky.

The teashop was crowded once again, a long line snaking around the weeping fig tree and not a free seat to be seen at the tree-ring tables. And as Dorian had anticipated, the glass counter of treats was nearly empty. I couldn't catch Blue's eye because of the crowd, so I waited impatiently in the line.

"You look terrible, Zoe," Blue said once I reached the counter. "Did you catch Max's cold? Let me make you your friend's cayenne tea."

"Tobias has been arrested," I whispered.

Her eyes grew wide.

"Or at least he's being questioned," I added. "Nobody will tell me anything."

"Give me one second," she said, and disappeared into the back room.

"Hey." The muffled sound of a young voice came from the back room. "My break isn't over yet. Oh, hey Zoe." Brixton appeared behind the counter with Blue.

"Sorry, Brix," I said. "I need to borrow Blue. It's important."

"No problem. I get overtime for this, right?"

Blue tousled his hair and he scowled at her.

"Come with me," she said, and led me to a back room opposite the kitchen.

Whereas the front of the cafe had high walls that stretched to a ceiling painted blue like the sky, including wisps of white clouds, I doubted anyone over six feet tall could have stood comfortably in Blue's backroom office. But like the cafe, the office had a cozy feel. Blue had made the boxy little room a comforting sanctuary, with a tiny desk that had space for a laptop and a reclining cushioned chair with a reading lamp and a side table with coasters. A large corkboard covered one wall, filled with photographs she'd taken of friends and of plants from her wildcrafting.

"If you're willing," I said slowly, "I need some informal legal advice. For what to do about Tobias. He has some things in his past that would be better if they didn't come out. But I swear it's nothing bad. Just ... complicated."

Blue nodded. "First, what are they accusing him of?"

"Detective Vega mentioned a fake ID. But the thing that worries me the most is that it's the detective looking into Logan Magnus's death. She said she had questions for Tobias about the case."

"I thought the poor man killed himself."

"The detective doesn't think so."

"I'll be right back."

She returned a few minutes later with two steaming mugs of tea. "Better for thinking." She smiled as she inhaled the scent of her spicy cinnamon chai.

"How can I help Tobias? Should I get him a lawyer? I know you don't practice law here, but do you know someone I can call?"

"If your friend is arrested, he'd be allowed a phone call. Who would he call?"

"Probably me."

"And he hasn't called?"

Why couldn't I get used to these damn things? I hadn't thought to check. I pulled my cell phone from my bag, but I hadn't missed any calls. I tried calling Tobias, but his phone went directly to voicemail. So he was most likely still talking to someone at the station.

Blue reached over and took my hands. "They're probably just talking with him. The police won't arrest someone unless they've got good evidence. That was the problem in my case, that there was too much false evidence against me. But unless someone has set up your friend, anything 'suspicious' doesn't mean much."

"Then why do I feel so wretched? And so helpless."

"Because he's your friend. And because I've always known you were an old soul. Even though you're young, you understand the importance of old friends. How did you two meet? No, let me guess. Was he one of your teachers? He has that vibe."

"That he does. But no. We met in a small playhouse production for a play about the Underground Railroad." It was the cover story we'd come up with. A lie is always best when it's as close to the truth as possible. "We lost touch until I saw a picture of him online last year."

I'd found Tobias because I was trying to locate another true alchemist and saw a familiar face. I hadn't known that the young man I'd met when he was an escaped slave had become an alchemist. If he hadn't been photographed as a speaker at a spiritual alchemy conference, I never would have found him again. The discipline of spiritual alchemy uses the same principles I use to transform plants into purified essences for healing. In practice it means looking inward to find your flaws and transform them, to become a better person and more accepting of the world. It was how alchemy survived publicly in the last century.

"Those unexpected reunions are the best," said Blue. "As much as I hate that our identities are everywhere for the world to see, there are silver linings if we're open to them."

"I'm glad you're getting more business at the teashop thanks to that article."

She took my hands in hers and said, "Don't worry about keeping up with demand. We'll be fine. Focus on taking care of your friend."

When we emerged from the back room, Brixton's mom was helping him behind the counter. At the sight of me, Heather squealed happily, set down the pumpkin muffin she was holding with metal tongs, and enveloped me in a hug. Even though I saw her several times a week, this was her standard form of greeting. Half of her long blonde hair hung down her back, the other half was braided with daisy chains encircling the top of her head. Her white sundress, covered by a short jean jacket on top, swished around my legs as she hugged me.

Brixton had been born when Heather was sixteen. In many ways she'd grown up quickly, but also she had missed her youth, so at thirty-one she often acted more like an adolescent than her son did at fifteen.

"You dropped this customer's muffin, Mom," Brixton said, retrieving a fresh muffin for a man with a handlebar mustache and aviator glasses.

"No coffee?" the man said. "You're serious? This place only serves tea?"

"Tell me what kind of coffee you like," Blue said, taking Brixton's place behind the counter, "as well as why you like it, and I promise I'll find the perfect tea for you."

"Zoe," Heather said as she took my hand and led me to a table that had just opened up near the weeping fig tree, "you're looking really stressed out. Come with me to an essential oils workshop later today. I know you already know all about herbalism, but it might get you out of your funk. It's with a group of women participating in the upcoming Autumn Equinox Fair. I know you've got a table at the fair, so it would be nice for you to meet some of the others. Since you're a little younger than me, I hope you don't mind that I feel like a bit of a big sister to you." She beamed at me.

"Thank you for the offer," I said, amused that someone nearly 300 years younger would think of me as a little sister, "but I need to help a friend today."

EIGHTEEN

Before going back to the Logan Magnus gallery, I had a stop to make first. Tobias was in the most immediate danger, but someone else I cared about might have been as well.

I found Dorian in the attic, reading a 1970s issue of *Ellery Queen Mystery Magazine*.

"Where did you get that?" I asked.

"Garage sale." He closed the newsprint magazine. "Do not worry. Since *someone* lost their library card privileges, Brixton bought me a box of these old magazines. They are *très bon*. Have you read them?"

"Many of them, yes. But I don't have time to reminisce right now. Tobias is in trouble." I filled Dorian in on what had happened.

"Not to worry," Dorian said. "You should recall, I have broken out of police custody before. I can help Monsieur Freeman do the same."

"Nobody is breaking anyone out of jail," I hissed. "And I think being mistaken for a statue and held in an evidence room is different than being locked up in jail."

Dorian narrowed his eyes. "If you did not wish my assistance, why did you tell me this?"

"I wanted to warn you. The police might come back with a search warrant. If that happens you'll need to go out through your skylight window even though it's daytime. Have your cloak at hand so you'll be prepared."

———————

The sky crackled with thunder and lighting as I drove to the gallery. Outside, the storm was still a few miles away. But inside the memorial exhibit, light from the tall, off-white candles flickered wildly, making it look as if a storm was raging inside.

I headed straight for the desk at the back of the gallery but was greeted by an empty chair. The woman who'd been there earlier was nowhere in sight.

I looked up at the self-portrait of Logan Magnus. It was representational rather than stylistic, showing a close likeness. Dressed in white, the figure sat cross-legged with a paintbrush in one hand and a candle in the other. His eyes held a vibrancy and also ... was it a trick of the light, or did they also hold a deep sadness?

I'd learned a great deal from the people I'd met throughout my life, but one thing I knew I'd never be able to understand was what it felt like to grow up under public scrutiny, on the edges of the spotlight of a famous parent. I had been nobody special in Salem Village, which my parents made sure I remembered. Only when I was thirteen did my skills with plants begin to attract attention. But what must it have been like to grow up as a darling of the art world from the time you could walk? I'd witnessed Lawrence Magnus's fame while traveling around in my Airstream and selling antiques at flea markets. Mass produced prints of his modern art paintings were quite popular for a time before he was forgotten in favor of the next art trend. Logan's career had started slowly, but in the past two decades his fame had far surpassed his father's.

I stepped closer to the hypnotic self-portrait. The background of the painting was black at first glance, but even in the candle-lit room it was possible to see that the color of the darkness was made not with black ink, but through a combination of colors that mixed into black yet also swirled in the shadows with hints of images. Both Philippe Hayden and Logan Magnus knew how to use color to dramatic effect.

Subdued voices spoke around me. As before, the candle-lit atmosphere demanded reverence and respect. It was more effective than a sign requesting quiet.

"It's like the early Renaissance," an elderly woman near me said softly to her friend. "This is how art looked by candlelight. The gold leaf is what makes the colors dance like that."

"Since when do you know about art history?" her friend asked. "I thought I knew all of your secrets."

She held up a half-sheet of paper. "Picked this up at the door. It has the obituary of Logan Magnus on one side and his artist statement on the other."

I smiled at the women, wondering if they'd been friends all their lives.

Dozens of people filled the narrow gallery. I made my way back to *The River of Flames*, where the largest crowd was gathered. There I saw the young woman with the tear-stained face I'd spoken to earlier that afternoon. She wasn't looking at the painting but surveying the crowd, as if she was searching for someone.

Her eyes still red from crying, she raised an eyebrow at me. "I hope your friend is all right."

"It was a misunderstanding," I said. "I'm Zoe. And I'm sorry for the disturbance we caused earlier today."

"I'm Cleo," she said. "Cleo Magnus."

I cringed. This was Logan Magnus's daughter.

"And now I'm even more sorry for the disruption we caused," I said. "I'm so sorry for your loss."

"Thank you. Though if one more person tells me my dad will live on through his art, I'll scream."

"You should go ahead and scream. It can be very therapeutic."

She smiled. A genuine, happy smile, though it looked like it could turn to tears at any point. "I should probably try it tonight after I lock up. Nothing else has worked."

I hated to ask her about the painting again, now that I knew she was the grieving daughter. But I didn't have time to be polite. That painting could lead me to Nicolas.

"When I was here earlier I mentioned the painting of the man with intense eyes that was in the window yesterday. I know you said it was a mistake and not one of your father's, but I'd still love to see it."

"I'm sorry," Cleo said, "but it should never have been shown publicly. I'm sorry I can't help."

"You still can," I said. "Can you tell me ... is it a Philippe Hayden?"

Her smile was back. "You can tell too? It is. At least I believe it is. I'm an art dealer, and I found it myself for Dad. It's called *The Alchemist*. The artist wasn't identified, but I *know* it's a Hayden. So does Dad. He loves it." Her smile disappeared. "I mean, *loved* it ... "

The Alchemist.

"You have a good eye," I said, "realizing that it was a Philippe Hayden. That painting means a lot to me. It—"

"It's not for sale," she snapped. "And this is a memorial to my father, not an art sale."

"I only want to see it. It stirred a memory from when I was young. I know the timing is bad, but that's why it would mean a lot to me."

"You say you know the painting?" Her unnerving, penetrating stare was back. I could tell she was a keen observer but had also cultivated the look because she knew how it affected people.

"I think I do. From a long time ago."

She nodded slowly, but the skepticism remained in place. "I didn't realize it had been catalogued elsewhere."

"This might sound sentimental and foolish, but if I could see it again, it would help me have closure. And also maybe help you figure out more about it. Since it means a lot to you too."

"That decision," she said, "will be up to my mother." She scribbled text onto the back of a business card and handed it to me.

I groaned inwardly. Isabella Magnus. The woman who'd accused me of murdering her husband.

Cleo brushed a tear from her cheek, then gave a curious glance behind me. "I think you have a young admirer, Zoe."

I turned and saw Brixton hovering a few yards away, near one of the towers of candles. I thanked Cleo and walked over to him.

"What are you doing here, Brix?"

"The teashop ran out of pastries so there's less of a line now. People keep requesting avocado toast, but Blue is refusing to give in to pressure. I didn't want to stick around."

"That doesn't explain why you're *here*."

Brixton rolled his eyes. At least I'm fairly certain he did. It was awfully dark in the gallery. "Blue guessed this is where you'd be, and I needed to find you. Dorian called to tell me what was going on."

"He did what?" I hissed.

"He said you needed my help."

For the second time in twenty-four hours, I wanted to strangle the gargoyle. Over the summer, Dorian had asked for Brixton's help spying on a dangerous man during the daytime when he couldn't do it himself. Brixton had only been fourteen years old at the time.

I admired my young neighbor's loyalty, especially since it had been hard-won. When he'd accidentally seen Dorian the day I found the gargoyle stowed away in my moving crates, he was understandably freaked out and had tried numerous times to get people to expose Dorian. Until he'd realized the implications of what exposing Dorian's secret would mean and became one of the gargoyle's fiercest protectors. And one of his only real friends.

"What exactly did he say I needed help with?" I asked.

"Well, at first he said it was"—Brixton lowered his voice—"breaking Tobias out of jail. But when I pointed out that this didn't make any sense, since we don't even know if Tobias has been officially arrested, he told me you were searching for your old mentor who went missing. He said it was really getting you down, since, you know, Nicolas was like a dad to you."

Though I was touched that Brixton wanted to help, he was still only a kid. "Thank you, but I'm all right."

"I know what it's like, you know." The boy's words were hesitant now. "Not having a dad around, I mean. I couldn't ask for a better stepdad than Abel, but for most of my life it was just me and Mom. I don't know what I'd do if Abel disappeared without me knowing what happened to him. From how you talk about your past, the little you tell me, it seems like Nicolas meant a lot to you when you were my age. It just … I mean, it doesn't seem right for me not to help."

I stopped myself from embarrassing Brixton by giving him a hug in the gallery. I was wrong about him being a child. At fifteen, he was more mature and understood more of the world than I gave him credit for. He was right that Nicolas had once been like a father to me. For those four years when it was me and my brother against the world, Nicolas had not only taken us in and given us food, shelter, and an education, but most importantly, he'd believed in me.

"I promise I'll let you know if there's something you can do to help," I said. "And if your mom is still working later this evening, you're welcome to come over for dinner."

"Nah, I've got plans with Ethan and Veronica. But you promise?"

"I do." But only if it was safe. I'd never forgive myself if anything happened to Brixton.

NINETEEN

WHILE I'D BEEN INSIDE the gallery, the clouds had let loose. Rain pelted down and lightning crackled above. Brixton wasn't yet old enough to drive and had arrived on his bike, so I drove him the short distance home. His stepfather, Abel, was gone for long stretches of time with his oil-rig job, so Heather was spending more time at home than she had in the past.

Brixton and his mom had previously lived in a tiny apartment, but after Heather sold a few paintings, she started to take her art more seriously and wanted a proper studio. The one-car garage of a small rental house not far from Hawthorne Bridge served perfectly. It also served Brixton's growing interest in music. He could play his instruments in a house more freely than in an apartment. The guitar had been his favorite until Abel brought him a banjo.

By the time I'd dropped Brixton off with his bike and was back at my house, Tobias had returned as well. I'd missed two text messages from him. The second one was from only a few minutes before, telling me that he was in the attic playing chess with Dorian.

"You're okay?" I asked once I reached the attic. "You don't need a lawyer or anything?"

"They had no reason to hold me," Tobias said, standing up from where he was sitting cross-legged on the attic floor.

Dorian sat on the opposite side of my antique chess set. He barely glanced up at me, instead keeping his liquidy black eyes focused intently on the chess board.

"Not even your fake ID?" I asked.

"It's not fake. It's an official Michigan license. More real than I am, in the eyes of the law. I'm prepared for needing to show my ID to the police."

"What about what she said about confirming where you were when Logan Magnus was killed? That was strange."

Dorian glanced up at the two of us for a moment, and I thought he was going to say something, but he instead went back to studying the chess board.

"I wasn't expecting that," Tobias said. "She was also peppering me with questions about your online business. She asked what I thought of the fact that some of your inventory was small but some of the items were priced unexpectedly high."

I sighed and looked around the attic at the antiques bursting from the shelves. I'd finally finished cataloguing nearly everything I owned, but I didn't have the heart to put all of them for sale on my business website. Elixir was less a profitable business model and more a way of getting by. I didn't want to spend my days filling orders and collecting new acquisitions. I had several items worth a lot of money that collectors would buy every month or so, which kept me going, and the rest of my orders were small and infrequent.

"She asked me about my business as well," I said. "But why would she care about antiques? I only have a couple of paintings." My eyes fell on one of Isaac Newton. He'd hidden his alchemical experiments during his lifetime to avoid ridicule.

"It's not the art connection," Tobias said. "Running an online business in general can be cause for suspicion. Apparently it's a good way to cover crimes. Like I said, the fact you don't do a brisk business is suspicious. The expectations of capitalism in the twenty-first century, I suppose."

"I can't win," I said. A storefront drew too much attention in the modern age, as did selling herbal concoctions. I'd thought selling antiques remotely was my safest option.

"She was only fishing," Tobias said. "Your business isn't a front for anything, so you're fine. Same for me. She had no real evidence to hold me, only vague suspicions, so she let me go."

"One thing you have not told us," Dorian said, standing and clasping his hands together, "is how you explained the inconsistencies in your life, Monsieur Freeman. I expect this is why an intelligent detective would harbor suspicions."

"I told the detective the truth. Or at least as close to it as is possible. My father was the famous singer the Philosopher. He fell off the grid and went to Mexico after his big hit in the late 1950s. That's why my records are spotty and she suspected I stole someone's identity to get my ID—because I lived with Pop, off the grid in Mexico, until he died. And if a fifty-year-old man can marry a twenty-five-year-old woman, why not the reverse? Rosa was a young soul, so we fell in love. We told people in Detroit I'd moved home to be the caregiver to my mom because we thought it would be easier to get by if people weren't constantly judging us."

"You just left out the part about her being about a hundred years younger than you," I said. That part always got awkward. Tobias's cover story was similar to my own—that I looked very much like my

French grandmother, whom I also was named after—and to the convincing story we used for how the two of us had met.

"Dorian is luckier than us in that regard," Tobias said.

"Simply because I can turn to stone at will and am a beautiful specimen," Dorian said, "does not mean I am luckier. I am social by nature, yet am trapped in the house all alone."

"I'm here with you," I said. "And Brixton comes over all the time. He spends more time with you than he does working in the garden. And you're out all night exploring and you have your cooking—"

"*Oui*. It is only years of hard work that have made me the Michelin-star-worthy chef you see before you today. I am innately talented, but hard work is *très nécessaire*."

Tobias stifled a laugh. "I meant you're lucky with your cover story. Your references are in order, and nobody you work with has seen you."

"Working for blind chefs was a brilliant idea, yet one I cannot take credit for. It was my father's plan."

When Notre Dame restorer and architect Viollet-le-Duc had realized his gargoyle prototype was too small for the new gallery of gargoyles he was building, he'd given the stone carving to his friend, the famous stage magician Jean Eugène Robert-Houdin—who became Dorian's "father." The magician began reading from a book of alchemy that he thought was only a dramatic prop but was actually imbued with the alchemy that brought Dorian to life. After recovering from the shock of the gargoyle being alive, the magician had raised Dorian in secret like a son, and before his death made sure Dorian would have a place in the world.

"And now that we are all safe in my attic," Dorian added, "we shall set aside our game of chess. It is time for a council of war."

"Is that a line from one of the novels Zoe has been getting for you?" Tobias asked.

"Many of them," Dorian said with a straight face. "It is such an apt phrase in times of crisis, no? We have many items of importance to work through."

"Nicolas is being held captive in parts unknown," I said, "and I need to examine the Philippe Hayden painting that holds the clue without getting myself or Tobias further implicated in Logan Magnus's death. Which is going to be tricky, since his wife is the one who has it and she's accused me of murder. *And* we need to do it without getting Brixton involved. Are we agreed, Dorian?"

Dorian ignored me as he took my laptop in his clawed hand. "*Oui, mon amie.* You must also relax, so we may think with clear heads." After a few taps on the keyboard, Tobias's song "Accidental Life" began to play on the laptop speakers.

"1959," Dorian said. "That year, I was cooking for a blind man in Lyon. He was a vegetarian, and I did not yet know how to cook vegetarian meals properly as I do now. Such a wasted opportunity." He shook his head. "That was followed by working for a man who'd lost his sight from cancer. He later underwent chemotherapy, when it was a new treatment. He appreciated my cooking all the more once his body had recovered from the poisons used to save his life. I appreciated his praise, yet I did not understand at the time how differently foods can taste depending on one's own body. But now, it is quite like my own situation, no? Now that I am truly alive, the flavors themselves are—"

"Stop changing the subject away from Brixton," I said. "I'm happy that you're enjoying food more. But we are *not* getting Brixton involved in a potentially dangerous investigation. You need to promise you won't tell him we need help again."

"*Bof,*" Dorian said, pushing away the laptop and crossing his arms. "I bow to you. I will not use a good resource, simply because 'convention' says he is still a child."

My life was certainly a strange one. A living gargoyle and a former slave were gathered around a laptop computer surrounded by alchemical wares I'd collected over the centuries. But it felt like the most natural thing in the world, working together with friends to solve a problem. I hadn't realized how desperately I'd missed that while living out of my Airstream. I'd had freedom and more safety, but I wasn't truly living.

"I wrote this to commemorate my hundredth birthday," Tobias said as the chorus of "Accidental Life" danced through the attic. "I count my birthday as the day Minty saved me and several others. Not the day I was born on the plantation. I'd say I was 'celebrating' but that's not the right word."

"No," I said, "it's not. But neither is commiserating. We've had some good times—"

"—and helped some good people," Tobias added.

"Yes, yes." Dorian waved his hands through the air and flapped his wings. "I did not realize I was signing up for the maudlin party in the attic." He stood to his full height and puffed up his chest. "I am sorry I found the song, as it has brought out the worst in you both. Truly, you are far too sentimental. Now is not the time. You will never be ready for battle."

"Hold on," I said. "We're not going into battle to find Nicolas. I need to see the painting to find its clues. Isabella might not give me permission to see it, but if there's a good photograph, I might not need the painting itself. I was already thinking of ways we can look at it. First—"

"This," Dorian said, "is why we need our council of war. I have already taken the liberty of conducting research from my attic, both online and speaking on the telephone with an art historian. This portrait you speak of by Philippe Hayden … It does not exist."

TWENTY

"THAT CAN'T BE RIGHT," I said. "The painting clearly exists. It's just that nobody knows what Nicolas Flamel really looked like, so art historians don't know who the man in the painting is. You can't search for it by using his name."

"*Non,*" Dorian said, his strong French voice echoing off the sloping ceiling of the attic.

I shivered, but I didn't think it was because of the rain pelting on the skylight window above us.

Dorian sniffed. "You think me this careless? *Non,* I have sought out Philippe Hayden works of art. There are many, many photographs of his paintings. Several of his works of art are similar to each other. Yet none of them resemble what you described in the slightest."

"So Cleo could have been wrong about it being a Philippe Hayden," Tobias said. "People see what they want to see. It's not just vanity. Many forgers are damn good at painting in the style of another artist. Like Van Meegeren. Nobody would believe he painted the 'Vermeer' masterpiece until he painted a new one while in jail. Ironically he was caught *not* for forgery—"

"—but for selling Dutch masterpieces to the Nazis," I said. "Selling national treasures to Nazis was treason, a far greater offense. I remember that trial."

"I know he was a scoundrel," Tobias said, "but I can't help respecting anyone who put one over on the Nazis."

"He was most likely a collaborator too, you know. Or at least a sympathizer."

Tobias swore. "Seriously?"

"I'm afraid so. Not the folk hero he wanted people to think he was."

"I forgot you lived through part of the occupation in Paris."

"*Allo?*" Dorian said. "Do I need to separate you two children so you'll stop reminiscing?"

"I'd hardly call talk of Nazis 'reminiscing,'" Tobias mumbled.

"Dorian is right." I sat down on the hardwood floor in front of the old chess set, which had been carved by hand around the time I'd studied under Nicolas. "It's hard to focus because there are so many ways we could go about this. The painting is key. Because of Nicolas's note, I'm certain it's a Philippe Hayden. Nicolas had to have been referring to the one and only painting of himself. It's the only thing that makes sense."

"If only living through history made us experts on all things from the past," Tobias said.

I smiled at him. "I know an art historian we can contact. One who also knows about how to find lost works of art."

"Yes," Dorian said, "I have already taken the liberty of calling him."

My smile vanished. "You did what?"

"I mentioned this a few minutes ago, no? I shared with you that I have spoken with an art historian. I found his contact information in your Elixir records."

"You were going through my—"

"Lane Peters was quite charming—he sends his regards, Zoe— yet he did not have high hopes for me. Philippe Hayden is an artist whose body of work is much debated. But Monsieur Peters told me something most interesting. Much like the case of the Vermeers you spoke of, many of the paintings art historians once believed to be Hayden masterpieces are in fact modern forgeries."

"It's not a forgery," I snapped. "I'm not disputing the fact that there are Hayden forgeries out there. But that's not the case here. It can't be."

"Instead of arguing," Tobias said, "let's think about how we find out."

"Truce," I said. "I have an idea. One we should have thought of immediately. Even though the painting was misattributed, the auction house that sold the painting will have *photographs*. We know the name given to the painting from Cleo: *The Alchemist*. We can find the auction house."

Tobias threw his head back and chuckled. "Damn. You're absolutely right."

"She is a wise one," Dorian said, "our alchemist."

We found the auction house online through the name of the painting and the date of sale, but no image accompanied the listing, so we had to contact the auction house.

"Dorian should call," I said. "His male French-accented voice will get us to the right person more quickly."

"An undercover assignment! *Très bon*."

Dorian sweet-talked his way through two low-level employees who couldn't help us but who hoped Dorian would join them at a meal if he ever came to New York, and within minutes was transferred to the head of the company.

Dorian had insisted on using the antique rotary dial phone he preferred, instead of my cell, so I wasn't able to catch all of what was being said on the other end of the line.

"But surely there is something you can do, *Mademoiselle*," Dorian said into the receiver. "Yes … I understand it is the end of the day … But it is of utmost importance … I see … I gave you my phone number … I look forward to hearing from you. *Merci beaucoup.*" He hung up and drummed his claws together.

"They giving you the run-around?" Tobias asked.

"*Oui*, it is the 'run-around,' as you say. She promises she will call back, but … "

"What?" I asked.

"It is most strange. I had the strongest feeling she was hiding something from me … *Alors*, we must explore other options." Dorian flapped his wings. "I know what we need to lift our spirits. I will cook a feast to celebrate old friends. Food will help us think."

"But—" Tobias began.

"Don't argue," I said. "When it comes to food, you've already lost."

"Then I'll help," Tobias said. "I've got a few culinary tricks up my sleeve."

Dorian looked back and forth between us. His mouth opened, then snapped shut.

"He's worried about letting you into his kitchen," I explained. "He's trying to think of something to say that isn't rude."

"You must understand, it is nothing personal," Dorian said. "I welcome you to keep me company with a glass of wine while I cook, but I can sufficiently handle the meal on my own."

"I beg to differ," Tobias said. "I saw turnip greens wilting on the kitchen counter. You were going to toss them and just keep the turnips. I can't let that happen on my watch."

Dorian nodded slowly. "Zoe has many turnips growing in the yard. It is a challenge to figure out the best use of them. I can spare one burner, Monsieur Freeman. One."

"That'll do."

I wished I could have joined them in the kitchen, but thoughts of murder and a missing alchemist were in the forefront of my mind. While the two of them cooked, I searched online to double-check Dorian's research. Unfortunately, I confirmed that my gargoyle friend was right: an online search wouldn't yield any references to our painting. My next idea came up blank as well: tracing Nicolas himself.

I knew why I hadn't begun with that line of action. It would be a massive undertaking on any level. I could look for a modest French country home that had once existed in 1704. I could sort through references to Nicolas Flamel over the centuries, most of which would be fictional. Or perhaps look back on what was going on in the early 1700s that might have involved danger—which was pretty much most of life in 1700. Even something as innocuous as women's makeup was dangerous back then, poisoned with toxic substances including lead. All paths of historical research were theoretically viable, but each could easily involve years of effort—whereas the painting might reveal the clue I needed as soon as I was able to see it.

When the spicy scent of jalapeño peppers and the sweet earthy fragrance of roasted sweet potatoes and corn reached me in the attic, I climbed down the stairs.

"How is it possible neither of you knows any alchemist whom you can ask for assistance?" Dorian said as I walked into the kitchen. "I cannot believe this is truly the case."

"Can't you?" Tobias said. "Neither Zoe or I are your textbook alchemists. A woman and a black man don't exactly fit into the secret societies practicing alchemy."

"And they're a secretive bunch to start with," I added.

"Alchemists…" Dorian shook his head and untied his apron. "At least you have a good sense of smell. You have perfect timing. Dinner is served."

Dinner was flawless. When Dorian had seen how well Tobias's stewed turnip greens were turning out, he made a spicy jalapeño corn bread and stuffed sweet potatoes to perfectly complement the greens.

This was to be the first autumn I'd lived with Dorian. I'd brought home the season's first harvest of apples, and that night for desert, Dorian baked an apple pie. Since we both believed in cooking with seasonal ingredients, he'd never made one for me before. I took a bite. And was overcome by memories.

"Something is wrong?" Dorian asked, watching me. A look of horrified embarrassment swept across his face before he took a bite of pie himself. "But there is nothing the matter with my pie! The coconut oil worked well to replace butter… True, it is not overly sweet, yet this is the style of pie I was striving for. It perfectly elevates the apples themselves."

"This recipe," I said. "Where did you get it?" The tart flavor and the crisp texture of the pie transformed the apples into something much greater than Dorian could have realized: a memory of my childhood.

"It is my own recipe," Dorian said, "based on ideas from cookbooks from the library. The Pacific Northwest has many apples, so I wished to learn their secrets."

"New England is filled with apples," I said. "I grew up surrounded by orchards. Your apple pie tastes like a freshly picked apple on its best day of the year, eaten after a hard day of manual labor." Though my childhood hadn't been an easy one, there were some good memories too. And Dorian had given one back to me.

Dorian beamed. "*Bon*. Enjoy the pie, because then I fear we are back to our first option. We have come up with no better ideas. You must get a closer look at the painting."

Which meant I had to speak with the woman who had accused me of murdering her husband.

TWENTY-ONE

IN THE MORNING, I packed up leftovers from Dorian's feast and went to see Logan Magnus's widow, Isabella. I was hoping she would open the door for me because of the ostensible reason I would offer for visiting: that I wanted to offer an apology for the grief I'd caused her by having her husband's phoenix charm. Though it wasn't my main reason for visiting, my heart did go out to the woman.

I was on my own; Tobias had an important errand to run for Dorian. The gargoyle had his usual list of ingredients delivered directly to the Blue Sky Teas kitchen, but with the new and bigger demand, he'd run out early.

I had Isabella's phone number from the card Cleo had given me, but I knew she would be able to turn me away too easily over the phone. Luckily, it was public knowledge that Logan Magnus had lived at a house the locals called the Castle, situated in the hills on land that had been owned by his artist-father. The house itself was Logan's own, built when he catapulted into stardom with his first million-dollar sale. The old house in which he'd grown up was now an in-law unit dwarfed by the Castle.

From the front—the portion visible in the distance from the highway—the Castle did indeed look like a medieval castle, made of stone and featuring two turrets. But I knew from media photographs that in back, it was an industrial, modern-age castle of steel.

The entrance of the driveway was blocked by a locked gate with an intercom. Cool raindrops fell onto my face as I rolled down the window of my truck.

"Go away," Isabella's disembodied voice crackled from the speaker.

"I wanted to apologize for causing you any grief when I found your husband's pendant," I said into the speaker. "I brought a basket of home-baked pastries as a peace offering."

After several seconds, the iron gate buzzed and slid open and I drove up the curving driveway lined with wrought-iron sculptures. They glistened a bright black in the rain. At first, I thought the elegant shapes were abstract art rather than representational, but when a nearby bolt of lightning lit up the yard more sharply than the drizzly morning sunlight, the sculptures cast shadows over the concrete that showed them as birds taking flight.

Isabella Magnus was waiting in the open front door. She held herself with a proud beauty that wasn't marred by the dark circles under her eyes. Even barefoot, she was nearly a head taller than me.

"Logan could never refuse a peace offering," she said. "You have him to thank."

"Like I said at the gate," I said as I handed her the basket of Dorian's creations, "I have to apologize for causing you more pain. I know what it's like to lose someone." I touched my hand to my locket.

"I don't want it on my conscience when you catch your death of cold out here. Come on inside." She led me to a sunken living room decorated almost entirely in white. The L-shaped couch, the mid-century modern chairs, and even the tables were bright white, contrasting with the darkly colored modern art on the walls. Isabella's steps wavered as she walked. It wasn't even noon, but had she already been drinking? As she had just lost her husband, I couldn't blame her.

"The sculptures that follow the driveway up to the house are amazing," I said. "I didn't realize they were birds taking flight until the lightning cast their shadows."

A small smile formed on her lips. "Those are mine. They never caught on. People in this day and age don't like to wait for a payoff. They only work with spotlights at night—or during a storm—and even then you have to catch them at the right angle to see their true form."

"You're a welder. That's what you meant when you said that you'd made the phoenix charm I found."

"My studio is out back." Isabella's balance faltered and I took a step forward, but she steadied herself and looked at me with a frightening intensity that stopped me in my tracks. "Though I can't imagine ever making art again right now." She sank into a chair.

"It will pass," I said. "That feeling. It took many years after my brother died for me to feel whole again, and I'll always feel like there's a small piece of me missing, but I promise it gets easier. That's why I loved the phoenix charm you made. It felt like wearing it next to my locket was giving me permission for a rebirth in my life. Not forgetting, but moving forward."

"You're so young to have lost a brother. You can't be any older than my Cleo." She hesitated. "The police told me where you found Logan's pendant. I just hope they'll give it back to me someday."

"I'm sure they will. After the investigation is over ... "

"Thank you." She stood and moved toward the front door. "And thank you for dropping off the comfort food."

Damn. I was being dismissed. "I know this is bad timing, but I wonder if I might see the Philippe Hayden painting that was in the memorial gallery for a day."

She stared at me. I couldn't read her expression. "That wasn't what I imagined you were going to ask."

"What did you think I was going to ask?"

"For a peek at Logan's studio. That's what most people want from me."

"I appreciate art, but I'm not an artist or a collector."

Isabella cocked her head, and her black-and-silver hair shimmered. "Then why on earth do you care about the painting?"

Double-damn. "My stepfather," I said, thinking of Brixton's words. "The portrait by Philippe Hayden reminds me of a portrait he used to have. He disappeared many years ago. It's been hard for me. But I'd feel like I had a piece of my family back if I could see it again."

She nodded and slipped on a pair of black sandals. "Come with me."

We walked outside into the modern backyard, keeping underneath an awning that shielded us from most of the rain. She unlocked a set of tall, natural-wood double doors and stepped into a high-ceilinged studio that reminded me of the inside of a cathedral. The arched ceiling was buttressed, though it must have been for aesthetics rather than function. The back wall held a stepladder next to a welder's torch and was flanked by two fire extinguishers.

The left-hand wall was windowless, but the view inside was more impressive than the hillsides beyond the confines of the walls. Metalworks of all shapes and sizes, and at different states of finality, lined the wall, in front of a row of floor-level lights that cast their shadows at different angles. On the opposite wall was a smaller space for both painting and jewelry-making. Thick pieces of wire and larger chunks of metals filled glass jars. An in-progress oil painting of a rose morphing into a butterfly lay on an easel. Though it was technically competent, the painting didn't hold the same life as the metalwork pieces. Next to the easel was a tray of homemade paints, resting atop a pile of old art books.

"This is my workshop," she said. "Logan's is across the patio."

She slid aside a landscape painting of Oregon's Mount Hood, revealing a safe built into the wall. The metal safe was long and narrow. Isabella turned her back to me so I couldn't see what she was doing. She must have been attempting to open the safe, but it didn't appear to be going well. She swore in frustration, but a few moments later swung open the heavy metal door.

"That's odd," she said.

"What is it?"

"I thought this is where it was ... It's not here. They must have taken it back out already."

"Taken it?"

"That damn painting ... Cleo thought she'd found something special for her father. But it's fake. At least that's what the 'art experts' say—that it's not a Philippe Hayden. But I'd like to think it was fated for Cleo to win the bid anyway." Isabella closed her eyes and smiled to herself. She turned her face upward toward the high ceiling, her silver-streaked hair falling over her shoulders. "Lost money and found love," she whispered.

I was glad she wasn't looking at my face to see my panic. "But who's taken it?"

Isabella opened her eyes and blinked at me as if she'd forgotten I was there.

"You said you're not a collector," she said. "How much do you know about the art world?"

"Enough to understand the skepticism in your voice when you said 'art experts.'"

"Most of them mean well, of course. But their livelihood is tied to being right, so the first whiff they get that you're questioning their judgment, they dig their heels in. Did you know that most authenticated paintings are never tested with scientific methods? Most authentications are done purely by a so-called 'expert eye' looking at the painting. And because Cleo's Philippe Hayden was once declared a fake, it's tainted and nobody will agree with her that it's real."

"What did Logan think?"

"He loved it regardless of who painted it. The fact that his beloved little girl went to so much effort to find him something beautiful, something that reflected his new interest in alchemical art, that was all that mattered to Logan."

"That's beautiful," I said, because it was. "How did he become interested in alchemy? It's such an … esoteric subject."

"You mean alchemical art? He saw a painting last year that intrigued him—trees with hidden faces transforming the forest into a living being. He frequently got bored, and Taylor's paintings invigorated him again."

"Heather Taylor?"

"You know her art? I hadn't heard of her before, but she certainly has talent. Logan bought one of her paintings. He loved art regardless of whether or not a famous artist painted it. So it didn't matter if the painting from Cleo was authentic, because it was real to him. That's why I can't understand why they'd care … "

"Who?"

"Cleo and Ward. They must have sent the painting away for authentication."

"Sent it *away*?" And who was Ward?

"They talked about sending it to someone in the Czech Republic. By courier, of course."

I clutched my locket. I'd lost my brother and Ambrose. I wasn't going to lose Nicolas as well. But with the painting with the clue on its way to Europe ...

"The brother you mentioned," Isabella said, her gaze following my hand. "He's in your locket?"

"He is. We had a miniature portrait of him made." I lifted the long chain and opened the locket to show her the picture.

"I can tell how much you care about your family, so maybe I could ..." Isabella's face contorted as she lifted the locket closer to her eyes. "Is this a joke?"

"No, of course not."

"I don't know what you're after, or why you're lying."

"About my locket? Oh, you were looking at the photo of my first love. The portrait of my brother is on the other side. It's—"

"It's fake, is what it is. Or rather, it's *real*. Unlike you and your story." Isabella's face was so close to mine I could see the veins in her bloodshot eyes and smell the earthy scents of coffee and liquor on her breath. And there was something else ... "Best not to lie to someone who knows a thing or two about antique art."

"I'm not lying about Thomas." A frenzied fury bubbled up inside me. I could weather whatever was thrown at me in this life, but I couldn't withstand someone sullying my brother's memory.

"There's no way that portrait was done within the last two hundred years. Where did you find it? At an estate sale, and then you thought it was trendy to wear it in a piece of Victorian jewelry? Perhaps to match your dyed white hair? It'll turn white for real soon enough, and then you'll wish you hadn't spent your youth chasing trends and lying to strangers. God, sometimes I hate Portland. You could have just said you wanted to see what you believe is a famous painting."

"You're wrong."

"Get out!" she screamed. She picked up a mallet and clutched it in her hand.

I stumbled backward, disoriented under the Gothic arches and unable to remember the way to the door. I rushed past the easel with the half-finished painting. That's when the real disorientation hit. It was the scent that did it. I was transported back to 1692, when the hysteria began. When I had to flee Salem Village after I was accused of being a witch. Ergot.

The fungus, found in moldy rye bread, caused hallucinations and odd behavior such as paranoia. Only later did I learn that ergot poisoning was why people on both sides had been acting so strangely in Salem, where my former friends had accused me of witchcraft simply for being good with plants.

The scent wasn't strong, but as a plant alchemist I was especially attuned to scents. Especially this one. I could never forget the tart, astringent smell, because ergot had ruined my life. That wasn't something you forgot, no matter how long it had been.

Ergot was the type of hallucinogenic poison that could render a person open to a suggestion to swallow toxic paint. And Isabella had this poison in her studio.

The painting of Nicolas was gone, and with it my hope for finding him. But this new insight was even worse. Unease wrapped its way around me as I realized I could be in the presence of Logan Magnus's killer.

TWENTY-TWO

1597, Prague, Bohemia

EDWARD STEPPED BACK FROM his hiding spot. He needed a few moments to compose himself after realizing he was in the presence of a man far more powerful than he'd expected. Edward was normally calm under pressure, but this turned his worldview upside down: Alchemy was real, and Philippe Hayden was a true alchemist.

So that was what had called the funny little man to Bohemia. Clearly Philippe preferred solitude to company, but Prague Castle was bursting with people. Edward himself didn't mind the stench, which seemed blissfully fresh compared to the fragrances he'd experienced while locked up in foul dungeons. And he didn't mind the crowds. He knew he was a natural charmer. He could read people's expressions more clearly than words and reflect their desires back to them, endearing himself to them and acquiring patronages across the land.

Yes, he claimed to be an alchemist and scryer with the ability to speak with angels. But Edward didn't actually *believe* in either of those things. He simply told people what they wished to hear. After finding a small quantity of gold in a mine, he had realized he could live off that gold for a much longer period of time if he got patrons to support an alchemy lab. In his lab, he would "create" a small amount of gold for the patron, which bought him at least another year of work. And writing words that were supposedly dictated by an angel made him seem more trustworthy. People were so gullible. But now…had he been proven wrong by a dirty little Frenchman?

Edward knew he would be removed from Rudolf II's court if he did not continue to show results. But what if he were to become a real alchemist? He stepped forward again and watched the artist at work. A plan formed in his mind for how to solve all of his problems.

———

The following day, Edward Kelley knocked on the door of Philippe Hayden's rooms, confident his plan would be a success.

When the artist opened the door, Edward showed him the scroll clutched in his gloved hands. "You have been given a great honor, Monsieur Hayden. We have an audience with the Emperor."

Philippe frowned. "I have not yet completed my latest painting."

Edward smiled his most radiant smile. He had unusually nice teeth, and he used them to good effect. "Have I told you of my daughter? She is the light of my life."

Philippe's stiff stance relaxed. Good.

"Yes," Philippe answered. "You've spoken of her fondly. I would be pleased to paint her portrait if given the opportunity."

"It would be a great honor. I wish to see her again soon, and if I'm not mistaken, you wish to return to your family as well. Do I recall that you have a wife waiting for you in France?"

Philippe gave a noncommittal tilt of his head. "I should get back to work on this canvas before my paints dry."

"I apologize for the bad timing, but we do not wish to disappoint our patron, do we?"

"He understands the artistic process more than most. A little more time—"

Edward leered at the small man as he strode up to where the artist stood at his easel. It was time to change tactics. "Did I not mention that it is not art the Emperor is interested in seeing today? Rudolf was quite interested when I conveyed the message that you would be able to give a live demonstration for how to create gold."

The painter stood perfectly still. He was outwardly calm, but Edward could see the man's hands shaking. "Why would you say such a thing?"

Tucking the scroll into his coat, Edward walked to the wall and tapped on the uneven stones. "When I remove a stone from this outer wall, I can see everything you do." He shrugged. "I know your secret."

Philippe's eyes widened, yet he remained silent.

"I know," Edward continued, "that you can transmute lead into gold. It is no use trying to hide the truth."

"Why would I hide the truth?" Philippe said. "We are all alchemists, are we not?" He gave Edward a thin-lipped, defiant smile.

"Of course," Edward replied. "So it will not be a problem for you to perform your transformations in front of me and the Emperor."

"You know it's not so simple."

"Such a shame. We know what the Emperor does with people who lie to him."

Philippe narrowed his eyes at Edward. He remained still, yet his gaze flitted toward the door.

Good. Very good. Edward smiled, knowing he'd won. Philippe was looking for a way to escape. And Edward would give him exactly that.

TWENTY-THREE

I RUSHED DOWN THE driveway looking for my escape, not caring that it was pouring now. The rain obscured my view and propelled me further into 1692. Running blindly through the fields, then running desperately to escape.

I should have paid more attention. I slipped and went sprawling on the sloping concrete. I felt scrapes cutting across the palm of my hand and my knee, but a bit of broken skin and blood was nothing compared to the lightning bolt of pain that shot through my left ankle.

I had salves at home that would help. Now I just had to get there. I stood and limped toward my truck. With each passing step, a bigger stab of pain pulsed through my ankle.

I dropped my keys as I attempted to unlock the door of my truck. I finally got the door open, but it was a fruitless effort. I knew I couldn't drive. The truck was a stick shift, and the old kind of manual transmission that required a lot of force. I needed my left foot. I closed my eyes and tried to think how to get out of there, but I couldn't stop wondering about Isabella. If she was guilty of the crime as I now suspected, that would give her a good reason to accuse me of the crime, to turn suspicion away from herself.

I'd been assuming it was Isabella who had pushed Detective Vega to look into Logan's suicide as murder—but what if it was the *reverse*? If Isabella's plan to have her husband's death written off as the suicide of a temperamental artist had been ruined by the detective's suspicions because Logan's death was similar to other murders, Isabella would need a scapegoat, and I had offered myself up as the perfect person to blame. I was new in town, without an established past, ran an online business, and had Logan's phoenix pendant.

How did the painting of Nicolas fit in? Had it truly been sent away for authentication?

I sat in the bucket seat gripping the steering wheel. Rain streamed down the car windows. I didn't want to stay on the Magnus property any longer than necessary, but I couldn't drive. On the incline of the hill, I realized it might work to ease off the brake and coast down to the street. From there I could call someone to come and get me.

I kept my 1942 Chevy truck in good shape, and as close to its original condition as possible. But in Portland, modern windshield wipers were one thing I'd invested in. After a few more deep breaths, I started the engine and turned on the wipers.

And screamed.

A handsome man stood in front of the large green hood of the truck. He held an oversize black umbrella in his hand, which kept him dry. He walked up to the driver's-side door and knocked on the window. The knuckles of his hand were swollen with what looked like arthritis. My fear evaporated as I thought about which salve might help him.

"I'm sorry to have frightened you," he said with an English accent as I rolled down the window a few inches. "And I'm terribly sorry about Isabella," he continued. "I heard her screaming and went to see what was amiss. That's when she told me what had happened. Please forgive her. She's grieving. I came after you and saw the nasty spill you took. I can't leave you like this. Let me get you some ice for your injuries."

I hesitated.

"Don't worry," he said. "Isabella went to lie down. I promise she won't scream at you anymore."

It wasn't the screaming I was worried about. With the poison on the grounds, someone else in that house was most likely a killer. But what choice did I have? Tobias and Dorian knew where I was, so they'd know where to look if something happened to me. I rolled up the squeaky window and opened the car door.

"I'm not sure I can make it back to the house."

"Take my elbow. I'm Ward. Ward Talbot. We half-met at the gallery yesterday."

"Zoe," I said as I accepted his arm. "Zoe Faust."

"Are you an artist?"

"No. Antiques dealer by day, herbalist and cook by night."

"Shame. With your style and that name, I could sell your art in a heartbeat."

"You're an art dealer?"

"Your day job's less-talented cousin." The laugh that followed made him sound even more like an upper-class Brit. The wavy hair that fell to his shoulders was the one rebellious feature on his otherwise formal yet charming face. In the darkness of the gallery, I hadn't gotten a good look at him.

"Ouch."

"Sorry. Almost to the door now."

Isabella's daughter, Cleo, appeared in the doorway and took the umbrella from Ward. She held a bag of ice in her other hand. It was only as I stepped through the doorway that I noticed this wasn't the Castle itself, but the smaller house off to the side where Logan had grown up.

"I apologize about Mom," Cleo said. She was perfectly put together today, in black clothing cut at severe angles that felt incongruous with her quiet, tentative voice, like a dubbed movie gone wrong. "And it looks like I'll need more than one bag of ice."

"I should be well enough to get going in a few minutes," I said as Ward helped me onto the couch. "I already texted my boyfriend to come get me."

That didn't get a reaction out of either of them. A good sign.

"Sorry Mom freaked you out so bad," Cleo said.

"Isabella is an incredibly talented artist," Ward said, "but like Logan, she's..." He looked at Cleo and lowered his eyes.

"It's okay," she said, squeezing his hand. "If you were going to say Mom isn't especially stable, you're right. And when she gets an idea in her head, there's no stopping her. She told us you were lying to her about a portrait of your brother who passed away."

"I came over to apologize for finding your father's phoenix charm," I said, "and all I did was make things worse."

"Did you get her to show you the painting before she kicked you out?" Cleo asked.

"Wait..." I said. "You mean you didn't send it away for authentication?"

Cleo and Ward exchanged a glance. "Did you?" she asked Ward.

"Of course not." He rushed from the room.

I gasped. "You mean the painting is *missing*?"

"Mom can be spacey," Cleo said, "especially now. I'd better check."

Before I could reply, she'd disappeared from the room, leaving me alone with my fear that I would never see the painting again.

While I waited for Cleo and Ward to return, I tried to ground myself by focusing on the pain of my swollen ankle. I looked around at the art that adorned the living room. Sculptures were placed among the books on the built-in bookshelves, and three six-foot paintings of birds adorned the walls, with smaller canvases between them. I didn't recognize the pieces, but they were beautiful and fit together. The newest painting depicted roses. I could still smell the lingering scent of varnish.

One of Isabella's sculptures had a place of honor in front of the fireplace. I wondered what animal shadow it would cast on the floor when the fire was lit. On the mantle above it was a photo of a smiling Ward and Cleo. He must have been at least twenty years older than she was, but they clearly loved each other. I could see the need for each other in their eyes.

Cleo was the first to return, with Ward a few steps behind her. She picked up a red throw pillow from a voluminous chair by the fireplace. The bright, comfy chair fit into the cozy room, which struck me as so unlike the modern interior of the main house. Ward stood behind her and wrapped his arms around her. "I'm sorry, darling," he said softly and kissed the top of her head. He stood there for a few moments, rocking back and forth, giving her the time she needed.

"What's happened?" I asked.

"My ex," Cleo said. "Another 'joke' of his, I imagine."

"Archer didn't take our marriage well," Ward said to me. "But this is ridiculous. We should tell the police—"

"No police." Cleo's shout echoed through the room.

Ward and I stared at her in stunned silence.

"Give him a chance to call me back," Cleo continued, her voice nearly a whisper now.

"You can't keep blaming yourself," Ward said. "Who wouldn't want to fight for you? But I wonder how much of his anger is ego." Ward turned from Cleo to me. "He walks around with paint-blotched skin on purpose, so people will know he's an artist."

"Ward, don't," Cleo said.

"What? It's true. He has red all over his fingers because it stands out the most and doesn't make him look like he's simply dirty, even though red rarely shows up in his paintings."

"Archer … " I said. The memory of the young man with paint-stained hands who'd asked if I was okay came back to me. "Is he in his twenties, with long blond hair?"

"You know him?" Cleo asked. "But you said—"

"I think I saw him at the gallery a few days ago. I didn't know his name, but remember the paint on his hands."

"I knew we should have gotten a better security presence," Ward said.

"For all his faults," Cleo said, "he's not a thief." She looked at her phone.

"Then why isn't he calling you back?" Ward asked. "I'm telling you, we should call the police."

"At least give him a few minutes," she said.

Ward looked as if he wanted to press her, but held his tongue.

"That painting made Dad so happy," Cleo said to me. "I was searching everywhere for a worthy fiftieth birthday present for him. He'd fallen in love with paintings that depicted alchemy and transformation, after seeing a local artist's work last spring and buying one of her works."

I wondered why Heather hadn't mentioned this. But then I knew. Heather didn't care about celebrity. She'd been giddy the first time a few of her pieces had sold, but the fame of the buyer wouldn't have mattered to her.

119

"Where did you find this painting of—" I stopped myself before saying Nicolas's name.

"An auction house. Listed as *The Alchemist* by an unknown painter. No provenance beyond that it had been in the California family's care for generations. It—" Cleo broke off and answered her buzzing phone. "This isn't funny, Archer," she hissed. "Especially now, after what happened to Dad."

Holding the phone, she walked into the other room. Ward followed. I heard raised voices, though I couldn't make out what they were saying. But when the two came back into the room, the words on Cleo's lips were clear. "Yes," she said. "I'd like to report a stolen painting. A painting and the ownership papers that went with it."

TWENTY-FOUR

MAX CAME TO PICK me up. His jeep had automatic transmission, so I could drive it with my working right foot while he drove my truck. Ward found a bandage that Cleo used to wrap my ankle. And once I reached home I could make myself a poultice of garlic and olive oil for swelling, and then a rub of frankincense and peppermint oils for the pain.

Max and Ward helped me to the jeep. But after Ward said farewell and left to return to the house, Max remained standing at the side of the road with me, the driver's-side door open.

"I know there's gotta be a good reason you're at the home of the man you were falsely accused of murdering, covered in blood, at the same time a burglary was reported at the house."

"You heard about the stolen painting? And I'm not *covered* in blood. I came to apologize. It went horribly wrong."

"I can see that."

I hesitated before saying more. I didn't know how sensitive the speaker system at the gate was. I had to tell Max about the ergot I'd smelled in the studio, but not here.

"Why aren't you walking to your car?" I asked him. "I'm getting soaking wet. Again." The rain had let up, but it was still sprinkling.

"Your friend Tobias, is he staying with you?"

"For a little while, yeah. I thought you two had bonded. You're not jealous, are you?" I joked. Tobias was a handsome guy, but *no*. After what we'd been through together, he was like a little brother to me.

But Max didn't laugh. "I know more about him now. About his … proclivities."

"Proclivities? What's that supposed to mean? That he likes the spiciest food of anyone you'll ever meet—"

"That woman he married. Rosa. She was in her seventies when she died."

"Too young, I know."

"That's not funny."

"I'm not being funny. I'm sad she died so young."

Max shook his head. Raindrops flung from his hair, and more stuck to his long black eyelashes and ran down his face.

"Either your friend was running a scam to get her money, or—"

"Or what? He fell in love with an older woman? And would you give it a second thought if their sexes were reversed? A fifty-year-old woman with a seventy-something husband? I thought you liked Tobias and understood his grief at losing her."

"I did. I feel like I still do. But now I know why. He's a con man, Zoe."

"They were married for decades, Max. Decades. That's a really long con."

Max took a moment before speaking. "You're right. I don't know what it is ... but something is off about his story. How well do you know him?"

"Better than I know you," I said, and immediately regretted it. But it was too late. The look on Max's face showed me I'd shoved a knife into his heart. He stepped back and nodded, then slammed the car door.

———

When I pulled the jeep up in front of Max's house, my green pickup truck was already parked on the street. As I turned off the engine, Max came over to help me out. Instead of lifting me to the ground, he pulled me into a hug and buried his head in my shoulder.

"I'm sorry," he whispered. "I don't want to fight."

"I'm sorry too. I know you were angry because you care about me and don't want to see me get hurt. But I won't. Not by Tobias."

Max pulled back, but his lips hovered an inch from mine. "I don't want to get you sick."

"You seem well to me."

He laughed and rested his nose on mine. "I don't know what magic was in that soup you made me, or in Tobias's tea, but I do feel so much better."

"It's not magic," I said. "It's old medicine we've forgotten. And besides, I wouldn't care if you did get me sick."

Max's lips brushed mine as the rain began to fall harder, pelting nearly as hard as hail.

"We can't get a break, can we?" he whispered.

"It's only a few yards to the house."

I expected him to help me limp to the house at his side, but instead he swept me up, carried me inside, and set me down on the couch.

"I'm dripping water and blood all over your white couch," I said, trying to move.

"I don't care," Max said and crawled on top of me.

It was a kiss that reached every part of me. I have no idea how long it lasted, until he finally said, "As much as it pains me to say this, I should probably be the sensible one and get you some ice for your ankle. Then we can pick up where we left off."

"And as much as it pains *me*," I said when he returned with the ice pack, "I need to tell you something I couldn't while we were at the Castle. I need you to call Detective Vega."

"I'm sure she's busy with the stolen painting, since it relates to the Logan Magnus case. And I'm kinda hoping she doesn't hear you went to see Isabella. You were just being nice, not anything related to the case—"

"That's the thing. We need to tell her there's ergot at that house."

"Ergot?"

"It's a poison."

"She already knows there are a bunch of toxic paints at the Castle. She took them for testing. The question, of course, is whether Logan killed himself or whether someone somehow forced him to swallow the paint. Which doesn't seem likely. But that's what Vega is working on."

"Ergot is a poison that can cause hallucinations and leave people open to suggestion." My throat tightened as I thought of my former friends, so quick to claim I was a witch. "It's a way someone could have convinced Logan to swallow the paint … "

Max swore. "How did you see it?"

"I smelled it."

Max swore again.

"You know I'm sensitive to the scents of plants and organic matter. It's a fungus. What? You thought I was going to say Isabella had a bottle lying about labeled 'Ergot Poison'? Sorry. I'm not making this simple. But I know what I smelled."

Max pinched the bridge of his nose. "You're right. You should tell her."

"I can't go anywhere." I pointed to my ankle. "Can't you just call her?"

"She needs the details from you." Max's cell phone rang. "Speak of the devil," he said as he looked at the phone. He went into the kitchen to take the call. I didn't hear most of what was said, but I heard his voice rising in frustration. After a few seconds of silence, he came back to the living room.

"As I expected," he said, "Isabella called Luciana after your visit. But she had a crazy story about you having an old portrait you claim is new. I wonder if Isabella is taking something to dull the pain of her husband's death."

"Wait, who's Luciana?"

"Detective Vega."

"Oh. So you told her about the ergot?"

Max shook his head. "Games of telephone are a bad idea in my line of work. She's working the case, though. She knows you hurt your ankle, so she's going to swing by … "

"You sounded like you were about to say something else."

"I'm going to have a really busy week with a case I caught. So I don't know how much I can take care of you and your ankle for the next couple of days. You'll be okay?"

"I will, but that's not what you were going to say."

Max smiled. "Do you think you can take a day off from baking for Blue? Oh—it's okay if you can't. Never mind."

"No. That's not what my expression meant. I ... there's something I should tell you about that."

"I've been waiting for you to tell me."

"You have?"

"I've suspected for a while now, but I knew it wasn't your secret to tell. It's his, isn't it?"

My heart thudded in my throat. Why was Max so calm if he knew about Dorian? Was this the calm before he exploded? "Um ... "

"Your French friend. The guy who's disfigured and doesn't want anyone to see him. I've been noticing the French themes in 'your' baking." Max grinned. "He's the real chef, isn't he? And you're his cover."

I smiled back at Max. "I don't know what to say."

"It's okay. Like I said. I know it's not your secret to give away. Don't say anything. Not about that. I want you to say yes to something else. Come to a birthday dinner for my mom tomorrow night. She lives out in Astoria. It's a few hours away and it's easiest to stay overnight. But I need to warn you, my family is ... ah ... not the most normal bunch."

"Whose is?" I know everyone says that, but with Dorian, I'm fairly certain mine makes the final cut for weirdest families.

"I didn't want to scare you away ... But I'd like for you to meet them."

I smiled. "Detective Vega told you she brought up your family yesterday?"

"She's good people. And she likes you. She didn't want me messing this up."

"I don't either," I said, and kissed him.

TWENTY-FIVE

FROM MAX'S COUCH, I told Detective Vega about the ergot I'd smelled in Isabella's art studio. I wouldn't want to play cards with the woman; she had the world's best poker face. I couldn't tell what she thought of the information I gave her. Since she knew undisclosed details about how Logan Magnus died, did ergot poisoning seem like something that could be involved? I doubted they'd tested for it. Was she happy I'd given her evidence that might confirm a theory of murder? Did she believe me at all?

After she left, Max drove me home in my truck. Tobias came out the door as we pulled up.

"What happened?" he asked.

"Zoe hurt her ankle," Max answered. He pretended not to see Tobias's outstretched hand and helped me to the house. "I've got her," he added curtly.

He lifted me to the green velvet couch, then stood hovering over me, struggling with his own internal dilemma. Did he trust me enough to trust Tobias too? I was injured, and home (supposedly alone) with a strong man who had a strange past.

"I'll be in the kitchen," Tobias said. "Making tea. It'll take a few minutes."

I raised an eyebrow at Max after he left the room. "You didn't have to be such an—"

"You're sure you'll be all right?"

"I'm one thousand percent positive."

Max winced. "I hate that expression."

"And I hate it when my friends don't trust each other. Or me."

"I trust you. It's not the same as not worrying."

At the sound of the front door shutting behind Max, Tobias came out of the kitchen. He walked over to it and locked it without me needing to ask.

"He found out about Rosa's age?"

I nodded.

"But he still left you here alone with me. And while a helpless, injured damsel in distress as well."

I threw a pillow at him and stuck out my tongue. "He still likes you. He's just struggling to reconcile his feelings with how he thinks the world works. The rational part of his brain still wonders if you're a con man who tricked an elderly woman out of her money."

"You going to tell me how this happened?" Tobias pointed at my knee and ankle. "Do you want me to take a look?"

"No. You'll sprinkle cayenne in my wounds. And that'll hurt even more."

"I only use that in emergencies, you know. You're not bleeding nearly enough. I'll even stick to basic EMT training, starting with cutting your jeans open to the knee. They're ruined anyway." Tobias had worked as an EMT rather than going to medical school to become a doctor because there was far less chance of being found out if he didn't pursue a degree.

"I hate these jeans anyway," I said. "Good riddance to my only pair. I don't know why people love them so much. They're not nearly as comfortable as tailored slacks." It continued to amaze me that modern people found an abundance of off-the-hanger clothing better than a few handmade clothes fitted to one's own body. "It's really just my sprained ankle that's not doing well. If you bring me that tea you promised, plus garlic and olive oil so I can make a poultice for the swelling, I'll tell you and Dorian everything."

"*Bon*," Dorian said, coming down the stairs.

"Gargoyles must have great intuition," Tobias said.

I pointed to a corner of the wall next to the kitchen. "The old pipes of this house lend themselves to eavesdropping. As long as people aren't whispering, from the attic it's possible to hear what's going on in the kitchen and living room. You have to listen really carefully for it to work."

"I am a great listener," Dorian said, hopping from the last step onto the hardwood floor of the open living room/dining room. "And I have just heard news. I—*bof!*—what has happened, Zoe?"

"You have news?" I asked.

"Not as dramatic as yours. Someone has attacked you? Who is the monster who—"

"I wasn't attacked. Not exactly. But I have a lot to report."

"As do I," Dorian said. "Monsieur Freeman. If you can help Zoe to the dining table, we can each share our news."

"We can't do that from the couch?" Tobias asked.

"We need sustenance," Dorian said. "And Zoe cannot eat properly while lying on the couch."

Tobias helped me to the table and then went off to make a poultice for my ankle while Dorian brought me a platter of homemade, salted, dark chocolate caramels, which he insisted were perfect for healing both body and mind.

"I have bad news to report," the gargoyle said as I bit into a gooey caramel. "The auction house returned my call. It is now public knowledge that they suffered a burglary."

The mouth-watering melted sugar felt as though it was transforming on my tongue from sweet cream to burnt sludge. My throat dry, I forced myself to swallow.

"The records of the painting?" I asked, already knowing the answer.

"Gone," Dorian said. "All the records pertaining to *The Alchemist* are gone."

Tobias swore. "That can't be a coincidence."

"It's not," I said. "Because that's not all. The painting itself has been stolen. That's what I discovered when I was visiting Isabella at the Castle."

I filled them in on erratic Isabella, the stolen painting, and the ergot poison. By the time I was finished, the chocolate caramels were gone and Dorian's gray mouth hung agape. Tobias stood from the table and pushed open the swinging door leading to the kitchen. He returned a moment later with a bottle of wine in one hand and three long-stemmed glasses tucked between the fingers of the other. In silence, he poured us each a glass, then swallowed his own in two gulps.

"We must ask ourselves," Dorian said, "what is so special about this painting?" He held up a clawed hand. "*Oui*. I know the painting is important to *us*. But what do *others* care of it?"

"Cleo believes it's an authentic Hayden," I said, "in spite of what the experts have said. It could be worth a lot of money."

"Or it could be proof of the art forger in Portland," Tobias said. "Either way, fake or authentic, there's a motive for murder and theft."

"There has to be a record of the painting somewhere," I said.

"*Je suis désolé,*" Dorian said. "I am sorry, but my internet research has also failed."

"What research?"

"Provenance. The history of ownership of a piece of art."

"I know what provenance is," I said. "I have to worry about it for the higher-end items I sell with Elixir. Especially the ones I had in storage in Paris for a while, to account for where they supposedly were when they were really just sitting in storage. My 'grandmother' had a lot of art."

"But all is not lost. We know a hacker—"

"You know a hacker?" Tobias asked.

"Veronica is *not* a hacker," I said.

"You diminish her incredible mind because she is only fifteen?" Dorian said.

"Brixton's friend Veronica is smart and good with computers," I explained to Tobias. "She built the new website for Elixir. That doesn't make her a hacker."

Dorian waved a clawed hand through the air. "Semantics. You should call Brixton to ask for the assistance of the hacker."

"What's she supposed to hack?" Tobias asked. "There's no magical database of where all paintings are at all times. And I'm sorry, am I the only responsible adult here? If she's only a kid—"

"Actually … " I began.

"You can't be serious," Tobias said. "You've been rooming with the gargoyle for too long if you think—"

"I don't mean that she should do hacking," I said. "I wonder if we're making this too complicated. If it's modern experts who've declared this Philippe Hayden painting a forgery, and it's not in current books and online databases, what we need is *old* art history books from the library. Even if my ankle was up for a trip, my library card has been revoked. Dorian can't get his own library card, and you've got an out-of-state ID. We need someone—or multiple some-ones—who can check out art history books at the library."

"It's Sunday," Tobias said, "so the kids aren't at school."

"If there's no way I'm going to find the painting itself," I said, "I need to find the best reproduction I can, to see if I can identify the clue that way. With the painting and its modern records stolen—"

"We go old school," Tobias said.

"Perhaps," Dorian said, "you have more gargoyle in you than I gave you credit, Zoe Faust. This is a brilliant idea from your little gray cells."

TWENTY-SIX

LIKE JOSEPHINE TEY'S DETECTIVE who solved a famous historical crime from the confines of his hospital bed, I was stuck on my green velvet couch with my ankle raised on a throw pillow. I hated not being able to walk, but that novel gave me hope that I could still achieve something from my sick bed. With the help of my friends.

Brixton had enlisted his friends Veronica and Ethan to go with him to the library to get as many art history books as they could—books that mentioned the painter Philippe Hayden and his contemporaries as well as those on art forgery.

Later that afternoon, they arrived with bags full of books. Tobias let them in. He'd offered to pick them up in my truck, but the kids insisted they could carry the books in their backpacks on their bikes. Dorian had left snacks on the dining table and then gone to hide in the attic, asking me to be sure to speak loudly so he could hear the conversation.

"Hey, T," Brixton said to Tobias, giving him a fist bump and dropping a heavy backpack at his feet. "We got as many books as we could before the library closed. They had a limit on how many we could check out, so we couldn't just take everything."

"Hi, Ms. Faust," Veronica said, smiling shyly at me and then Tobias as she set down a backpack of books that looked like it weighed more than she did.

Brixton had been best friends with Veronica Chen Mendoza since they were little. She was taller than either of the boys, though this year they were catching up. When I'd first met her, she'd stood awkwardly in her thin, gangly frame, always wearing ballet flats to look as short as possible. But this year she stood tall, with more confidence, and was wearing shiny gold rain boots with chunky two-inch heels.

"Veronica and Ethan, this is my old friend Tobias Freeman."

Veronica shook his hand. "Nice to meet you, Mr. Freeman."

"Hey Zoe," Ethan said, heaving an even heavier backpack onto the coffee table. "Good to met you, Tobias."

Ethan was the newest addition to Brixton's group of friends, his parents having moved to Portland a little over a year ago, before his freshman year of high school. He used to dress as though trying to emulate James Dean, with jeans and a white T-shirt and black leather jacket. This fall he'd switched to a Victorian style and wore a long black coat that fell below his knees.

"I really appreciate you bringing the books," I said. "Please help yourself to snacks before you go."

"We can stay and help," Veronica said.

"That's generous," Tobias said, "but Zoe and I have got it covered."

"Really, we'd like to help," Ethan said. "Brixton told us about this crazy idea of your stepdad's."

Brixton raised his eyebrows at me in a theatrical manner. He was trying to convey something, but what that something was, I had no idea. He'd said he would tell his friends a cover story similar to the one I'd already told to Cleo: that my stepdad had once owned a similar painting, so it would mean a lot to me to see it again. It was as close to the truth as we could get. So what was "this crazy idea"?

"I know Brix wasn't supposed to tell us, Ms. Faust," Veronica said, "but we didn't understand the urgency until he did. I was going to study this afternoon, but then he told us what we'd be looking for."

"What you'd be looking for?" I repeated.

"The clues," Veronica said. "The clues to the treasure."

Brixton coughed. His wavy black hair fell over his eyes and he looked away.

"Don't worry," Ethan said. "We know it's confidential. That your stepdad had a theory about clues to a treasure being hidden in this *Alchemist* painting."

"It's so romantic," Veronica said as the boys helped themselves to apple-stuffed pastries. "A secret message in a missing centuries-old painting…"

I smiled at her. She was at an age where she thought everything was romantic. When she'd learned about my French friend who didn't like to be seen because of his deformity, she began to see him as a tragic figure from literature, which was of course very romantic.

"Looks like you should get some of the apple fritters before Brixton and Ethan have devoured them," I said to her. "And Brixton—you forgot one of your gardening responsibilities. Come outside with me for a minute."

"Shouldn't you stay inside with your injured leg?" Brixton asked.

"You can help support me."

Ethan clicked his tongue at his friend as Brixton helped me through the kitchen and into the backyard.

"What on earth—?" I began once we'd reached the back porch.

135

"Veronica was going to do homework instead of coming to the library," Brixton said, "and Ethan wanted to watch a movie. Anyway, it was the only way I could convince them to help."

"By telling them there's a clue to a treasure?"

Brixton rolled his eyes. "It's true, isn't it? You're looking for Nicolas, and there's a clue to where he is inside that painting. You know, you've got a total mom-look on your face right now. *What*? It's a good idea, Zoe." He paused and grinned. "Now Ethan feels like he's in this classic '80s movie Max recommended to us. Admit it, you and Tobias couldn't read all those books as quickly without us. If you want to find your mentor, you need our help."

I resisted the impulse to tousle his hair.

Back inside, Brixton and Ethan spread books out at the dining table with Tobias, and Veronica sat on the floor in front of where I was sitting with my foot up on the couch.

"We're looking for a painting called *The Alchemist*, which you might find by name in an index, or look at the images in the books to see if you spot a portrait of a man in the foreground and shelves with small glass bottles behind him."

"Do you know what the clue looks like, Ms. Faust?" Veronica asked.

"If Zoe could tell us that," Ethan said, "it wouldn't be a clue, right?"

"It's a great question, Veronica," I said. "Philippe Hayden liked visual codes." I flipped through one of the art books and showed her a full-page photo of a narrow bottle that had words on it that were visible only when it was viewed nearly flat.

"That's so cool." She took the book and grinned. "I think I saw something like this at a science museum exhibit."

"Why aren't there any photos of Philippe Hayden in these books on him?" Brixton asked, flipping through an art history book on Renaissance artists.

"Um, because there were no cameras then," Ethan said.

Brixton rolled his eyes. "You know what I meant. There are no *portraits* of Philippe."

"I'm not sure how famous he was during his lifetime," I said. "So he might not have had a formal portrait done of himself, and any self-portraits he did might have been lost to history. Lots of artists didn't become famous until they were long dead. Like Van Gogh."

"Seriously?"

"I'm afraid so."

For half an hour, we read in silence. The hardback coffee-table books and dog-eared art history paperback textbooks were filled with memorable paintings that drew the viewer in, even as small reproductions. How many brilliant artists hadn't been discovered or had their masterpieces remembered after their deaths? Given that some unattributed works of art made their way into books, I was hoping that this would be the case with Philippe Hayden masterpieces that hadn't been attributed to him. After all, someone had believed *The Alchemist* was worth saving, even though it hadn't been attributed to Hayden. It had to be represented here somewhere.

Veronica was the first one to move. At first I thought she was taking a stretch break, but she placed two books side by side on the coffee table.

"This is a strange type of optical illusion," she said. "I know this painting isn't the one you're looking for, but this Hayden painting called *Roses with Bees* is photographed in this book and described in the other. But the descriptions don't match. In the really old book, the one that has just a description, it says there's a stack of gold on the table next to the flowers."

"A clue to the treasure?" Ethan said. "A code meaning the boring painting of flowers leads to a hoard of gold even though there's no gold in the painting?" He picked up the book with the description.

"Or an optical illusion," I said, taking the book with the photograph. "Maybe we can only see the gold from a certain angle." I looked more carefully at the painting, tilting the book again. The perspective didn't reveal anything. I shook my head.

Roses with Bees didn't look like one of Hayden's alchemical paintings. The only thing related to alchemy was the bees, which were symbolic in alchemical art—especially in backward alchemy. After the year I'd had, I hated bees. Bees had been drawn to the backward alchemy book that had initially brought Dorian to life. As the book had aged, it had aged backward, emanating the sweet scents of honey and cloves instead of the putrid smells of mold and decay.

The book itself changed through alchemy … I looked more closely at the *Roses with Bees* painting. There was no hidden perspective, but there was an imperfection where the stack of gold should have been.

"Good catch, Veronica," Tobias was saying.

Her stomach grumbled and she blushed. "I guess scholarly work makes me hungry. Are there more chocolate chip and pumpkin muffins?"

I slammed the book shut so hard that Veronica and Ethan both jumped. Brixton scowled at me. I couldn't have seen what I thought I saw, could I?

"Tobias can pack up some muffins for all of you," I said. "You've done more than enough for today. I didn't realize how late it was. This isn't the painting we're after, but these books are a great start."

Everyone stared at me but complied.

"Why'd you want to get rid of them?" Tobias asked after sending the confused kids home with their backpacks filled with food and locking the door.

"Get Dorian."

"I am coming!" the French voice called from above. A moment later he appeared on the stairs. "Did you save me any food?"

"We sent you to the attic with enough food for two," Tobias said.

"I was bored and lonely," the gargoyle said. "But I believe Zoe is unwell. Look at her. Does she have an illness? You studied *les médicines*, you can diagnose her. She is too pale, even for her usual palor." He turned to me. "*Mon amie*, can you hear me?"

"The gold," I whispered. My voice shook. "Don't you see? The gold!"

"Zoe cannot make gold," Dorian said to Tobias, his horns scrunched with concern. "She is hallucinating."

"I'm not hallucinating," I said. "There was once a stack of gold in this painting, *Roses with Bees*, but now it's gone."

"You spotted another forgery?" Tobias asked.

"No," I said. "Something worse. *The Alchemist* doesn't contain a clue to *where* Nicolas is being imprisoned. He was trying to tell me he's imprisoned *inside the painting*."

TWENTY-SEVEN

1597, Prague, Bohemia

Philippe licked the edge of a thin-tipped squirrel-hair brush and began painting a stack of gold coins onto the sunlit side table in the painting of the alchemy lab. The narrow bristles were needed to paint the delicate lines for the perspective shift that served as a second layer of the painting.

No, this painting was lacking depth.

It was difficult to focus after Edward's visit. Although Edward had explained to the Emperor that he'd been mistaken about Philippe's ability to produce gold in public, now Philippe was forced to not only produce more gold in private, but to tutor the charlatan Edward Kelley in true alchemy! He did not wish to hide the secrets of alchemy from anyone worthy, but Edward was not worthy. The saving grace was that unworthy people did not come easily to alchemy. Edward would have to work harder than he ever had in his ill-spirited life.

Philippe smiled at the thought and returned to the painting. It was not the best idea to work while in a foul mood and without the right planetary alignments, but after Edward's coercion, time was short. One had to act now.

With focused pure intent, a fresh brush was dipped into the gold leaf and gum, and then Philippe looked at the gold nuggets on the table, carefully replicating the image. Lost in the work, the painter paid no attention to the passing of time. Hours passed, or perhaps an entire day.

Thirsty, with a rumbling stomach, and exhausted nearly to the point of collapse, Philippe set down the paintbrush and picked up a cup of water with shaking hands, nearly knocking over the small table with the pile of gold. Or rather, the table that once held gold.

The painter blinked. Was this a hallucination from fatigue? No. It was real. This was truly happening. The pieces of true gold had been transformed from their place on the table—into the image in the painting.

After many years' work in alchemy labs and artist workshops, Philippe had theorized that this was possible but hadn't truly believed it would work. Not until coming to Prague Castle, with the energy of creativity and alchemy all around. How many years had it been, wondering if such a transformation was feasible? And here it was!

Philippe dropped the clay cup of water. It shattered into dull gray shards that scattered across the floor as the artist ran a shaking hand through short curly hair, now standing on end as if it had been struck by lightning. A great silence descended over the room, as if the whole world had ceased in both motion and the passage of time. This was a discovery of a new form of alchemy—one that combined it with art.

Alchemical Painting.

TWENTY-EIGHT

"WE'VE BEEN LOOKING AT this all wrong," I said. I tried to stand, but my ankle wasn't having it. Tobias helped ease me back down onto the sofa.

"*Mon Dieu.*" Dorian flapped his wings, knocking over a pile of books. But he didn't seem to notice. "Monsieur Flamel is trapped inside the painting. This is terrible. Terrible! I cannot bear the thought." He tucked his wings around his body.

"It's all right, Dorian," Tobias said in a soothing voice. "If that's what's happened to him, we'll find him and figure out how to get him out."

Dorian's lower lip quivered. "But he has been trapped in the painting for centuries. All those years … " He rocked back and forth.

"Uh, Zoe," Tobias said softly. "Does he do this sometimes?"

"Dorian," I said, standing with all my weight on my right leg and putting my hands on the gargoyle's shoulders. "Your situation wasn't the same. You were reverting to stone but still wide awake. We don't know that's what's happened to Nicolas." I hoped my voice conveyed a confidence I didn't feel.

Dorian looked up at me with his watery black eyes. "I could not bear it for a good man to suffer such a fate."

"We don't know what it's like to be trapped in a painting."

"Or," Tobias cut in, "if that's where he is at all."

"I don't know. But if you'd seen that painting. The way he looked at me … it was like he saw me." I shivered. "I thought at the time it was just the skill of a talented artist. I can't believe it didn't occur to me before that *he* was inside the painting."

"Because he might not be," Tobias said. "It's a nice theory, but it's just that: a theory."

"It was *him*, Tobias." I could barely contain my excitement, and I felt my voice shaking as I spoke. "As someone who practices both spiritual and physical alchemy, you know better than anyone how alchemy is about transformation. Philippe Hayden painted alchemical secrets into artwork. Real alchemy, not like most artistic representations of alchemy. Don't you see? He was an alchemist. One more skilled than us. Philippe Hayden figured out how to use his intent and alchemical ingredients to move objects like gold into paintings."

"And then people," Tobias murmured. "Sounds dangerous."

I gasped. "I wonder if Philippe Hayden was the person Nicolas wanted help fighting, if he was the one who trapped Nicolas into one of his own paintings."

"Monsieur Hayden was not a backward alchemist," Dorian said. He seemed to have snapped out of his catatonic state. "Those were stupid, stupid men. They could never have painted a masterpiece."

"Nicolas was always fearful of losing his humanity as he grew older," I said. "It was something he warned me of. " I groaned. "If Philippe Hayden was an alchemist who lived for centuries, that would explain why the experts disagree about which of his works are real. Because they don't know that Hayden was painting for hundreds of years."

"Zoe," Tobias said quietly, "if this Philippe Hayden is an alchemist, and a brilliant artist who knows how to trap people in paintings, he'd be a dangerous, dangerous man."

"I know."

Tobias spoke slowly, and so softly I could barely hear him. "Do we know for sure that Logan Magnus is dead?"

Dorian clicked his tongue. "Yes, yes, this is all very dramatic and you two should cowrite a Gothic novel that will make lots of money so you can buy me many truffles and other delicacies. But this does not work in reality. The police have a body. They know he died of poison."

"And Logan Magnus grew up in the public eye because of his artist father," I said. "There are lots of photos of him growing up."

"That's what I always thought," I said. "But what if he switched identities with Logan Magnus because they looked so much alike? Even without plastic surgery, Hayden could have altered his appearance with tricks that play on what people expect, the way stage magicians do. And the man who died could have been the real son." But I knew I was grasping at straws.

"A trick that fooled all his family and friends?" Tobias said.

"Logan was an only child," I said, "and his father died a long time ago." Dorian looked as if he was about to suffer an apoplexy, so I quickly continued. "I know, I know. I don't believe it either. I don't think Logan Magnus is Philippe Hayden. There's too much we don't know. I keep coming back to the fact that Nicolas wanted my help with something. He wanted me to stop someone. Was it Philippe Hayden?"

Dorian scampered to the kitchen and came back with the translated note we'd deciphered.

"*I might not survive,*" he read, "*but if I do, I will be imprisoned ... I am not afraid to die. But I fear for the world if I do not complete this important task. I must prevent ... You must ... stop them ... You will find ... in the Philippe Hayden painting.*"

"'Them,'" I repeated, "What were 'they' doing that Nicolas thought needed to be stopped? Oh no ... "

"What are you pondering?" Dorian asked. "Tobias, I believe our friend might be in need of smelling salts."

"I'm not swooning," I snapped. "We've been forgetting Perenelle. But Philippe Hayden and Perenelle Flamel together ... Two people make a 'them.'" My heart was racing so fast I could barely breathe. I shook my head. "No, I can't believe Perenelle would hurt Nicolas."

"And I can't believe," Tobias added, "that the great Nick Flamel would say he fears for the world because of an affair his wife is having. That's beyond overdramatic. I don't buy it."

"She loved Nicolas way too much to have an affair. I don't think that was her relationship with Philippe. But what if she was advising Philippe to do something dangerous with his art? Or helping him herself?"

"Such as teaching alchemy to a painter," Dorian said.

"Perenelle loved art. While Nicolas would write the steps of alchemical processes, Perenelle preferred to sketch them. She never learned to paint, but with her interest in art ... "

"She could have been swayed by a dangerous man with ill intentions," Tobias said.

"The Flamels' home was filled with art by Philippe Hayden and other painters," I said. "It was one of the many things I loved about my time with them. Do you think Philippe Hayden could have been one of their students, like I was, and that's how he met Perenelle?"

"Isabella Magnus," Dorian declared. He puffed up his chest before continuing. "The mysterious woman who is a metalworker yet cannot paint. Who possesses ergot poison, which has been manipulated for many centuries. Who was the last person in possession of *The Alchemist* before it disappeared."

The gargoyle paused, straightened his wings, and drummed his claws together. If he wore glasses, I was sure he would have adjusted them for effect.

"Isabella Magnus," he said, "is Perenelle Flamel."

TWENTY-NINE

"You're forgetting one very important thing," I said. "I know what Perenelle looks like. And Isabella Magnus is not Perenelle Flamel."

"But as you admitted," Dorian said, "plastic surgery and psychology—"

"Neither can make people a foot taller."

Dorian's nostril's flared. "But... But I was so certain! It was such a perfect solution. Are you quite sure?"

"I am. I haven't seen Perenelle Flamel anywhere since 1704. Not over the years, and not here in Portland now."

"That is a long period of time," Dorian said, his wings slumping. "You could have forgotten, no?"

"No. But she could be trapped inside a painting as well. That would explain things, if they were both imprisoned. If I can get him out of the painting and help him with the important task he wrote of, I can also help him find her again. He was never happy when she wasn't at his side."

"I hope she wasn't involved with whatever Nicolas was trying to stop," Tobias said, grabbing his leather jacket from the coat rack. "Perenelle has got to fit into this somehow. You said she and Nick were inseparable. So where is she?"

"Where are you going?"

"I'm the only one who can do something beyond play armchair detective today," Tobias said. "Looks like it's up to me to figure out whatever else I can from the Magnus family. What other alchemy-related paintings do they have in their mansion?"

"You can't go back there. Isabella had poison—"

"You're not the one the police are most suspicious of, Zoe."

"Exactly. You can't go investigating—"

"It's *my neck* on the line. I know the cops mean well, and that I explained away my past, but there are some blank spots and inconsistencies that won't be so easy to explain if they go digging … I want the murder solved as quickly as possible, as well as help to get Nick back to you."

"He makes a good point," Dorian said. "I am less clear on why Monsieur Freeman refers to the alchemist as 'Nick.'"

Tobias and I looked at one another. "Do you remember, Zoe?" he asked.

"What does she remember?" Dorian asked, jumping up and down.

"The man who once owned Tobias," I said softly. "His name was Nicholas."

"*Merde*," Dorian said.

Tobias grabbed my keys from the glass bowl next to the door. "I promise I'll take good care of your truck."

"But you can't just barge in—" I began.

"She'll let me in," Tobias said. "I have a good reason."

Before I could ask what he meant, he was out the door.

"He is an enigmatic one," Dorian said once the front door had shut behind Tobias. "What do you presume he has in mind?"

"I don't know. But I've learned not to doubt him."

"*Bon.*"

"Could you help me up?"

"If you can wait a few moments," the gargoyle said, hopping onto the first step of the stairway leading to the second floor, "I have a better idea."

He returned a few minutes later holding a stack of my clothes and an ornate wooden cane that I hadn't thought about in years.

"Now you understand what it is to be housebound," Dorian said as he handed me the antique Chinese cane. "Yet you also observe how it gives your little gray cells more incentive to work. But this cane will help you move around the house. At least on the ground floor."

"You know my inventory better than I do," I said, smiling at the dragon carved into the smooth handle. It reminded me of the phoenix pendant. Fierce, symbolic creatures that rose from flames.

"Where are you going now?" I asked, noticing Dorian was already halfway up the stairs again.

"My work station is set up in the attic."

"Your work station?" I'd been wondering why he'd set up my old printer in the attic.

He pointed at the books surrounding me and the laptop on the coffee table. "You should get to work as well."

Before returning to the books, I took a bath in the downstairs bathroom to give myself a chance to think about what we'd learned. I couldn't get it out of my mind that Perenelle was a missing piece of the puzzle. Why hadn't I thought more about that? I knew a big part of the answer. Perenelle and I had never been close. Nicolas was the mentor I needed, but Perenelle had never seemed fully comfortable with my presence in the house. I don't think she was jealous of me. It was something else. Something I never understood at the time, and didn't have a chance to learn before I fled.

I'd also been terribly selfish. I hadn't thought about how worried Tobias must be feeling, knowing the police were looking into him.

Tobias shook me awake from where I'd accidentally fallen asleep curled up on the couch.

"You could have texted," I said, stretching my kinked neck. "I was getting worried."

"I didn't realize how late it was. But it looks like the gargoyle took good care of you." He pointed at a tray of food on the coffee table. I hadn't even realized Dorian had brought it out. "That spread explains why you're dressed like this. Couldn't fit into your other clothes? No judgment. I've been there."

I looked down at my pink sweatpants, hand-knitted green sweater, and yellow sun-and-moon socks and laughed. "No. Actually I'm wearing these because Dorian went upstairs to get fresh clothes for me before I took a bath downstairs. I didn't want to try the stairs yet."

Tobias laughed so hard a tear rolled down his cheek.

"It's not funny," I said, gasping through my own laughter. "I think he might be color-blind."

"Where is the little guy, anyway?"

"He should have heard us talking. I expected he'd be down by now."

Tobias hefted a satchel onto the floor. I hadn't noticed it in the dim light. I would have assumed it was more baking supplies for Dorian except that it bulged at sharp angles.

"What on earth?" I asked.

"Gift from Isabella." He lifted a two-foot metal sculpture from the canvas bag. Like the ones I'd seen in front of the Castle, it was a series of twisted iron beams.

"A gift? You're friends now?" I couldn't take my eyes off the sleek and beautiful lines of the sculpture.

"It's two intertwined crows," he said, following my gaze. "When the light hits them just right, they look like they're flying."

I sniffed the air.

"What are you doing?" Tobias asked. "Do you need a tissue?"

"I'm making sure there's no poison on the statue or in the bag. Stop looking at me like that. I just don't want to see you get hurt."

Tobias sighed. "Why is it so hard to believe she'd be generous?"

"She's a murder suspect."

"So are we. Crows were Rosa's favorite. They're arguably the smartest non-human animal." He paused and gave me a pained look. "And loyal."

"Rosa. That's why you two bonded."

"We both know what it's like to lose a spouse. Especially so recently."

I'd felt that pain before, but time had done its job healing the sharp edges of grief.

"That's why you guessed she'd see you."

"I gave Isabella my condolences and told her about Rosa. She already knew who I was. She knew the police had questioned me in relation to the case because of the misunderstanding at your house. She was horrified about it, especially since I'd been coming to visit after Rosa's funeral. That detective questioned her about me as well. Wondering if I'd crossed paths with Logan at some point in my 'spotty past.'"

"I'm sorry."

"For what? You didn't know I'd be arriving in Portland so soon. You had no way to know they'd pick me up."

"I've failed spectacularly at giving you the relaxing break you needed. And for not trusting you."

"Zoe." Tobias scooted my feet on the couch over to make room to sit down. "We need to talk."

"Conversations beginning with those words never end well."

Tobias nodded. "You know there are these rumors that an art forger was somehow connected to Logan Magnus? Isabella says she found information proving that an art forger murdered her husband."

THIRTY

"Did she go to the police?" I asked. "Who—?"

"Two problems." Tobias cut me off. "First, she doesn't know who the person is—if it's the forger Neo who's on the run, or someone else. Second, she doesn't *have* the proof. It was something Logan found, which she discovered in their safe after he died. When she went back to look more closely at what she realized it was, she says it was gone, just like the painting."

"That's an even better reason to go to the police."

"Without any hard evidence, and without even knowing who the documents implicate, she's worried nothing will come of it except for scandal—that there'll be headlines saying Logan Magnus was in league with an art forger. The police already know about the possible art forgery connection."

"You realize she could have made up the whole thing to get false sympathy from you."

"And to draw suspicion away from herself," Tobias added. "Yeah, I know all that. But my gut is telling me Isabella is good people. One of the lessons I've learned from alchemy, especially spiritual alchemy, is that you've gotta believe your gut. Even when there's no rational reason to do so. You're certainly keeping my mind preoccupied, Zoe Faust. For that, I thank you. Shall we solve this thing or what? Where *is* Dorian? I have to admit he's good with coming up with plans under strange circumstances like these."

Tobias went upstairs to fetch the gargoyle, but returned a minute later shaking his head. "This is weird. He must've already gone out for the night. It's a bit early."

"He needs to spend even more of the night baking at Blue's to meet the new demand."

"Are you sure that's what he's up to?" Tobias asked.

"Why do you say that?"

Tobias handed me his phone and showed me a photo of the attic. Only it looked nothing like the space I knew. I couldn't believe what I was seeing.

"You took this just now?"

He nodded.

"Help me up the stairs," I croaked.

"You sure?"

"I have to see this with my own eyes."

With the railing, I barely needed Tobias's help on the first set of stairs. The steep, narrow stairs leading to the attic were trickier, but I had to see for myself…

I didn't recognize my attic. Dozens of printouts were taped to the walls, with yards of red yarn strung between the pages. The room had been transformed from a cozy sanctuary to the lair of a conspiracy theorist.

I yanked one paper off the wall. A picture of Isabella Magnus from a newspaper, taken at an art gallery. "This area is a dossier of the whole Magnus family," I said. "Logan, Cleo, Ward, and Cleo's ex the mysterious Archer. Even Logan's parents, Isabella's sister and parents, and Ward's family back in England. We're surrounded by everything publicly available on the family that Dorian could find online and print. Plus the paintings of Philippe Hayden that might be relevant ... and clippings about the Portland art forger who escaped after his studio was raided."

"Look at this side," Tobias said. "Here on this wall, we've also got a few references to Nick and Perenelle—though I'm guessing most of these are wrong. The little fellow has lost it."

I shook my head and picked up a 1970s spy novel sitting on top of a garage sale box of books and magazines. "He's simply impressionable. What do you want to bet the characters in this spy novel constructed a suspect chart like this?"

Tobias ran his hands across his face and stifled a laugh.

"It looks like he's not finished," I said. "The section above the chess set stops abruptly. He must have realized he needed to leave to start baking—"

I broke off when I saw the note Dorian had left for us: *Arrêtez! Stop! Mes amies, I will explain my system once I have returned. There are clues here, but I cannot yet see the forest for the trees.*

————————

I woke up at sunrise with my heart beating furiously, the echoes of a dream fresh but fading. I struggled against the image seared into my mind of Philippe Hayden and Perenelle Flamel as partners in crime, laughing as they imprisoned Nicolas in the painting.

If Philippe Hayden was an alchemist who'd discovered the Elixir of Life thanks to Perenelle, could they have worked together to trap Nicolas in a painting? Why would they have let the painting out of their control, and why steal it back now? How was it related to the death of Logan Magnus?

I cautiously stretched my toes, bent my ankle, and stepped softly onto the hardwood floor. Thankfully, my ankle didn't give way. I felt it twinge, but the ice, poultice, and rest had worked. I could walk with only a minor limp today.

I watered my kitchen window box herb garden and got myself a glass of water with a squeeze of lemon. I slipped on sandals and sat down on the back porch steps, drinking the water as I looked over my garden coming to life with the sun. The plants were covered in dew and the soil was damp from the rain, so I only needed to water the plants in containers on the covered back porch. Max had given me lavender clippings that I'd planted in old tomato cans.

Mint, thyme, and blackberry brambles were taking over the yard. I'd shown Brixton how to safely cut back invasive plants, but he'd resisted cutting down plants that were healthy, asking why we couldn't simply let the yard run wild as long as everything was doing well. He couldn't see the underground network of roots that would squeeze out other plants, choking the life out of them. And he wouldn't believe what he couldn't see.

In the planned part of the garden, kale, parsley, mustard greens, and mizuna were interspersed with fall squashes. The pumpkins were doing especially well. Only a little bit of powdery mildew touched their leaves.

Back inside, I started hot water for tea and rooted through Dorian's misshapen creations to see what I'd like for breakfast. Even with the influx of customers, Dorian still refused to serve anything that looked less than perfect. The misshapen pastries tasted every bit as good—arguably better, for having character and more nooks and crannies for the natural sweetness of crisping in the oven—but of course Dorian believed presentation was an essential part of stoking the palette.

I decided it was late enough that I could knock on Tobias's door to see if he wanted to join me for breakfast. The door swung open as I knocked. The bed was made and the room was empty.

He wasn't in the bathroom or backyard either. I even checked my Airstream trailer.

"Dorian," I called as I carefully climbed the attic stairs. "Do you know where Tobias went? Dorian?"

The attic was empty of life as well. My truck was still in the driveway, so they must have walked to wherever they went. Where had they gone?

Only belatedly did I think to look for a message on my cell phone. But there were no messages. I texted Tobias and he wrote back immediately: At breakfast. Back soon.

I sighed. I'm much better at picking up local languages, including accents and dialects, than adapting to new technology. I prefer landline phones that don't drop a signal and classic cars that can be fixed by hand, and I firmly believe that kitchen tools were perfected in the 1960s. That's when gadgets served multiple purposes and were built to last. I had the same blender I'd used for fifty years. Like my Chevy, all it needed was a new engine every so often.

Tobias's text didn't explain everything, though. Dorian couldn't go out to breakfast. So where was Dorian?

I had a cup of green tea, a fruit and vegetable smoothie made in my blender, and a misshapen carrot cake breakfast cookie Dorian had rejected the day before—the cookie looked like the state of Florida—all before Tobias walked in the front door.

"How are the teashop crowds?" I asked.

"I wasn't at Blue's."

"You weren't? I thought you said you were at breakfast? Don't tell Dorian you've found a better spot."

"I called a car to take me to the Castle to see Isabella again," Tobias said. "She invited me over for an early breakfast. I thought I'd be back sooner."

"So last night wasn't just a one-time sharing of grief…"

"I can take care of myself, Zoe. And so what if there's a risk? What good is living for so long if we don't help people? You used to know that."

"You think I'm not?"

"Hey, where's Dorian?"

"He's not here."

"What do you mean? It's daytime. He should be back here."

"I know."

Tobias picked up his phone.

"He doesn't have a cell phone," I said. "It doesn't work well with his clawed hands. He can only use a proper keyboard and the landline phone in the house."

"That's not what I'm doing. I'm looking to see if there are any news reports of a strange creature sighted." Tobias broke off and pointed at my phone resting on the dining table. "Your phone is blinking. You've got a message."

It was a text message from Brixton, letting me know he'd gone to school and that Dorian was safe at his house for the day.

"Why is Dorian at Brixton's house?" Tobias asked.

"Well, they're friends…" I said, but there was no reason for Dorian to have taken the risk of going to Brixton's. No *good* reason. Not when Brixton was due to come over to our house to work on the garden after school. What were they up to?

The phone rang. The voice on the other end was a whisper. A whisper with a French accent.

"Dorian?" I said.

"Shh!"

"Um ... you're the one who called."

"Yes, yes. Can you drive yet? Because I need you to pick me up at Brixton's home."

"Uh ... "

"Heather was supposed to be working at the teashop," he whispered, "but she felt like painting instead, because the muse struck. She is here! It is difficult for me to stay in stone form for long periods of time now. I will be waiting if you pick me up. We will need a distraction. Perhaps a fire alarm?"

"No fire alarm," I said quickly. "I'll make it work to drive. You can assume stone form for a few minutes when I arrive, and we'll tell Heather that Brixton borrowed my gargoyle statue to draw you for art class and that I'm picking you up."

"This is not very believable, no?"

"Hopefully Heather will be so involved in following her muse that she won't notice."

I hung up.

"What was that about?" Tobias asked.

"Apparently I'm a gargoyle soccer mom."

THIRTY-ONE

I RETURNED HALF AN hour later, safe but with a sore ankle, and set the satchel containing my "statue" on the living room floor. Dorian climbed out and stretched. He flapped his wings and wriggled his horns.

"Now that we can talk," I said, "what were you doing at Brixton's house?"

"I do not suppose you would believe I was assisting him with his mathematics?"

"No."

"You are right." Dorian giggled. "I was helping him with history."

"Before dawn?" Tobias said. "What kind of teenager gets up before dawn?"

Dorian sighed. "You are correct. I had many misshapen pastries last night, so I wished to bring him extras. He is a growing boy, after all. When I was leaving the bag on his window sill, he woke up. We are friends. *Alors*, we conversed. And then it was too late to come home."

I eyed the gargoyle. "What aren't you telling us?"

"You are such a serious, suspicious person, Zoe Faust. I worry for your blood pressure. You are not immortal, you know."

I pinched the bridge of my nose.

"Can we get down to business?" Tobias said. "The conspiracy room in the attic."

"Ah, so you discovered my research. It is not yet complete, so I hope you heeded my note."

"We did," I said. "Otherwise we would have been up all night trying to figure out your methods rather than considering what you'd actually discovered."

"*Bon.* I will meet you in the attic."

"You're not coming?" Tobias asked him.

"You don't know him as well as I do," I said. "He's going to the kitchen."

"Dorian, buddy," Tobias said, "isn't this research more important than cooking? And I've already eaten breakfast. I don't need anything."

Dorian stood to his full height of three-and-a-half-feet, plus a few added inches of wings that stretched past his horns. "You know not of which you speak, Monsieur Freeman. If we do not have regular sustenance, our brains cannot function properly. And if we do not take the time to savor—"

"We'll meet you in the attic," I said, hooking my hand around Tobias's elbow. "You need to pick your battles," I whispered.

"I heard that," Dorian called over his shoulder from the swinging kitchen door. "And yes, this is yet another reason we need food. We must prepare for battle."

While Dorian cooked, Tobias and I cleared space in the attic for the three of us to sit around a table. I moved the chess set from its perch, careful not to move the pieces from Dorian and Tobias's in-progress game, and Tobias hefted the steamer trunk and an ottoman to the table.

"I can barely see these articles with the lines of red yarn covering so much of the walls," Tobias said.

"I have an idea." I reached for my laptop.

Dorian arrived in the attic a few minutes after I'd completed my task. He carried an apple-themed tray: freshly cut apples from the farmers' market next to small dishes of homemade nut butters; mini fresh-baked baguettes filled with thinly sliced apples, figs, and cashew cream; and a pot of jasmine green tea, which I recognized as the batch Max had made.

"A simple mid-morning snack," he said, expertly spreading a white tablecloth with one hand while he balanced the tray in the other. "*Bof!* What is this?"

"He's noticed your contribution," Tobias said.

I'd printed out two dozen pages of what looked like the most relevant articles on the members of the Magnus household, as well as references to art forgery in Portland, and taped them to the bookshelf. I'd been forced to limit myself to that small number because the printer was running out of ink. No red threads connected the information. They were simply there for us to read.

Dorian frowned. "This is not how proper investigators make connections."

"At least we can read the text and see the photos," I pointed out. "But we never would have found all of these articles without you."

Dorian grinned. "I am quite adept at internet searches. My fr—I mean, I have taught myself many things in this strange new world. I prioritized high quality photographs, as you can see. You are certain none of these people are Perenelle Flamel?"

I shook my head as I limped across the attic, lifting pieces of yarn to study each face in the hundreds of images on the walls. "None of these people look like anyone I know."

"Let's take it from the top," Tobias said, pointing at the top left paper. "We've got Logan Magnus, the famous Portland artist who grew up the only child of a famous father, who died by swallowing toxic paint—either by his own hand, which is unlikely, or by force."

"What's not on the walls," I said, "is that Logan had an interest in alchemical artwork and owned Hayden's painting *The Alchemist*."

"Purchased by Cleo Magnus," Dorian said, scampering to the section of wall focused on Logan's daughter. "I have included the auction house in my notes. You see? The auction house is legitimate. I do not believe they are lying about the burglary in which all records of the painting were stolen. There must be a conspiracy afoot. This is why I conducted such thorough research."

"Why the red yarn?" Tobias asked.

"This is how connections are made," Dorian said, pointing his clawed index finger at the intricate red spiderweb.

"But you've got every single paper connected. How does that help—"

"I didn't know Cleo was an artist herself," I said to preempt an argument. I was reading an old article on Cleo I'd taped to the bookshelf. "Or that she owned a lot of waterfront property that she's been renting out as art galleries. I thought she was only an art dealer."

"*Oui*. She studied fine art during her college years."

"And," Tobias said, "Ward Talbot, Cleo's husband, was previously swindled by an art forger. His career as an art dealer was nearly ruined. Damn. That's gotta sting."

"Looks like his English baron father got him back on his feet," I said.

"Even worse for his ego, I'd expect," Tobias said. "You think he could have hated art forgers enough to kill one?"

"We deal in facts here in my attic, Monsieur Freeman," Dorian said. "Such as the fact that I find no signs that any of these people could be an alchemist. They all have families. This is why I have done such extensive research. I fear that we have no leads on Perenelle Flamel and Philippe Hayden. Wherever they are, they are in the shadows."

"The shadows…" I said. "Archer. He's the only person who doesn't have family connections here. And remember, Cleo suspected him of stealing the painting. She thought it was a joke, but—"

"First instincts are often the right ones," Tobias said. "Even if we don't know where they come from."

"Archer, Archer…" Dorian mumbled to himself as he followed incomprehensible lines of yarn. "Ah! Here. 'Artist Archer.' A rather self-congratulatory moniker, is it not? This is how he signs his artwork. Therefore I do not know his surname, so there is no way to find his family."

"He's just a kid," Tobias said, looking at a photo of Archer.

"I felt the same way when I saw him at the gallery," I said. "I don't think he could be as old as Philippe Hayden. Not simply his looks, but the way he carries himself. He's a twenty-something finding himself. Not a 450-year-old painter."

"Unless," Dorian said, drumming his fingers together, "he is a master of disguise."

"We deal with facts in this attic, Monsieur Robert-Houdin," Tobias said, looking at a photo of Archer from a zine. He picked up a sketch of another young man. "This doesn't look like Archer, but this guy doesn't have a name."

"Ah yes," Dorian said. "This is the person presumed to be the art forger who fled the city after his studio was raided earlier this year. I found it in relation to my research on art forgery in Portland. He goes by the name Neo, but his real name is unknown."

Tobias leaned over the gargoyle to get a better look at the photo. "It's a rather generic image. Could be almost anyone."

"If my olfactory senses are not mistaken," Dorian said, "you have been eating bacon. You did not find my leftover breakfast options satisfactory? I know bacon is superb, but I have been surprised not to miss it at all after learning how to cook differently—"

"I went to see a friend," Tobias said.

"She's not a friend," I said. "You can't think of her like that."

"Zoe, don't start."

"Start what? I'm trying to make sure my dear friend doesn't get hurt."

"Isabella?" Dorian said. "The metal-sculptor wife of Logan Magnus? The beautiful woman we see before us on these very attic walls?"

"The murder suspect," I said, "who tried to deflect suspicion off herself by accusing me."

"What happened to trusting me?" Tobias asked.

"It's one thing to let you accept a gift. It's another if you two are bosom buddies now."

Dorian cleared his throat and flapped his wings. "If you would stop bickering, you would see we must send Tobias undercover at the Castle."

Tobias and I stared speechlessly at the gargoyle.

"*Bon*," Dorian said. "I take your silence as agreement. You, Tobias Freeman, will be our mole."

Tobias raised an eyebrow at me. "You weren't kidding about that spy novel."

"I will bake fortifications," Dorian said. "Have you discerned what type of foods are Isabella's favorite?"

"None are needed," Tobias said. "I've already made plans to go to the gallery with her later."

"You—" I began, but Dorian silenced me with a hand on my arm.

"Get yourself invited back to the Castle," Dorian said calmly. If I didn't know better, I would have said he was practicing his hypnosis voice. His stage magician father had unwisely taught him the basics of mesmerism, which he'd tried to teach Brixton.

"I'll see what I can do," Tobias said. "Because whatever I discover will help *both* Zoe and Isabella. That painting of Nick is somehow tied up in her husband's murder."

It made me uneasy to see how much Tobias trusted Isabella Magnus. But he could make his own decisions. And Nicolas's fate might depend on what he could learn.

THIRTY-TWO

It wouldn't do any good to sit at home and wait for Tobias's reconnaissance, and I didn't see what further armchair research I could possibly do, so I went ahead with my plans to go with Max to his mom's birthday dinner in Astoria. Much like Dorian's sense that we needed to slow down and eat good food for our minds to operate at full capacity, I knew that being in the presence of nature and loved ones could have the same effect.

It gave me a shiver to realize how easily I thought of Max as a loved one. But I did. If I got through this mess and rescued Nicolas, I wanted to build a life here in Portland with Max.

Dorian was in the kitchen cooking. Tobias wasn't meeting Isabella at the gallery until later, so he kept me company in the attic as I rooted through my Elixir inventory. I had two online orders to fill before leaving for Astoria, one of them an unusually large one.

My business model was the opposite of what it had been when I was on the road. Then, I'd sold a high volume of small items at flea markets and antique fairs. My postcard bin had been especially successful, featuring World War II trading cards, Victorian food trading cards, and vintage postcards from all over the world that I'd bought when new. Now, since Elixir was focused on selling higher-end items to real collectors, business wasn't as brisk. Some of my more in-demand items included authentic apothecary shop memorabilia, first edition cookbooks, and quirky pieces of miscellany related to healing. My modest income from the online shop was enough to pay my mortgage and bills, and the money generated from Dorian's baking for Blue Sky Teas paid for our groceries.

"Let me know if you need help getting this box to the post office," Tobias said as we wrapped and lifted two large eighteenth-century oil paintings into a shipping container.

"I won't object to you carrying it down the attic stairs."

"Eddie O'Kells of Beaverton must be decorating his house," Tobias said. "This spirit holder and alembic are too old to be used. You do give that disclaimer, right?"

"They're popular these days as ornamental display items. I wish I'd saved more of them."

I thought briefly about emailing the buyer back to ask if he would like to pick up the items to save on postage, since he didn't live too far away, but decided against it. Soon I'd be leaving for the birthday party and Tobias to meet up with Isabella. It wouldn't do for a gargoyle to meet Eddie O'Kells when he picked up his order.

Thinking of Max's mom …

"If only I could make gold," I grumbled. "Then I could buy something nice for Max's mom's sixty-fourth birthday."

"I'm sure she's not expecting anything."

"I want to make a good impression." I ran my hand through my hair. Why was it there were some things in life that made you feel like a self-conscious teenager no matter how old you got? So I was meeting my boyfriend's mom. Why was I nervous? It was silly. I grinned at Tobias. "How's your alchemy these days? I've got a base-ment lab set up for my spagyric tinctures, so it's prepped for working with plants to create herbal medicines. But I don't have any projects going, so my own spirit won't mess with anything you do with min-erals. You know any secrets to get gold-making down from months to hours?"

"I'll be right back." Tobias walked down the stairs to the spare bedroom I'd given him.

"I was joking," I called after him.

He returned a minute later and set a muslin drawstring bag in my hand. I untied the twine bow that held the small package shut. Peering inside, rough chunks of shimmering rocks caught the light. Gold.

"I really was joking," I said. "I can't take that."

"I know you were kidding. And that you don't need it. But think of it as rent."

I looked at the pure gold, the metal that had been held in high esteem above all others. It had never been my favorite, though. Per-haps that's why I'd always been so bad at creating it. There's some-thing about impure lead that speaks to me. Lead is the beginning of an alchemical journey; the world is still wide open to possibility when you have a chunk of lead. Even though you haven't succeeded, you also haven't yet failed.

"I didn't know you were actively practicing physical alchemy," I said.

"When Rosa got sick, I wanted to have enough money to take care of her, whatever she needed. We did a round-the-world cruise too." He chuckled. "The women we met at sea loved the fact that I was taking my elderly mother on a cruise. Rosa *hated* that. But at the same time she loved that I didn't give them the time of day. It was a good trip."

"I'm glad you did it."

"I don't need this leftover stash. And besides, unlike you, I can make more." He grinned. "But I was serious—you don't need it for Max's mom. Pick her some flowers from your garden."

"You're right. Save the gold for an emergency. I have everything I need right here." The antique artifacts of Elixir were objects I'd picked out as special items that I hoped would stand the test of time.

I began collecting after I saw how many people across cultures valued historical objects, and how museums would feature something that was once insignificant but had been given meaning by time. Victorians knew how to do this especially well, bringing back whole fads but ruining them as they did so. The Victorian era is when alchemy got a bad rap, when its true historical applications were skewed to be edgy and cool and look far more like magic than science. That's when the chemists broke off from the alchemists, and I can't say I blamed them.

"I'll pick out something small from my collection." I looked over the homey objects from around the world, from the framed frontispiece of a famous book of alchemy that had fallen apart long ago to a set of handcrafted puzzle boxes.

"I still think flowers are safer. How do you know what she'll like?"

"She's Max's mom. I'll make a guess."

THIRTY-THREE

"I should warn you," Max said.

"Really, there's no such thing as a 'normal' family, Max. They don't exist."

We were nearly to Astoria. As the sun approached the horizon, the rocks off the Oregon coast reminded me of the natural formations common in the Southwest, but these rocks were in the ocean. The US Southwest had been an easy place for me to fit in wherever I parked my Airstream. I didn't attract much attention there, and it also offered me as much solitude as I wanted. Even sharing the national parks with hikers, it was impossible not to feel at one with nature.

"My sister in particular. She's . . . She's going to try and fix you."

"Fix me?"

Max lifted a hand from the steering wheel and reached over to tuck a lock of my white hair behind my ear. "She's going to notice your hair isn't dyed."

"So? It's fine, Max. Really." People with keen observation skills noticed my hair wasn't the white-blonde of some northern Europeans and that I didn't have albinism, so they assumed I'd fried my hair by dying it.

The faint sound of thunder rumbled in the distance. Only half the sky was filled with storm clouds, but the wind was moving quickly. We pulled up at a sprawling two-story white house with a monumental Atlas cedar tree in the front yard. One of its hulking branches bore the marks of hammocks and tire swings.

"This is the house where you grew up?"

"Yup." He grabbed our bags from the back and helped me out of the jeep. My ankle and his cold were nearly better, but not quite perfect.

"I love it."

"Zoe?" Max hesitated before starting up the path to the house.

"What is it?"

"You know this is my mom's birthday…"

"Of course."

"It feels absurd that I don't know this, since I've known you for nearly a year, but… when is your birthday?"

I laughed. "You didn't miss it. It's January first."

January 1 wasn't the day I was born, but it was the birthday I liked to celebrate. I was born under the Julian calendar, where the new year began on March 25. That was decades before the current Gregorian calendar was adopted, and in a community that didn't celebrate birthdays. My old life in Salem felt so far removed from the life I'd been living when I met Ambrose that we chose that day of new beginnings as my symbolic birthday.

"Come on inside before the rain hits," a woman's voice with a thick Texas accent boomed from an open front window. "I know these skies. It's breaking any second."

Sure enough, as we walked past the cedar tree, two fat raindrops fell onto my face.

Max's mom came through the front door and enveloped me in a hug. "I can't tell you how happy I am to finally meet you. I was beginning to think you were a figment of my son's imagination. I'm so glad you could make it tonight."

"Zoe, this is my mom, Mary Jasper. Is Mina here yet, Mom?"

"She's inside cooking." Mary squeezed my hands before letting go of me. She wore steel-tipped cowboy boots over leggings and a blue tunic. Her black hair was cut nearly as short as Max's, giving plenty of room to her radiant smile and freckle-covered nose and cheeks.

"I'm so happy to meet you, Mary," I said as she ushered us inside with the rain pelting behind us. "Happy birthday."

The house was stuffed with the cozy furniture of family life, much of which I guessed had been there since Max's childhood. The side table next to the door, as well as most of the free surfaces, were covered in framed photographs of an extended family.

"You two arrived just in time." A woman who looked very much like Max, from her features to her smart style of dress, stepped out from the kitchen, wiping her hands on an apron with an illustration of a cactus. "There's no way the storm is letting up tonight. Hi, Maxi. This must be Zoe."

Mina shook my hand warmly, then her expression changed. "Your hair ... " she murmured.

"Don't," Max said.

"What?"

"Why don't I get everyone drinks?" Max said, shooting his sister a look.

"Let me show you around the house while the kids get our food and drinks ready," Mary said to me. She grinned as she began the tour with the staircase lined with framed photos. "I swear those two act like kids when they're in the same room together. I almost expect them to stick out their tongues at each other. But they know not to mess with me." She laughed and paused at a photo of a young girl at the gates of a ranch.

"Texas, 1960s?" I asked.

"Max told you about my childhood?"

I shook my head. I'd seen similar ranches during that decade when I was traveling across the country.

"That's me at twelve or thirteen," Mary said. "I grew up in a rural area. My dad's family were Texan farmers and ranchers for generations, and my mom was first-generation Chinese American. I grew up learning to live off the land. I'm a crack shot. Maybe that's what keeps the kids in line." She laughed again. It made her look so much like the girl in the photo.

"I taught Max to shoot as well," she added. "From the start, he hit a bull's-eye every time. Though when he was young he refused to shoot anything besides zombies at the shooting range."

As we proceeded up the stairway, I learned that Mary hadn't had many Chinese friends and had no interest in learning to speak Chinese because she just wanted to fit in. When she met Max's dad in college, she'd found another second-generation immigrant unsure where he fit in. That connection was so wonderful that it had eclipsed the fact that they didn't share the same life goals. They'd been divorced for decades, so Mary used her maiden name, Jasper.

Her twenty-minute tour of the house was mostly focused on telling me about the people in photographs. We returned to the living room and I picked up a photo that had caught my eye when I'd first entered the house.

"This is Max and Mina as kids?" The picture was of two cute kids silhouetted against a boulder with the ocean behind them.

"Did Max tell you why I named her Mina?"

I shook my head.

"She has a birthmark on her neck." Mary's expression grew more serious than I'd thought her happy face capable of. "Two small marks that look like puncture wounds."

I leaned in closer as she pointed at a shadow in the portrait.

"You know what I'm talking about," Mary whispered, "don't you?"

"Dracula?" Was this why Max had warned me?

"Ma!" Mina's voice came from behind us. "Zoe, is she telling you the Dracula story? That's *not* why I'm named Mina."

Mary laughed. "She speaks the truth. That's not why I named her Mina. She's named Willamina after my father, William. Mina has a beautiful ring to it, doesn't it?"

"Except for the fact that my brother is named for a warrior," Mina said, "and I get the diminutive of a patriarch."

"Bite your tongue," Mary said. "You loved your grandpa."

"He was a great man, but that doesn't mean he wasn't a patriarch."

Mary sighed. "She really does have a birthmark on her neck, so she loved to tell kids that story to scare them. Mina has always been the dramatic one of the pair. I grew up reading southern Gothics, and have a beautiful old copy of *Dracula* that Mina found on the bookshelf when she was a bit too young. She loved that it had a character with her name, so she made up that story about herself when she was little. I just borrowed the story once she was old enough for it to embarrass her."

Mina kissed her mom's cheek. "Ma, will you talk some sense into Max? He won't take the zinc I offered. He's got a cold. He's not taking care of himself."

"I heard that," Max called from the kitchen. "Your collards are burning."

Mina swore and rushed back to the kitchen. Mary and I followed.

"I guess I should expect you not to care about your own health," Mina was saying to Max as she stirred the pot, "since you're someone who doesn't care about taking care of people."

"Mina, don't start," Mary said. "And Max, since it's just us, we should have rescheduled. Do I need to make you some chicken soup? And I think we have cokes in the pantry."

"I'm fine," Max said, handing me a glass of sparkling wine. "Truly. It's just the tail end of a cold. Zoe has been taking good care of me."

"Then why are you still sick?" Mina asked.

"He's doing a lot better," I said. "I made him homemade nettle soup the day he got sick. Along with a cayenne tea that seemed to do the trick."

"Nettles?" Mina slipped her phone into her hand and looked up something on the screen. "I specialize in integrative medicine and I've never seen nettles suggested for—"

Max threw his hands in the air. "I only got sick three days ago. I'd say I'm doing pretty well."

Mina's brow drew together. "That's awfully quick a recovery. What else are you taking?"

"I told you, Zoe's been taking good care of me. She found the nettles in my backyard and used what I had on hand."

"Food smells delicious," I said. I breathed in the scents of various chili peppers. I'm usually good at identifying scents, but I didn't recognize all of these.

"Mom's favorites," Mina said. "I hope you like spicy food."

"I love it."

Mina grinned and showed me the range of southern-inspired dishes sitting on the counter, from corn bread to collards, all seasoned with Chinese chili pepper sauces. We sat down to dinner at a round dining table. In the warm house, I'd taken off my sweater and was wearing a short-sleeved silk blouse. I caught Mina studying my arms as I reached for the salad.

"I've never seen a condition like yours," she said.

"Mina, please—" Max said.

"What? I'm a doctor. I could help her. Zoe, have you ever seen a specialist? I've never heard of someone without albinism who has white hair all over."

"A toast to Mom," Max said. "Happy birthday." He stood and toasted, then retrieved a small gift wrapped in newspaper.

"My favorite of your homemade teas!" Mary kissed his cheek.

Mina handed their mom a much more formally wrapped present. Inside was a cookbook holder made of copper.

I handed her a small package as well.

"You needn't have brought me anything," Mary said, but she looked touched. Her face lit up as she opened the kraft wrapping paper to reveal a Victorian vampire hunting kit: a small wooden box containing a stake, mallet, and crucifix.

A wide grin spread across Mary's face. "This looks antique. Is it what I think it is?"

I nodded. "It's over a century old, and it is."

"Had Max told you that story about Mina already?"

"I didn't." Max shook his head, a baffled look on his face. "How did you know?" he whispered to me.

"I have my secrets."

THIRTY-FOUR

AFTER DINNER, MAX'S MOM insisted she and Mina would clean up and they'd join us on the covered back porch. Max and I took cups of chamomile lavender tea to the warm room filled with plants that overlooked the backyard.

"Sorry about Mina," he said. "I warned you she'd try to fix you. She's like that. She's a great doctor, but most things don't interest her. It's only rare cases that make her pay attention. She likes to know the exact mechanisms that make things work."

"That's why she was grilling me about nettles."

"That's just her way."

"I know. I like her. And your mom is the sweetest person on the planet."

"Mom? *My* mom? Mary Jasper Liu? I love her more than anything, but 'sweet' isn't a word I'd use to describe her."

"This house is great," I said as I sipped the tea. Max's special blend. "I bet you have some great memories from this place."

"Before my parents got divorced, my dad's parents spent a lot of time here with us."

I knew Max had been close with his grandparents. He'd spoken of them often. His grandfather had gone back to China after his grandmother passed away, and Max had gone to his grandfather's hundredth birthday celebration earlier that year.

"My grandfather used to take me treasure-hunting along the coast nearby," Max continued. "When I was little I was obsessed with this kids' movie, an adventure about a pirate's treasure that was set here in Astoria. You ever see *The Goonies?*"

I shook my head.

"Really?" Max asked. "I guess you're too young. For my birthday one year, Granddad really buried a treasure for me to find."

"What was the treasure?"

"A treasure chest filled with blocks to build a castle. Which I built here in this room. This is also where ... "

"Where what?"

"It's silly. Never mind."

"Come on." I set down my steaming mug of tea and took Max's hand in mine.

"This is also where my grandmother showed me how to take care of plants."

"Why is that silly?"

"Grandmother had the greenest thumb of anyone I've ever known. When I was a kid, I believed she could truly bring dead plants back to life. It was like magic." He shook his head and squeezed my hand. "Now I know they were only false memories of a child, blending my imagination with what I'd really seen."

"It's not magic," I said. "It's alchemy. The science of transformation. We both coax plants in our backyard gardens back to life from unhealthy states."

"I know. But it was the way she talked about it too. She believed it was magic, and I believed her. Mina was closer with our mom's parents than our dad's, even though she's the one who went on to become a healer. Mina hates that I became a cop. She thinks she's the only one who helps people."

"There's more than one way to help people," I said, as much for my own benefit as Max's. Since giving up my Paris apothecary shop, I hadn't been helping people as directly as I used to, and I'd even begun to wonder if I was moving away from my humanity, the danger for alchemists. That was one of the reasons I was eager to sell my tinctures at the Autumn Equinox Fair the following weekend. My prices were on a sliding scale, as they always had been, charging however much people could afford.

"You never talk about your family," Max said.

"I lost them a long time ago. Even the couple who took me in … I lost them too."

"They all died?"

"My biological family are long dead, but … " I thought of Nicolas, who'd shown me more fatherly affection and guidance than I'd experienced in my life. "I ran away and lost touch with the surrogate parents who saved my life and mentored me."

"Sorry. I can tell it's painful for you to talk about. It's okay. You don't have to tell me."

"You're lucky to have your mom and Mina."

"I know. And as much as we disagree, Mina's partly right about me. About why I became a cop. One of the reasons I wanted to be a detective had nothing to do with helping people. I love the feeling—the personal satisfaction—of catching the bad guys. In that pirate treasure movie I loved as a kid, the scrappy bunch of teenage friends come together to defeat the bad guys at the end. I always wanted to be like them."

I laughed and Max looped his fingers through mine.

"What do you say we watch the movie before bed?" he suggested. "It's a silly kid's movie, but …"

"I'd love to."

Sitting there on the Oregon coast in a cozy covered porch with a wild storm swirling around us, I knew it was the calm before the storm I'd return to in my quest to rescue Nicolas. But I let myself enjoy it. Just for the night.

———

In the morning, mist surrounded the seaside house but no rain was falling. Mina had left before dawn so she could make it back home in time to start the day at her medical practice. Max's mom packed half a dozen mason jars of leftovers to send home with us. She also handed a second bag to Max. He peeked inside and smiled.

"What is it?" I asked, looking over his shoulder.

"Homemade chicken soup and Sprite. What she gave me as a kid when I was sick." He gave his mom a hug. "This is why you got up so early."

"Of course," Mary said. "But I forgot one thing. Zoe, can you help me get it?"

I followed Mary into the house.

"You know, all three of us are both right and wrong," she said. "Me, you, and Mina. We each have different ways of taking care of Max. I'll tell you a secret I learned from my in-laws. It's not the method and medicine that matters—it's the love behind it. We all love him. It's the love that cures."

She gave me a hug and walked me out.

"What did she give you?" Max asked after his mom helped me into the jeep and waved goodbye.

"Advice," I said with a smile. It had been a magical evening of family and pirate treasure, convincing me anything was possible. I had survived wars and witchcraft trials. I almost believed I could get Nicolas out of the painting, and also have the nearly normal life I wanted to have with Max.

"Are you going to tell me how you picked out the perfect gift for my mom?"

I leaned over and kissed him. When I pulled back, I held up two small bundles in my hand. "I didn't," I said. "I picked out three. Once I met her, I selected the one that seemed most appropriate."

Max laughed and started the engine. "Even narrowing it down to three, you're still pretty magical, Zoe Faust."

As we drove away from Astoria and headed closer to real life, I felt less and less magical. The unanswered questions about Philippe Hayden, the Flamels, and the Portland art forger who might have been a murderer began to weigh on me again.

We rounded a curve in the road and the clouds transformed from leaping rabbits into columns of trees swaying in the wind. But it wasn't the clouds that had changed. It was my perspective. Just like in a Philippe Hayden painting, this was an optical illusion. Everything was connected to Philippe Hayden. I needed to figure out how.

Max had a long day ahead of him, so he dropped me at home. I would have been disappointed to part with him if I hadn't needed to do so much that day.

I found Dorian and Tobias in the attic playing chess. Tobias was winning.

"Monsieur Freeman learned very little with Isabella Magnus yesterday," Dorian said, not looking up from the board.

"Sorry, Zoe. I didn't get any closer to finding the stolen painting."

"Then it's a good thing I have a plan," I said. "You up for a trip to the library?"

The kids had checked out as many art history books as they could, but there were still more in the library. With all his red yarn, Dorian was looking at present-day connections, but I knew there was more to find out from the past.

Tobias and I walked under the ivy-covered walkway that led to the library. I needed the help of a librarian, but my heart sank as we stepped into the building. The librarian at the information desk was the one who'd revoked my library card. He looked up with a smile, but his helpful expression turned to a deep frown when he recognized me.

Before the desk librarian could berate me, another librarian with bright orange hair swooped up to me from where she'd been shelving books. "You're the chef at Blue Sky Teas, aren't you?"

"You recognize me?" I tucked a short lock of hair behind my ear and reminded myself the paper had only come out a few days before. Public attention was fleeting. People would forget about me soon enough. I hoped.

"Of course." The librarian beamed. "Your breakfast carrot cake cookies are to die for. It was rad to see you recognized in the weekly. Are you here looking for cookbooks? If so, I'm sorry to tell you that a library patron defaced most of them, so they're in storage being evaluated for repair."

"I'm sorry to hear it," Tobias said. He steered us away from the other librarian seated at the desk. "There's something we could use your help with."

Tobias and I sat at the most secluded table I could find, looking through the stack of books my librarian fan had brought us.

I've never fully grasped why some artists become famous while others languish in obscurity, but I understand all too well that much of life is the accidents of history. If Nicolas hadn't found me, what would I have become?

My stomach gave a loud rumble. I was about to suggest we take a break at the teashop to nourish ourselves, so we'd remain effective, when Tobias's breath caught. I looked up at him as he began to chuckle.

"I've found your museum doppelgänger," he said, pushing a book across the table.

On the center of a page was a painted portrait of two young people, a brother and sister, done in the style of Philippe Hayden. Time stopped. I stared at the portrait and forgot to breathe.

"Everything okay?" Tobias asked. "It was a silly joke. I'll get back to work—"

"It's not that," I said with a shaky voice. "I know the subjects of that portrait."

How could I not? I was one of them.

"This," I said, "is me and my brother, Thomas, in front of the hearth at Nicolas Flamel's house."

I now knew who Philippe Hayden was. And I didn't know why it had taken me so long to realize it was her.

THIRTY-FIVE

1597, PRAGUE, BOHEMIA

THE MORE BEAUTIFUL A painting, the less likely it was to contain the true secrets of alchemy. That was the way it was—before Philippe Hayden. Alchemy *versus* art.

Alchemy had always been handed down through secret codes shared through secret associations. Those coded illustrations resided in woodcuts, not in paintings. Paintings with alchemy as the subject matter existed, but they were painted by artists who had no knowledge of alchemy itself. Those artists had patrons who envisioned alchemy as a romantic pursuit rather than the backbreaking labor it truly was. Therefore the artists painted the pleasing settings their patrons wanted.

Philippe, meanwhile, wished to hide alchemy's secrets in artwork that would be displayed, so that more worthy people might discover the science. Men and women, regardless of their stature in life, could have a chance to use alchemy if they so wished. Philippe knew what it was like to be kept outside, unable to obtain delicious knowledge.

Coming to a royal court was the best way the painter had found to attain the status of a great artist whose work might appear before the public, not only now but in future generations.

There was one last thing to try. Could such a transformation as had been achieved with the alchemical painting of the gold nuggets possibly work with something *living*?

Philippe hesitated, then stepped outside. Night had fallen and the moon had risen. That was a good sign. The moon held power—especially to someone with such gifts. The artist stepped back inside and lit additional candles.

With the outside world fading away, Philippe used focused intent, this time concentrating on a dying dandelion flower. Using arsenic and dragon's blood from the alchemy lab, the painter recreated the flower on canvas.

As had happened with the gold, the flower disappeared from the side table and appeared on the canvas. But at great cost … Philippe collapsed onto the floor from the exertion and did not awaken until first light.

Stiff joints did not detract from feeling exuberance at what appeared on the canvas that morning The dying flower had not deteriorated further during the night. *Its life force had been suspended.*

This was no time to be timid. Confidence was needed for the next stage of transformation to succeed. After several deep breaths, Philippe reached *inside* the painting. The canvas gave way. The flower and gold now sat in the painter's hand, exactly as they had been before entering the painting.

But in great excitement, the painter had failed to look around. Joy turned to horror as the shadow of a man appeared.

———

Edward had been watching the alchemist since daybreak. Now that Philippe was working for him, Edward had a key to enter the rooms at his pleasure, yet he still preferred to watch the artist secretly. At first he had considered waking Philippe, who was sleeping not in bed but on the stone floor. As the daylight from the one window woke the man, Edward was kneeling behind a row of canvases. He remained hidden until he understood what the alchemist was doing. This was the secret. Philippe had extracted a living flower and chunk of gold from within the painting.

"Hello, Philippe," said Edward, stepping out from behind the canvases. "You and I must speak. It appears I have been underestimating alchemy and you have more to teach me."

Philippe nearly dropped the flower, but had the presence of mind to quickly recover. His eyes narrowed and his chin thrust out defiantly.

That's when Edward saw it. Philippe had no Adam's apple. He wouldn't have noticed it had it not been for other subtle clues that Edward hadn't thought much of. The artist's diminutive size wasn't abnormal; many people had been malnourished in childhood. Philippe's voice had also not fully matured.

Edward's eyes dropped to the painter's chest. It was impossible to detect its form. The artist wore a loose robe, caked with dirt. Only it wasn't dirt. Edward realized that the air in this supposedly dirty room had a more pleasant odor than in other houses within the castle walls. The "dirt" was a carefully constructed mixture of paints. And Philippe's hair. It was not the hairstyle of a woman, yet the short hair revealed a petite head.

"Who *are* you?" Edward hissed. "*Mademoiselle.*"

He watched in awe as the painter's eyes grew wide. He'd been right. This was no man.

"You insult me, sir?" the painter said.

"If I send for a guard," Edward said, "he will most certainly have a less pleasant way of proving you are a woman. Tell me, who are you?"

Philippe's thin shoulders shook. With rage or with fear, Edward wasn't sure. He waited for the man—er, woman—to speak.

"Does it matter?" the masquerading woman asked.

"No. You're right. It does not." Edward took in the painter, seeing him—her—in a new light. "The only thing that matters is that you can trust me with your life. As long as—"

"There's always an *as long as*."

Edward arched an eyebrow. "As long as you agree to my plan."

The woman nodded. "I have already agreed to teach you the steps to true alchemy."

"I'm afraid it's too late for that," Edward said. "You had your chance. Now I desire more. You will show me how to move gold into and out of a painting."

She laughed without humor. "You have smuggling in mind?"

"Such a crass word for enterprising individuals who have faithfully served their king. You and I are going to be Rudolf's most favored artisans. And very, very rich."

There was no use pretending. She wasn't physically strong enough to resist the men who would tear her robe from her and see she was a woman. "Philippe" nodded.

She closed her eyes and breathed in the scents of the raw minerals she ground and mixed to transform into the pigments that would come alive as images of the natural world. Sulfurous dragon's blood, earthy ochre, metallic carbon, tinny chalk. Natural minerals she could command. She was not as powerful as Edward, but she was a force of nature with a brilliant mind, with an equally brilliant mind supporting her.

"If Nicolas Flamel doesn't hear from me within the week with a message that I'm well," she said, "there will be trouble. He expects regular letters from me."

"He knows you're a woman?"

"Of course. I'm his wife. Perenelle Flamel."

THIRTY-SIX

"Fire," I whispered, chastising myself for never seeing it before. "That's why Perenelle chose the surname Hayden. Flamel means *flame* in Old French, and Hayden means *fire* in Welsh. Philippe Hayden isn't working with Perenelle. He *is* Perenelle Flamel."

Tobias let out a whistle, raising the ire of the librarian who'd suspended my card. I couldn't check out the book, so I snapped a quick photo on my phone. We left the books and fled to my truck. The sky above had turned gray and oppressive. I pulled my silver coat around me as we walked through the parking lot.

"You're driving," I said, tossing Tobias the keys.

"Your ankle acting up again?"

I shook my head. "My memories are." I stole a glance at the image on my phone. *Brother and Sister, artist unknown, France, circa 1700.*

The painting, now in a small museum in France, was accompanied by a one-paragraph description. The curator speculated that the young woman might have been from a bourgeois family who had fallen on hard times because her green dress would have been unusual for a peasant girl of the time. I smiled to myself. Green had always befitted me. Perenelle had dyed the fabric so we could have the dress made for me. And I was neither peasant nor nobility. We had existed in a strange realm of society, creating health and wealth to help others but never enjoying Nicolas's gold ourselves. The description also noted the flattering way the faces of the brother and sister were featured, bathed in the light of the window in an otherwise dark room. It was true. Thomas's angelic face held a hint of mischief, as it always did, and his kind eyes were captured exactly as I remembered them. This painting was, the curator concluded, most likely painted by an artist who had familial ties to the young brother and sister.

"Why didn't the Flamels tell me she was Philippe Hayden?" I said once we were inside the truck. "I didn't even know she was a painter." Perenelle was the one who'd been especially drawn to the more colorful alchemical ingredients, though, and most appreciated the paintings in their home. She made no secret of the fact that she loved art, and I'd seen her sketch me and Thomas, but I hadn't known she'd also painted our portrait in secrecy. I should have suspected she would do such a thing, but I'd been too absorbed in my own foolish life at the time.

"I can imagine her reasons," Tobias said. "A woman in the late medieval era? You know what that's like."

"I'm from the Enlightenment, thank you very much." I forced a laugh, but it didn't take.

"This explains for sure how there are so many paintings attributed to Hayden over a longer period of time than one artist could have lived. They aren't forgeries. They're alchemy."

Tobias started the engine, and we drove home. We found Dorian in the kitchen, whisking lemon curd in a double-boiler on the gas stove.

"You missed lunch," he said petulantly. "And I am out of several ingredients. You left before I could give you my list."

"We found something more important," Tobias said as I held up my phone so Dorian could see the image.

"I have seen this meme," Dorian said, never missing a beat with his whisking. "It is very old now, but I appreciate the effort. You look very much like the woman in this old portrait. If the game were a contest, you would win."

"It *is* her," Tobias said.

"*Pardon*?"

"This woman in the dress—it's Zoe."

In silence, Dorian turned off the burner, jumped down from his kitchen stool, and wiped his hands thoroughly on the apron. He proceeded to take the phone from my hand, his liquidy black eyes looking from me to the screen and back again. "It is true. But how? I thought you did not sit for any portraits."

"Perenelle Flamel is Philippe Hayden."

"*Alors*, she is truly the one who has imprisoned her husband!" Dorian cried. "Perenelle Flamel and Philippe Hayden, one in the same, have trapped Nicolas."

"No," I said, shocked by how emphatically the word burst from my mouth.

"But you were the one who theorized—"

"Not this. Now that we know Perenelle Flamel and Philippe Hayden are the same person, we know there's more going on than we realized."

"I fear Zoe is hysterical again," Dorian said.

"Women throughout history have been called far worse," I said. "This is exactly my point. Perenelle had to disguise the fact that she was a painter."

Although Perenelle had been distant with me, I couldn't imagine her turning against Nicolas. Especially not after seeing this loving portrait she'd painted of me and Thomas.

"Zoe, it'll be okay," Tobias said. He said it in what I imagined was his bedside manner when he treated patients in his ambulance. "But you have to face the facts. She's been creating and selling Hayden's work for centuries—and stopping anyone who got in her way. Everything points to Perenelle."

"She imprisoned Nicolas because he wished to stop her nefarious deeds," Dorian said. "She is a bad woman, Zoe. Trapping someone in a work of art for eternity is a special kind of evil." He shuddered and folded his wings around himself.

"No," I said again. "You're both wrong. Look at this painting of Thomas and me. Look at the love she put into it. She couldn't have imprisoned Nicolas."

Tobias put a hand on my shoulder. "Max would tell you to follow the evidence where it led, wouldn't he?"

"The evidence only tells us she was Philippe Hayden, a brilliant and infamously reclusive painter. People believe Hayden's artwork was forged on a large scale for another hundred years, but now we know it was Perenelle the whole time."

"Why didn't Nick mention her in the note?" Tobias asked. "He didn't say he was imprisoned *with* her."

"He didn't say she had done it to him, either."

"Because you wouldn't have believed him. Just like you're not believing it now."

"*Excusez-moi,*" Dorian said, tapping his gray forehead. "My little gray cells have told me something both of you are forgetting. We are missing many words in the letter. This is why we failed to understand that Monsieur Flamel was trapped *inside* the painting, and believed instead that the work of art contained a clue." Dorian clasped his clawed hands behind his back and paced as he spoke. "There is most likely additional relevant information we will never be able to learn from the worn piece of paper. We must glean what we can from external facts in conjunction with the letter. First, we know Perenelle to be Philippe Hayden. We agree on this point."

Tobias and I nodded.

"*Bon*. Second, she is a woman of high intelligence. We know this from her clever paintings that are both visually pleasing and clever with optical illusions. It was also astute for her to take a similar name, so she would sign her signature properly and respond to the name." Dorian paused and clasped his clawed hands together. "Third, she is an alchemist who discovered the Elixir of Life long before Zoe was born. I have seen her faux grave in Paris. Now, what is always a lurking danger to alchemists when they live too long? Tobias, why don't you educate us?"

"Okay, Socrates. But Zoe already knows the answer as well."

I walked to the spot in the kitchen where light from the window was falling. Sunlight poured into the kitchen from a break in the clouds. Philippe Hayden paintings commonly captured morning or evening light coming through a window in an alchemist's rooms. "You both think Perenelle lost her humanity. You believe that's why Nicolas needed to stop her, so she turned on him and trapped him in the painting."

"Pretty much," Tobias said.

"Regardless of what we think she has done," Dorian said, "we must seek for her to get answers. She, and whatever it is she is hiding. For she is certainly hiding something."

"Of course she is," I snapped. "She was an intelligent woman trying to be an alchemist and a painter in a time when women were property. Of course she used deception."

"The question," Tobias said, "is how far she went."

"Yes, Monsieur Freeman. Has Perenelle Flamel been living her long life as a murderess? Is it she who has been in search of the painting containing her husband? Did she murder Logan Magnus when she found it in his possession and then abscond with his phoenix pendant, which I discovered while f... while ... um ... "

"Are you all right?" I asked.

"Of course. Why would I not be?"

"You stumbled over your words."

Dorian smiled. "You are worried the Elixir of Life is fading for me, as a gargoyle who is an untested subject for alchemical science. *Non.* I can assure you I am perfectly healthy. Even a gargoyle has a slip of the tongue now and again."

"We're getting off track," Tobias said. "Why would Perenelle kill Logan Magnus?"

"She wouldn't," I said. *Unless she'd lost her humanity...*

"So ... " Tobias said. "What do we do now?"

We looked at each other in silence.

"*Bon,*" Dorian said quietly. "Zoe has had a breakthrough. You can see it on our benefactor's porcelain, heart-shaped face."

"She has?" Tobias whispered as he studied my face.

"It's not really a breakthrough," I said. "Dorian has been telling me about all the books he's been reading. The Gothic novels are without value—"

"Bite your tongue," Dorian said.

"—but the detective novels suggest that when stuck, it's helpful to compile a list of what we know. Poisonous pigments, an artist in disguise, an imprisoned alchemist, and an art forger. Logan Magnus and Perenelle Flamel, two artists centuries apart, are the two threads connecting everything. Only I don't see how they're intertwined."

"Logan Magnus is no more," Dorian said. "*Alors,* we must find Perenelle."

"I wish I'd taken the time to get to know her better," I said softly. "I was so young at the time. I didn't make the effort to find out why Perenelle acted as she did."

195

THIRTY-SEVEN

1597, PRAGUE, BOHEMIA

THERE HAD ALWAYS BEEN fire in her. For her necessary male alias, Perenelle had chosen the given name Philippe so she could sign her name with the *P* flourish she'd always loved. And Hayden because, like Flamel, it meant fire.

When she'd married Nicolas more than two hundred years before, it had felt like the most natural thing in the world, in every way. Her whole life had clicked and fallen into place. Even when he told her about alchemy, it was as if she'd known it all along and was simply waiting for someone to teach her this particular language.

Before their marriage, her language had been paint. But she'd never been respected as much as her male contemporaries even though she was far more talented than most, and her paintings had been relegated to the farthest reaches of the ancestral home of her first husband. She was lucky he'd cared for her and indulged her interests, from books to art. He gave her the means to obtain the minerals to create her paints. She ground and added an egg base to the pigments herself, and contentedly settled into a studio on his estate, transforming raw materials into paints and performing what to her at the time was the greatest magic she knew: giving new life to a dying world by documenting it with pigments. She painted a portrait of her first husband before he died, and he told her she had a true gift. She made him look as he did, but at the same time more vibrant, less sickly. She'd captured his *essence*.

Grieving her first husband, Perenelle hung his portrait in the main hall. His sister immediately ordered it taken down, unwilling to have the ancestral home defiled by an amateur painting done by a woman.

That was the day Philippe was born. Perenelle packed her art supplies and took her substantial inheritance to Paris, where she sold her "invalid brother Philippe's" paintings through an intermediary, signed with an ornate *P*.

It was Paris where she met Nicolas, while sketching Notre Dame. Nicolas later told her that as soon as he saw the stains on her hands, he knew she was destined to be an alchemist.

"Why me?" she had asked.

"The minerals you chose to work with," he'd answered. "You sense the essences that represent life. That's why you're drawn to these substances. And why they respond to your touch."

He smiled so warmly and with such understanding that Perenelle knew that from that day forward she would do anything in the world for this man. She proposed marriage the following week. She feared if she didn't do it herself, Nicolas would be too proper to cross their differences in class.

Working with Nicolas, she found the Elixir of Life more quickly than most, because her own experiments with color had prepared her for the concentration, intent, and stages required in alchemy.

She used mineral extracts and salts from stones milled from the village where she was born to form the Philosopher's Stone, and she was superb at creating gold from graphite.

The two lived happily in Paris for many years, giving generously to charity with the true gold they both created. Nicolas wasn't close to the few alchemists they knew because the others weren't as accepting of Perenelle. She didn't mind. It gave her more time to paint.

After leaving Paris for the countryside, Nicolas built an alchemy lab and took on worthy apprentices who would go on to do good for the world, and Perenelle's painting flourished. "Philippe" began to gain recognition.

But Perenelle was restless. She wished not only to live up to her full potential but also to bring alchemy to a broader worthy audience through her art, reaching more people than Nicolas could through the pupils he found. And she had a wild theory of alchemical painting, which had never worked in her solitary laboratory workshop, but perhaps with the energy of more alchemists and artists it might be possible.

Nicolas brought word that Rudolf II's court was offering patronages to both alchemists and painters, and he encouraged her to go. They were already good at hiding, so he wasn't worried that his wife would be recognized as a woman, or as Perenelle Flamel. He cut her beautiful orange curls short himself.

If only she hadn't been restless … Nicolas never would have suggested it otherwise. And she wouldn't be in this mess now. It was as if fate were taunting her. Showing her what might have been, but making the achievement of it impossible. She knew she would never let another woman repeat her mistakes if she had any power to prevent it.

THIRTY-EIGHT

"I WILL NOT MAKE the mistake of leaving us unfed," Dorian said. "It is scientifically proven that the mind cannot focus at full capacity if one's body is starving. Zoe, would you pick a pint of blackberries from the backyard? I wish to make another dessert *papillote* to accompany a stuffed sweet potato as a late lunch."

"You want me to pick the blackberries instead?" Tobias asked. "Those brambles look a bit treacherous for that ankle, Zoe."

I put my foot up in the living room while Dorian and Tobias cooked, thinking about finding Perenelle's painting of Nicolas. Now that I knew Perenelle Flamel was Philippe Hayden, I was even more confused about the theory of a forger at work here. Perenelle lived a long life, so her artwork would span a longer period than art historians would accept as legitimate. The paintings that experts thought too modern to be painted by Hayden could easily be hers. But what did that have to do with the modern-day Portland art forger Neo, Logan Magnus's strange death, and the theft of Nicolas's painting?

If we were to believe Isabella, Logan Magnus had found proof of the identity of the forger. Had Isabella been telling the truth about Logan's discovery? And how was it related to the painting of Nicolas that experts thought was a forgery? Thanks to Dorian's research I knew someone who was knowledgeable about forgeries—and quite concerned about them, because he'd been swindled himself.

Ward Talbot emailed me back immediately and agreed to meet at the teashop. A nice, crowded space. But I'd never get there if I told Dorian and Tobias what I was up to. As I crept silently across the living room floor towards the door, I smiled at the sound of the gargoyle and former slave singing folk songs in the kitchen.

———————

I waited with a mug of chai and a mini loaf of cran-apple nut bread at my favorite tree-ring table in the corner, with a perfect view of the weeping fig tree and Heather's paintings. When Ward walked in, Cleo was with him. They were both dressed stylishly in black, as they'd been when I'd seen them before.

"Thanks for meeting me," I said. "I ordered a pot of chai and this cran-apple loaf we can share, or I can get something else."

"Chai and nut bread are perfect," Ward said, pouring two cups for himself and Cleo. His British accent and the tea service made me feel like I was back in England. "And I know what you're thinking. You wish I hadn't brought Cleo. Oh, I know you like her. But I bet you're worried I won't reveal my art purchase blunders in front of her."

Cleo laughed. "I know more about it than he does, so he knew he'd better bring me … " She spun her head around.

"Are you all right?" I asked.

"These paintings. This is the artist who got my dad interested in the art of alchemy."

"Have you met Heather?" I glanced at my favorite painting, which depicted a tree transforming into a person.

"I haven't had the pleasure. She doesn't do many shows."

"She works here." I nodded toward the counter. "If you'd like to meet her, she's at the counter right now."

"Really? A talent like this shouldn't be behind a checkout counter. But I know how it is to be an unrecognized artist."

I introduced them. Heather squealed and hugged Cleo, and the two were immediately immersed in conversation. Blue shook her head but took over the register, and I sat back down with Ward.

"I'm glad she's so happy with a kindred spirit," he said, looking fondly at Cleo. "She needs all the distractions she can get. She's already quite upset about her father's death, and now that the painting he loved has been stolen, that's made it even worse."

"No word on it?"

Ward shook his head. "But you wanted to ask me about my experience of being swindled by an art forger. I know you didn't put it quite as crassly as that, but when you asked about a potential forgery in an antique painting you had acquired, I knew it was why you asked me in particular. Tell me, how much do you know about this business?"

"A little bit, because of the antique books I sell through my business. I've encountered a few questionable items, and I know to look for provenance so I can have proof of an object's history to show the buyer. But I haven't encountered many forgeries."

I knew *in theory* how to look for provenance, though in truth I'd had little opportunity to put that theoretical knowledge into practice. Most of the items I sold had been new when I bought them. Put a Victorian canned food trading card in a box for a hundred years, save the original packaging, and it takes on new value. But it also meant I didn't have a lot of experience sleuthing for provenance.

"Forgers," Ward said, "often *want* to be caught. They do it for their egos, after being rejected by the art establishment."

"Isn't that an oversimplification? Van Meegeren didn't want to be caught."

"Didn't he? Look at how many risks he took. In the end, he loved the fame. But he's an outlier anyway." Ward ignored his tea and leaned across the table. "Forgers like Tom Keating and Shaun Greenhalgh purposefully painted anachronisms into their paintings, and used modern synthetic paints. Those two were screaming to be caught, to show up the art world snobs who'd rejected them as untalented. They wanted money, certainly, but that was secondary. And Lothar Malskat wanted to be found out so badly that he sued *himself* so people would believe him."

"You sound like you approve."

"If I hadn't been a victim myself, I'd say it was a victimless crime. Because it usually only harms the very rich or the very corrupt. The biggest problem is that it taints the way conservators view art. It plants the seed of doubt even when the art is authentic."

I refreshed our tea from the china teapot in the center of the table. "What happened in your case?"

Ward cringed. "I'm afraid it was my own ego that got me. A successful forger paints not what an original painting would have looked like, but what their current audience *wants to see*—subjects a modern audience has fantasized about seeing their favorite Renaissance painter portray, and that the artist theoretically *could have* painted during a period of unrecorded years while he was finding his style." He shook his head. "An added layer of the con is what convinced me: the seller. The man who gave me a 'great deal' was an elderly chap in a wheelchair who was downsizing and having his family estate in Lancashire cleared out. In the attic, low and behold, the house cleaner found a forgotten Philippe Hayden."

"Yours was a Hayden?"

"That's why I was so keen on attending the auction where *The Alchemist* was being sold. What's the situation in your case?" he asked me.

"Antique show find. Red flags from a similar story from the elderly saleswoman."

"That's a rather vague answer." Ward paused and appraised me. After a few moments, he laughed. "I didn't take you for a busybody. But apparently I've been swindled again. Why did you really invite me here?"

"I messed up the police investigation," I said truthfully, "by finding the pendant Isabella made for Logan. I want to help make it right."

"Ah. Guilt. A strong motivator. This all makes more sense now. Well, what I can tell you is this—Cleo's mom is hiding something."

"You don't think—"

"No, of course not. She loved Cleo's father passionately. But there's something making me uneasy..."

I was surprised by the emotion that covered his face. *Fear.*

"Hi you two," Cleo said, sitting back down at the table. "What did I miss?"

Ward leaned over and kissed her cheek. "Nothing more than an art forgery history lesson. You would have done a much better job, but it looks like you made a new friend." He ran his hand around her ear, where a fall flower was now braided into her hair.

"Isabella has a—" I began.

"Yes," Ward cut me off. "You were saying how much you loved her metal sculptures."

So Cleo didn't know of her husband's suspicions about dear old mom.

"Cleo," I said, "I really am sorry to have caused your family further grief by finding the pendant your mom made for your dad."

"Mom would have found something to obsess about, if it hadn't been you. She's like that. At least this way we'll get the charm back. Otherwise it might have been lost forever. Like Dad's painting."

"I don't know why the police won't return the pendant to her," Ward said. "It clearly has nothing to do with the case—if there is one."

"So you believe he could have killed himself?" I asked.

"What else? He had the most terrible mood swings."

"Mom doesn't want it to be true," Cleo said softly. "I just want to be able to mourn properly. Ward, I don't feel like anything sweet right now. Could you get me a black tea with lemon?"

"Of course." He popped a piece of nut bread in his mouth and headed for the counter.

"Did you want to tell me something?" I asked Cleo.

"That obvious?"

"Not to him. He adores you."

"He's a wonderful man, but he has his blind spots. That's why I wanted to tell you this alone. I'm not sure the theft of Dad's painting was really a theft."

"You're not?"

"Mom hasn't been herself since Dad died. Now that I don't believe Archer stole the painting, I wonder if Mom did something to the painting herself. Not on purpose. Just ... "

"What would she have done to the painting?"

"I don't know. She's just not herself." Cleo shook her head. "I guess it'll take her time to get back to normal. I can't imagine anything being normal ever again."

And I was keenly aware how far I was from the normal life I wanted here in Portland. In order to give myself that life, I had to rescue Nicolas, stop the police from looking into Tobias's past, and finally tell the truth to Max. *Right*. I could use the help of some little gray cells to figure out how exactly to rise to the impossible challenge.

THIRTY-NINE

WALKING HOME, I WAS slower than usual with my injury, but I still took the long way, along the waterfront by the Logan Magnus gallery. The walk provided a mix of trees along one side of the popular waterfront path, and industrial warehouses and homeless tents on the other. My ankle gave a twinge when I turned sharply, but walking on flat ground wasn't too bad.

Frustration threatened to overtake my emotions, but I reminded myself that he'd been in the painting for years, if not centuries. A few more days wouldn't make much difference. Normally, walking in nature would clear my head, but not that afternoon. I couldn't understand why I felt so nervous ... What was that noise?

I whirled around, wincing as my ankle objected to the unplanned movement.

There was no one behind me. Thunder rumbled in the distance. I decided the noise that had made me feel uneasy must have been just another crash of thunder, below my conscious awareness.

As soon as I walked into the house, I smelled the intermingled scents of sweet and savory but couldn't place the fragrances. The kitchen was empty, and a note from Dorian was on the counter. The gargoyle wrote that he and Tobias had eaten all the stuffed sweet potatoes and blackberry *papillote*, but he'd made me a small jackfruit and mushroom pizza that he'd left in the oven so I could reheat it for a late lunch. He knew me well. I have a tendency to single-mindedly focus on what I'm working on—a blessing and a curse for an alchemist—so I sometimes forgot to eat. But Dorian's note had no trace of admonition.

I peeked into the cool oven. The sweet scents of jackfruit meat and cashew cheese wafted out, cut with the sharp scent of red pepper. The crispy cornmeal crust looked delicious. I turned on the oven. While it heated, I stepped into the backyard garden. The cold rains of the week were making the arugula and mustard greens tougher, so I guessed Dorian would want to gently cook them instead of using them raw in a salad as I usually did. I picked some of the smaller arugula leaves to add to the pizza.

When I came back inside, Dorian was in the kitchen shaking his head. "If you reheat it at this low temperature, you will have a soggy pizza. Is that what you want?"

I gave the gargoyle a hug. "Don't ever change, Dorian."

He patted my shoulder with a wing. "Why so sentimental this afternoon? Has something else occurred?"

"Nothing. That's the problem."

"You are troubled."

I studied the gargoyle as he peeked into the oven. "You're uneasy as well."

"Of course. Monsieur Freeman is behaving strangely—"

"Not you too. I trust Tobias completely. That's not why I'm worried."

"I will leave you to your pizza. It must cook for seven more minutes. I will be upstairs. I was reading an excellent Gothic novel."

I watered the herbs in the kitchen's window box planters while I waited for the pizza to finish crisping. I sat down at the dining table with a slice of steaming pizza, but before I could take a bite, fists banged on the door.

I hadn't been expecting Brixton, but glancing out the window on the way to the door, I saw his bike lying askew in the driveway. He'd been working weekends at the teashop but still coming over to my house two afternoons a week to learn about gardening. Had I lost track of days?

I opened the door and Brixton blew past me. "He in the attic?" he asked, already halfway up the stairs. "Dorian!"

"What did he do?" My ankle protested as I tried to follow him up the stairs. I winced and sat down on the step.

Brixton turned back and helped me up. "He roped Veronica into helping him do research—"

"That was my fault," I said. "Checking out those library books was my idea, but it's harmless."

"That's not what I'm talking about. Art history library research is cool. But now? He's having her track down antique alchemy books kept in Europe. He's looking for that backward alchemy book that brought him to life—the one that almost got me killed."

My hands tightened around the bannister. "He wouldn't…"

Anger shone in Brixton's eyes. "He did."

"Dorian!" It was my turn to yell. I limped up the stairs and called his name again. "What's this about the book—"

Dorian flung open the small attic door and looked down at us from the steep second set of steps leading to the attic. "I have not defaced more library books. I admit, it was not solely my own will-power that prevented it from occurring, as you have also not brought

207

me more books, but I would like to think I would have the fortitude—"

"Dorian," I snapped, "you asked Veronica to help you find your backward alchemy book." I groaned. I should have known he was up to something when he'd subscribed to so many newspapers from across Europe. If he'd just been homesick, he would have simply continued the subscription to *Le Monde* he'd begun earlier in the year.

"How could you tell her you exist?" Brixton said. "You were the one who made me swear not to tell anyone. And now she says she's working with you—"

"If you two would calm yourselves," Dorian said, "I will explain everything." He beckoned us into the attic.

I took the steps carefully, which was probably for the best so I didn't rush into strangling the gargoyle.

"Veronica," Dorian said once we were in the attic, "has always wished to meet Zoe's 'French friend' who is shy because of his deformity. She feels bad that only Brixton has met me. I called and asked for her help to track down a special alchemy book I wished to find for Zoe for Christmas."

"But that book and the guys who stole it are dangerous," Brixton said. His cheeks flushed. "If they find out she's helping look for the book … " He swallowed hard. "Veronica will be in danger." His hands balled into fists.

Dorian's black eyes grew wide. "There is no danger. She is behind a computer."

"Are you stupid?" Brixton screamed. "Is this because you're not human? Someone who cares about their friends and knew anything about the world would never—"

"Brix," I said, "how about we go out into the garden. I want to show you something."

He shrugged off my hand and rolled his eyes. "I'm not eight years old. I'm not taking a time-out."

"I'm older than your great-great-grandparents, and I still take time in nature to collect my thoughts. I need to step outside for a few minutes too. It's the only way we'll think clearly, not in anger."

"Whatever."

"Go out back and I'll catch up with you in a minute." I watched him stomp down the stairs, wondering if he'd be waiting for me in the backyard or not.

"I believe," Dorian said, "young Brixton is in love with his best friend."

"You might be right, but his worry is justified nonetheless. You know they're dangerous, Dorian."

Dorian scowled at me. "Alchemists! First you say it is not necessary to find the book as it is not dangerous, then you say it is so dangerous we cannot enlist the help of children."

"It's not the book that's dangerous. It's those who have it. That's why we should leave it alone. They can't do any damage." I hoped. "But if they think someone is looking for them … "

"*D'accord.* You may have a point."

The phone rang. I'd plugged an antique black candlestick phone into a new jack in the attic so that Dorian could telephone without leaving the room. I picked it up, along with the separate earpiece receiver that fit in the palm of my hand.

"I'm trying to track down Mr. Freeman," Detective Vega said. I could hear the hum of the station behind her. That was a good sign. She wasn't at the front door.

"Is everything all right?" I asked.

"Just some follow-up questions."

"He's not here right now, but I can give you his cell number."

"We have it," she said, frustration evident in her voice. "He's not answering. Well, I'm sure he'll turn up." A pause, but she didn't hang up. "Zoe?"

The sound of concern in her voice threw me. "I'm still here."

Dorian gave me a quizzical look and came to stand beside me to hear.

"It's just … " Detective Vega's voice softened. "Be careful. Your friend Tobias … He might not be the man you think he is."

I gripped the receiver. If she was still concerned about Tobias's sketchy past, she might stay focused on him instead of looking for the true culprit. "He and I go way back. I know he can be eccentric—"

"Tobias Freeman arrived in Portland before he told you he did," the detective said. "Before that morning he was arrested at your house. We've confirmed it now. He was here two weeks ago—at the time Logan Magnus was killed."

FORTY

"You must be mistaken," I said.

Dorian gaped at me, watching as I gripped the phone.

"I'm not, Zoe," the detective said. "Watch your back, okay?"

"If you're honestly worried that my dear friend might have killed Logan Magnus," I said, "shouldn't I know what I'm up against? You really think Tobias is... *what?* A serial killer?"

A long sigh came across the phone line. "No. Not a serial killer. A copycat."

"Of what? I keep up with the news and haven't seen anything similar for him to copy." Since Dorian now subscribed to several newspapers from across the world, I read those too. "I haven't seen anything about people dying from ingesting toxic paint. Or is this one of those things where you need a mathematician to see random patterns—"

"Not a mathematician. A historian. He's copying crimes that began in the early 1600s."

Before Tobias and I were born. *Oh no ...* Not before Perenelle was.

"I've always been interested in solving crimes," Detective Vega continued. "In college I double-majored in history and criminal justice. The parts of history that intrigued me most were the cases detectives never managed to solve. I remember one night at the library looking at old newspaper archives—this was before they were digitized to read from a smartphone—and making the connection that in different places and times in Europe, people died from swallowing large quantities of toxic paints. They never had any marks on their bodies from having fought back. Why not? It had to have been incredibly painful to swallow so much noxious paint. If someone wanted to kill themselves, there were plenty of easier ways. I don't know how it was done ... "

"But you thought they'd all been murdered."

"Don't make me regret telling you my theory," Detective Vega continued. "But I couldn't in good conscience not. You might be in danger if Tobias Freeman is copying these crimes. I could tell from our conversation that he's a history buff too. The guys at the station don't believe me, but there's something to this. I can feel it. Call me if you see Tobias Freeman again."

I stood staring at the black lacquered phone before returning the earpiece to its cradle. Was Detective Vega lying to me about Tobias arriving in town two weeks earlier than he'd appeared to? The police lied to people to see what their deception would shake loose. She had to be doing that ... Didn't she?

"Dorian, do you know where Tobias went?"

The gargoyle glared at me, clearly still angry and thinking that Brixton and I had overreacted about his enlisting the help of teenagers to track down the backward alchemy book that had brought him to life. "You did not ask me to keep your friend captive."

"He's your friend too."

"Unless he is a murderer." Dorian crossed his arms and sniffed. "Then I will rescind my friendship."

"Have a little faith. There's got to be a mistake."

I left the attic and went to Tobias's room. I didn't have to knock. The door was wide open. So was the closet. And it was empty. His clothes and his bag were gone.

———————

Brixton and I worked in the garden in silence as I worried about Tobias and Brixton fumed about Dorian. Had Tobias lied to me? I had the strongest impression that the detective believed what she'd told me.

I reminded Brixton how much of a sprawling plant he should trim. The right amount of pruning would cause a plant to thrive, but too much and it would wither and die. In his anger, his snips were overly enthusiastic and he cut back more of the pea shoots than I would have liked, but they were hearty plants, plus it was good for his wellbeing so I let him hack away.

"How could Dorian betray me?" Brixton said finally, echoing my thoughts about Tobias.

"He didn't mean to. He misjudged the situation. I don't want you, Ethan, or Veronica anywhere near that book. I'll have Dorian tell Veronica he found another perfect Christmas gift for me so she should stop searching."

"Should we ask Max to have someone watch V's house? I mean, what if someone tries to hurt her?"

As so often these days, I stifled the overwhelming urge to tousle his hair. "She's not in danger, but I'll keep an eye on her."

We worked in the garden in companionable silence for the next hour, stopping as the sun dipped low in the sky. I drove Brixton home with his bike in the back of my truck.

"You don't have to wait," he called over his shoulder as he walked his bike up the driveway to the little house.

Of course I'll wait, I thought to myself. Brixton headed to the garage to put away his bike. Keeping one hand on the handle bar, he knelt to lift the garage door. The sound of rusty hinges squealed as the cracked wooden door swung upward, revealing darkness inside. In the moonlight, I could make out the outlines of the bike falling onto the concrete driveway and heard Brixton cry out as he ran forward.

I jumped out of the car, wincing at the pain in my ankle but pushing forward.

Brixton hadn't bothered to turn on the light, so I didn't see what had happened until I was almost upon them. Brixton sat on his knees, cradling his mom in his arms. A trickle of blood ran down the side of Heather's temple.

She wasn't moving.

FORTY-ONE

I'M A HEALER WHO hates hospitals. My fate was sealed the moment I'd encountered a doctor during the plague outbreak that killed my brother. The unnerving visage of a beaked mask covering an anonymous doctor's face did little to assure the sick or those of us who cared for the dying. The terrifying mask was worn as a precaution against disease, with the extended beak filled with straw mixed with rose petals, cloves, mint, and other herbs and fragrances thought to clean the miasma in the air.

Modern hospitals worked miracles compared to the fearful doctors who'd poked patients with sticks from afar, but my involuntary reaction of unease remained the same.

Brixton had ridden to the hospital with his mom in the ambulance. I'd followed in my truck. I was glad to have the space away from the teenager. I didn't want him to see how worried I was. It wasn't only the fact that his mom had been attacked—it was what I'd noticed before the ambulance arrived. Though a palette of fresh paint had fallen next to Heather, the easel in front of her was empty.

The person who'd attacked her had stolen the painting she was working on. This attack was related to the Logan Magnus case.

It took me a while to find where at the hospital they'd taken Heather, but I knew I'd found the right place when I saw Detective Vega in the waiting room. I wasn't the only one who'd seen the connection.

"Is Heather all right?" I asked her.

"She will be. What are you doing here?" the detective asked, looking at my grass-stained knees. I hadn't changed after working in the garden with Brixton.

"I was about to ask you the same thing." Her brown hair was down, and she was wearing an elegant red dress with three-inch heels.

"This isn't a job with regular hours." Detective Vega sighed and tucked her hair behind her ear, which sparkled with silver earrings in the shape of Celtic crosses. "Did the Taylor boy call you?"

I shook my head. "I was with him when we found her. Why did you get pulled out of your evening out? You think it's related to Logan Magnus?"

"Or the art forger who got away. I'm getting notifications of local crimes related to art. Her son told the investigating officer her most recent painting was gone, and I remembered her name from the Magnus investigation. He owned one of her paintings."

"Who was it that attacked her?"

"I haven't been able to see Ms. Taylor yet. If you'll excuse me, I'm going to check on that."

As I waited in the sterile waiting room, my nerves got the best of me. I imagined everyone was staring at me. It was only the fact that hospitals made me nervous, I knew, but I still didn't like it.

The sight of Brixton was a welcome one.

"Mom's awake," he said.

"I didn't see him," Heather was telling the detective when we got to her room. "I assume it was a guy. It was someone strong. I was working on my latest painting and all of a sudden a gloved hand was covering my mouth and nose. The smell of the cloth ... I tried not to breathe, but I had to, you know?"

"This was a commissioned painting?" the detective asked casually.

"What?" Heather crinkled her nose. "No. I always paint what inspires me."

"Never copies?"

Heather laughed. "Why would I do that?"

I couldn't imagine that Heather had anything to do with the art forger, and it wasn't only because I was biased on account of our friendship. I could see her optimistic naiveté leading to her being tricked, but I couldn't imagine her creative spirit being confined to copying the style of another artist. Why had Heather been attacked and one of her paintings stolen?

While the detective finished questioning Heather, I went into the hallway and called Dorian, asking him to stay home until I returned. We'd developed a special pattern of rings so he'd know if he should answer the phone. Only Brixton and I knew the pattern. I didn't tell Dorian what had happened or where I was, because I knew I'd never get him off the phone, but he agreed to wait—as long as I didn't take too long.

Then I called Tobias. He picked up on the first ring.

"You were in Portland before Saturday morning." I wasn't asking a question.

"What?"

"You heard me. Detective Vega told me."

Silence followed.

"Tobias?" I said softly, feeling a cold loneliness encase me. My oldest friend ... "Did you lie to me about when you arrived?"

"Not exactly."

"What does—"

"I was distraught after Rosa's death. You can understand that, right? After the funeral, I needed to get out of Detroit. I hopped on a plane. To Portland."

"But I've been in town this whole month." The sterile light blue walls of the hospital felt like they were collapsing around me. "You never rang my doorbell."

"As soon as I arrived, I knew I couldn't see you. I wasn't ready to see someone who'd understand. I know that doesn't make any sense ... "

But it did make sense. At least to me. "There's an isolation you and I have experienced that people who grow old together before they lose someone can't imagine. It's not necessarily worse, but it's different. I understand that."

"And I wasn't ready for understanding. I wanted to lash out. I needed to get it out. But I didn't want to do that with you in the vicinity."

"So you left."

"And when I was ready, I called you. But I doubt that reasoning will fly with the detective."

"So you lied to her when you first spoke with her and told her you weren't in Portland when Logan Magnus was killed? You didn't think she'd check?"

"Give me some credit. I told her the truth. But I didn't count on having the bad luck that the dates would coincide with when that artist died."

"We'll figure it out together. But where *are* you?"

Silence.

"Are you at the Castle with Isabella?"

"I'm fine, Zoe."

"Watch yourself. Heather has been attacked."

Tobias swore. "Is she okay? What happened?"

"Someone attacked her in her garage art studio and stole the painting she was working on."

"Is she all right?"

"She'll recover."

"I take it they don't know who attacked her and stole the painting, or you would have mentioned it right away."

"No, but the detective is looking for you. It's probably best not to ignore her for too long. That'll just make you look more guilty."

Detective Vega stepped into the hallway as I hung up. "Ms. Taylor asked for you," she said.

Heather was sitting up in bed, with Brixton in a chair beside her. "Give us a sec, Brix?" she said.

I expected him to object, but he agreed and closed the door behind him.

"Are you okay?" I asked.

"Oh, sure." Heather smiled, but it wasn't her usual bubbly grin. "They want to keep me under observation for the night." She frowned. "They aren't sure of all the chemicals used to knock me out. It might have been something bad, you know? Abel is out of town for work…"

"Do you need me to get a hold of him?"

She squeezed my hand. "I've already called him. He's going to come but he won't be here until tomorrow."

"Brix can stay with me tonight."

After taking Brixton to get his things, it was late when we got back to my house. Dorian hadn't stayed home as I'd asked. Since he didn't know what had happened, I couldn't blame him. He was taking his increased baking responsibilities seriously. But after tucking Brixton into bed—a term I was careful not to use with the teenager as I said good night—I was keenly aware of just how alone I was.

––––––––––

In spite of the late night, I woke up at dawn. Brixton was still asleep, so I crept downstairs.

Tobias hadn't taken the metal sculpture Isabella had given him. It was a stunning design even without seeing its true form in shadow.

I opened the living room curtains. The light from the rising sun shone into the room from the large windows I rarely opened because of Dorian. I turned the sculpture until it cast a shadow of two crows in flight. As the sunlight filtered into the room, the birds' wings moved as if they were flying into the distance.

It made me think of the phoenix charm Isabella had made for her husband. The lightning bolts intertwined in the flames looked as though they were flashing from the sky, like a separate piece of the form.

As shadows danced across the floor, I ran my hands over the metal that formed the wings of the crows. It was made of two pieces that had been welded into shape around each other but didn't quite touch, similar to the structure of the pendant. I hadn't realized it at the time, because the pewter shapes were so perfectly matched, but the pendant must have been made of two pieces too. That was how Isabella had achieved the detail. I'd never tried to open the pendant. There wasn't an obvious opening, but I now felt sure there had been two pieces.

Detective Vega had given me her cell phone number, so I called her.

"Faust?" Her voice was sharp. "Zoe Faust? Do you realize what time it is?"

I hadn't. But as soon as I told her my suspicions about the pendant, she perked up. She was her usual noncommittal self, but she thanked me for the idea.

I hung up the phone and watched the shadow of the crows dance from the walls to a faint shadow on the floor, and then disappear all together as the sun rose higher. Both this sculpture and the pendant were ingenious designs that left different impressions depending on how you viewed them. So similar to the gallery lighting that made Logan Magnus's art a success…

The last rays of direct sunlight disappeared from the room as it filled with the diffuse brightness of the day. The stark shadows were gone, and the sculpture was again the central piece of art. A signature had been scraped into the base. An ornate letter that looked familiar. I thought at first it was an *L*, but it was an *I*. The style was the same as in the paintings displayed in the Logan Magnus memorial gallery.

It was her.

Just as Philippe Hayden was Perenelle Flamel, I was certain Isabella Magnus was the artist who'd created the famous "Logan Magnus" paintings.

FORTY-TWO

1597, Prague, Bohemia

Perenelle hadn't anticipated the violence to come so quickly.

She awoke in the middle of the night with a cold, rough sack sliding over her head. She flailed her arms and legs, but to no avail. He was stronger. A rope pulled the sack tightly against her neck.

"Be still," the voice said, the acrid scent of his breath accompanying the words. It wasn't Edward. This was one of the men he kept in his employ, the one with very few teeth. "This is your only warning before I snap that little neck."

"We both know he doesn't want me dead," Perenelle said through the stifling fabric. As he relaxed his grip, she kneed him in a most unpleasant place.

The man grunted in pain but he didn't let her go. It was small comfort that the noose didn't tighten around her neck. Instead, a heavy object crashed onto her head. In spite of the darkness from the sack, Perenelle saw flashes of light from a million stars. The bright starbursts were so beautiful, an unexpected thought flashed through her mind: she wished she could find the right pigments to paint them. Then all became darkness.

When she awoke, she found herself in a cell, most angry at herself for underestimating Edward. A cup of foul-smelling beer, a torn stub of stale bread, and an empty bucket were her only company in the room with stone walls and a thick wooden door. The only light came from a narrow slit high above. The fact that she could see told her it was daylight.

The stone bore no identifying mark. She wasn't sure where she was. But it didn't matter. By the time someone came to check on her hours later, she had formulated a plan.

"When you're ready to cooperate," said the man with few teeth, leering at her from the cracked doorway, "I will send for him."

"Please, kind sir," Perenelle said, her voice cracking, "you and Edward have made your point. You have won. I will do as he wishes." She crumpled into a fit of sobs.

She dared not look up at him, fearing he'd see the malice in her eyes or that the tears were false.

She needn't have worried. Edward was used to bending people to his will. He easily accepted that he had broken her. He brought her the materials she needed to create gold and paint it into paintings. He would be watching her, to learn the secrets himself. Once he learned the secrets of alchemy, would he kill her or let her go? She wasn't going to wait and see.

Perenelle's plan was simple—she only prayed it would be successful.

The idea was to work Edward to the brink of collapse—alchemy was a painstaking, laborious process, after all. She waited for him to confess he needed a break to rest. Yet he carried on. Why wouldn't he stop for much-needed sleep? Ah! She knew the answer. Though

Edward's exhaustion showed in his tired eyes and unsteady hands, he would not confess to being weaker than a woman. She hid her irritation and feigned fatigue. The reprimand was a small price to pay to being left alone.

Perenelle had been able to paint the essence of a flower into a painting and physically move it into the painting. Why wouldn't it be possible to do so with a human being? The heart of alchemy was capturing the true essence of a person (the Elixir of Life), of a plant (apothecary healing powers), or of a mineral (the Philosopher's Stone, to turn base metals into gold).

The same principles applied here. She'd done it with the gold nuggets and the flower, so it stood to reason she could do it with a man.

She painted a scene, leaving room for a person, then pilfered a cloth from the guard's pocket when he brought her more foul food. This was not only possible, but child's play, because he always tried to caress her face. This time it worked to her advantage.

Collecting ashes and dried flowers, she carefully mixed in the grime from the guard's handkerchief. Next she mixed the powdery pigment with an egg binder.

Pushing away her food, she turned back to her artwork, focusing her intent on the guard. She worked in brisk movements, painting his cape in shadows. She sketched his face in charcoal from the fire—the essence of charcoal helped her capture essences, just as it was essential in alchemy—then painted his features.

She felt the energy as she painted his eyes. It was working. She was nearly done. Just the snarl of his lips to capture his personality and give him life.

She called out to him. He came grudgingly. As he opened the door, she looked from his face to the lips of the painting. They weren't quite right … With the finishing touch that captured his essence, he disappeared from the room.

Perenelle turned back to the canvas. The malicious eyes painted from soot and soul shone back at her.

She let out a breath she hadn't realized she was holding, twirled the tip of her brush into a sharp point, and painted her signature *P* in the corner.

She was free.

FORTY-THREE

It wasn't only the signature I'd seen in Logan Magnus's artwork that convinced me Isabella was the true genius behind her husband's work. It was the essence of the artwork. With what I now believed about Isabella Magnus, I called Tobias. I could tell he didn't want to hear from me, but he didn't hang up. I told him my suspicion that Isabella was the artist behind her famous husband. He listened, but didn't say whether or not he believed me.

I roused Brixton so we'd have time to visit his mom at the hospital before school.

I called the hospital first to make sure we could see Heather. The nurses had a request as well, which made me smile. Brixton rolled his eyes when I told him. I shouted up to Dorian that we were leaving, but I didn't have time to go up to talk with him.

"I'm not any good," Brixton kept saying as we drove to the hospital. He was sitting in my truck with both his backpack and banjo in front of him.

Heather squealed with delight when we entered her room. She gave Brixton a hug from her bed and squeezed my hand. "Now that Brix is here, I can declare that I'm one hundred percent well."

"You're really okay?" Brixton asked, looking at the machines in the room.

She grinned. "Abel will be arriving soon, and they'll release me when he gets here. Family spaghetti dinner tonight."

Proud mama Heather had told all the nurses about Brixton's love of his banjo, so they'd asked if he'd play for the kids' ward. Apparently a magician had cancelled that week after catching a cold.

Most illnesses were treated with out-patient procedures these days, so it was a small group of kids, and the surly teenager was met with initial skepticism, but by the time we left, they were asking for more songs and Brixton was late for school.

I was exhausted when I got back to the house after dropping Brixton off, but I climbed to the attic nevertheless to tell Dorian what had happened to Heather. By the time we'd had an exhaustive conversation that led nowhere, my energy was depleted. The week was catching up with me. I declined Dorian's offer of breakfast, over his fierce protestations, and after a glass of water with lemon, crawled into bed and fell asleep immediately.

I woke up with my heart racing. Someone was in the house. Someone besides Dorian. The gargoyle's feet would make a scampering sound on the hardwood floors, and this was someone heavy, wearing shoes.

A faint knock sounded on my bedroom door. I pulled on a green silk robe and opened the door.

Tobias scratched his neck and looked sheepishly down at me. "Taking naps these days, eh?"

"I didn't sleep well. I have one dear friend in the hospital and I've been fighting with another."

"One who never should have spoken to you the way he did."

"What's the point of friendship if we can't forgive each other? Join me downstairs for breakfast. We've got Aurora apple tarts, Mac-Intosh apple oatcakes, and green Ginger Gold apples for breakfast smoothies. I hope you're not sick of apples."

"Apples are fine," Tobias said without smiling. He slouched against the hallway wall, a defeated man. Even his hazel eyes that had always shimmered like gold had now dulled to the color of straw.

"What's going on? You didn't confront Isabella—"

"No. I didn't have to. The painting of Nick. I think it's at the Castle."

I stared at him. *The painting of Nicolas had been there the whole time?* "You saw it?"

"Not exactly. I'll go get Dorian. Meet me downstairs."

I threw on some clothes, and by the time I made it downstairs three minutes later, Dorian and Tobias were already seated at the dining table with the misshapen pastries that hadn't made the cut for Blue Sky Teas. Dorian was drinking espresso, and a pot of green tea for me and Tobias was steeping.

"I'm sorry," Tobias said. "I was fooled by Isabella because I needed someone who understood what I'm going through. But ... she's been acting so erratically. It made me wonder if you were right about her after all. So I opened my eyes and started paying close attention like I usually do. She's the artist, all right." He paused. "But she also has to do with this art forgery ring, or whatever it is."

"But of course!" Dorian said. "This makes sense that she killed her husband. This is how he trusted her enough to swallow toxic paints. A femme fatale. A—"

"Why do you say that?" I asked Tobias, ignoring the gargoyle's theatrics.

"It started when she showed me her art studio," Tobias said. "She's an amazing artist. I couldn't understand why she didn't become famous in her own right."

"Can't you?" I asked.

"You're right. It's not as bad as when Perenelle was trying to be recognized as an artist, but we've still got a ways to go. I was honored she showed me her unfinished work. What she didn't show me on purpose was the additional studio on the estate, beyond hers and Logan's. One the police didn't find either."

"How did they miss it?" I asked.

"The door is disguised to look like one of her metal sculptures. The police didn't take apart works of art. I wouldn't have figured it out myself if I hadn't been suspicious already and knew how she used shadows in different ways. I was paying more attention than she thought, just like I was when you were practicing alchemical transformations back when we first met and you didn't realize how closely I was watching."

"Wait," I said. "If you got in there without Isabella seeing you, that means you were able to take back the painting of Nicolas?"

Tobias shook his head. "I couldn't get inside. There's some sort of key that needs to be fitted into the lock of the sculpture."

I swore. "Should we call the police? Damn, is that even a good idea? Have you called them already? Did you ever call Detective Vega back? I'm going to stop for breath now and let you talk."

"I called her, but she hasn't called back."

"You did not tell her about the painting?" Dorian said. "*Les flics,* they would not understand."

"No, only about what I'm pretty sure is an art forgery studio. We don't want her stealing old Nick, do we? But once Isabella is arrested, you can ask Cleo about the painting. Time for some waiting. You and I are used to that."

"That's one thing that never gets easier," I said, "especially when it involves people I care about."

"Yes, yes," Dorian said. "If you two are in a maudlin mood again, I will clean the dishes." He scooped up the empty plates and scurried to the kitchen.

The rain had held off, so I stepped into the backyard garden. Tobias followed me outside with a cup of tea.

"You really forgive me?"

I looked at the lines of worry on his face. "Of course." I hugged him and held on to him like he was my oldest friend in the world. Which, if we didn't rescue Nicolas, he would be.

Someone cleared his throat. Dorian shouldn't have been outside during daylight ... But it wasn't him.

"Max," I said, turning to see him walking into the backyard.

"Sorry to interrupt."

"I'll be inside," Tobias said, taking his leave.

"I can't do this, Zoe," Max said.

"You don't think Tobias and I—"

"I know. I'm not jealous of Tobias. No, that's a lie. I'm jealous, but not for the reason you think. I don't think you're sleeping with him. He's handsome and charming, but I trust you. And I think you feel the same way about me that I do about you."

"You know I do—"

"But you can tell Tobias things you'll never tell me. I can see it in the way you two look at each other. This past year, getting to know you, has been the most wonderful year ... I love you, Zoe Faust, but you won't let me in."

"Okay."

"Okay ... what?"

"You want to see the real me?" I took his hand in mine. "Come inside."

I led Max to my half-put-together basement alchemy lab and lit one of the kerosene lamps I used to illuminate the space. I didn't like to use modern electricity in this room. The light from natural flames made it easier to get into the calm, meditative space I needed to practice alchemy.

"This isn't storage for extra goods for Elixir, like I thought." Max's eyes swept over the wooden tables, glass vials, and dried plants.

"No, it's not. This is my contemplative place."

Max smiled as he picked up a mason jar of dragon's tongue. "This place is beautiful. This is going to sound silly, but it reminds me of my grandmother's photos of her apothecary shop."

"It doesn't sound silly at all."

Max put down the jar and took my hands in his. "No, it doesn't does it? I've always felt you were an old soul."

"I am." I inhaled deeply, breathing in the scents from centuries of love that I'd brought here to this room. Dried herbs from plants I'd grown myself. The pulpy, friendly fragrance of old books. The faint bitter scent of sulfur balanced by the sweet hints of natural sugars from the plants I transformed.

"I didn't mean to start a spiritual conversation." Max traced his fingertips in my palm.

"No. But it's time for me to show you what I've been afraid to. That this is who I really am."

"I love that you've got a place for meditation. It's okay for you to have kept it to yourself—"

"This place isn't for meditation. Not exactly. You know how the two of us garden similarly? How plants respond to us? It's been that way since I was little. And it scared people. That's why my brother and I ran away." I felt Max's hand tense as I spoke.

"The bullying was that bad?"

"We were taken in by the childless couple I told you about. They were the ones who taught me how to turn my aptitude with plants into something more."

"That's why your herbal concoctions, and even your simple soups, seem almost magical."

"It's not magic. It's alchemy."

Max laughed. "Exactly. Transformation."

"*True* alchemy. I'm older than I look." I waited for a reaction, but Max remained silent. "You've always sensed it."

"So how old are you?"

"Far older than you."

Max's laugh turned to a nervous one. "Zoe … " His expression changed as he watched my face. "You believe what you're telling me? You do. You really believe it."

"Because it's the truth. Think about everything you know about me. And what you learned from your grandmother all those years ago."

"My sister knows some good doctors."

"A psychiatrist? That's what you think I need?" Tension seized my whole body, leaving me feeling like a stiff stone carving, not a person of flesh and blood. "Why do you think all the hair on my body is white? Why do my scars look centuries old?"

Max shook his head. "I have an interview for a case. I'm already late. I have to go."

"Max?" I called after him as he rushed up the basement stairs.

The door slammed.

"You shouldn't have told him," Tobias said when I reached the kitchen.

I ran my hands through my white hair, which Max had always told me was beautiful, even though he knew it was real rather than dyed, and held back tears. "How did you tell Rosa?"

"I had it easier. You've got yourself a strategically rational man there. He's consciously chosen to reject things he once believed, to help him make sense of the world. He's a *cop*, for God's sake."

"I have to try. If we don't want to lose our humanity—if we truly want to let people in—we have to take risks."

"He's a good man. I hope he comes around."

"I do too."

Tobias gave a worried glance at his phone.

"What is it?" I asked.

"Still no word from Detective Vega. Which is odd, considering how hard she was trying to reach me before."

"So where is she?"

FORTY-FOUR

PRAGUE, 1597, AND THE FRENCH COUNTRYSIDE, 1700

PERENELLE DIDN'T KNOW WHERE she was. She'd been taken to a cell with a bag over her head. But with Edward's cruel servant no longer a threat, she held her head high and walked out as if she had every right to do so. It worked. Nobody paid her any attention as she walked confidently with the painting under her arm. She had been in a small house inside the walls of Prague Castle, luckily not in the dungeons or an outpost.

She planned to let the guard go once she reached Nicolas. Her husband would be there if she had any trouble with the man, who would undoubtedly be confused when he was pulled from the painting.

Perenelle wished to collect her possessions and present her remaining paintings to Rudolf before returning home to Nicolas, but it was too big a risk with Edward on the castle grounds. She hoped that after she disappeared, the Emperor would find her finest work left behind in her rooms and take it for his library. His grand library would survive, and with it the knowledge contained within its walls.

She stole a cloak from a scullery, leaving a piece of gold in its place. With her face hidden, she heard two men speaking as they passed.

"They've imprisoned him at Most Castle," she heard. "Can you believe Kelley told the Emperor he could lift gold from a painting? I always knew he was a fraud. His ears and hands, you know."

It took all of Perenelle's will not to turn and engage the men for more details, but she couldn't draw attention to herself. This was an unexpected development. She couldn't help laughing. A few years of solitude would do Edward good.

Now that Edward Kelley was imprisoned, it was easy for Perenelle to send word to Nicolas that she would be returning home, and return to her rooms to pack her alchemical possessions. She could also finish her last painting and present it to the Emperor. It would only take a few days.

She worked quickly, using existing pigments she'd transformed into paint to create what would be her last masterpiece for Rudolf. On the third day, after staying up most of the night to capture the essence of the night sky, she was awoken by a sharp knock at her door.

"Edward's leg is broke, sir," the page said. "He was trying to escape. I don't expect he should live. The Emperor says you may take what supplies of his you want, sir."

She swore. The injury would most certainly be a death sentence. No medical treatment would be given to a prisoner. Edward might deserve his fate, but Perenelle remembered how he'd spoken of his beloved daughter. She could send his family gold … But when there was more that she could do, she could not live with herself if she did not at least try. She pressed a small coin into the page's hand, an idea forming in her mind. One that would also allow her to solve another problem.

Her plan was simple. At least it was supposed to be. She would paint a good amount of gold into the painting of Edward's brute of an associate. Once she had done so, she sent for the page, giving him a more than fair payment to ensure the painting would reach Edward in his cell. "I wished him to at least have a small bit of beauty for him to gaze upon as he dies," she told him.

The painting would be searched for hidden weapons, of course, but there were none that people would see. But Edward was smart. He would recognize his servant inside the painting and the stack of gold, and know what to do. He could pull both from the painting and bribe the guards.

With a clear conscience, Perenelle headed home to Nicolas.

———

Perenelle put that part of her life behind her for another hundred years—until she saw her former self in a young woman who wore a curious mix of fear, serenity, and wonder on her face. Zoe, who came to them with her brother Thomas.

Nicolas had a steady stream of apprentices in their homes. He'd never before taken on a woman, though not for lack of trying. Perhaps that was why he was so pleased when an acquaintance contacted him about Zoe and her brother.

Zoe reminded Perenelle so much of her old self. *Too much*, which is why she tried to distance herself from the young alchemist-in-training. Perenelle would have been happier if she'd never listened to Nicolas's advice that a woman could do anything she wasn't allowed to. It simply wasn't true in this world. Those who tried received only pain and suffering for their efforts.

She reminded herself that the girl could make her own choices. But Zoe was too curious too early in her alchemical training. She asked about backward alchemy. No good would come of that. Nicolas warned Zoe of the danger, and Perenelle hoped the girl believed it. They didn't dare tell her the truth that the backward alchemists were stealing the lives of other people to extend their own.

After Thomas died tragically of the plague and Zoe left them before her training was complete, Nicolas didn't take on another pupil. Not only because he was sad to have lost Zoe, but also because he saw the growing threat of the backward alchemists—men who used alchemical shortcuts and the deaths of others to steal life to give it to themselves.

The Flamels set out on their new mission. Perenelle hoped Zoe was happy, living out her natural life with people who loved her, wherever she was.

FORTY-FIVE

With my two best friends beside me, I couldn't help feeling hopeful.

"We cannot wait for the detective," Dorian said as he paced the floor, having convened a meeting in the attic.

"I know," I said.

"And what of Heather's unknown attacker? Moreover, can you risk the police confiscating the painting? Nicolas is ill-equipped to break out of an evidence room."

"It's not evidence," I said. "Police search warrants don't cover everything in a house."

Tobias swore. "Dorian is right. Isabella's son-in-law thinks that painting is a forgery."

I groaned.

"Monsieur Freeman," Dorian said, "did you blow your cover with the artist-forger Isabella?"

"Do you mean am I still on good terms with her? I should be. I didn't confront her about the secret workshop before I took off this morning."

"*Bon*. You must break into the secret studio you believe contains the painting—"

"How do you propose I do that?"

Dorian blinked at him. "You do not know how to pick a lock?"

"Why would I know how to pick a lock?"

Dorian shook his head and flapped his wings. "*D'accord*. This means you must take me with you."

Tobias turned to me with his eyes wide. "He's a thief?"

"His father was a stage magician who was originally a clock-maker," I said. "Dorian's claws are better than lock picks."

"I cannot misplace them," Dorian said, chuckling as he drummed his claws together.

"Damn," Tobias said. "I forgot Jean Eugene Robert-Houdin raised you."

"Shall we depart?" Dorian asked. "My plan is brilliant in its simplicity. I will turn to stone form. You can say you wished to show Isabella a beautiful gargoyle sculpture. She would appreciate this, no?"

———————

It turned out the answer really was *no*. Something must have raised her suspicions.

I'd accompanied Tobias and Dorian to the Castle, and was hiding in the bed of the truck with a tarp above me and my cell phone at the ready. But when we reached the front gate, Isabella's screaming voice sounded so loudly through the speaker that even I could hear her.

"Spies!" she shouted. The gate speaker distorted her voice, but the words she yelled were clear. And chilling. "The phoenix is rising. You can't be here. Leave!"

Though I knew the sound of her voice had been transformed by the crackling speaker, Isabella's words made me shudder. They rang of madness.

Since I was in back, I couldn't see the reactions of my conspirators. But I felt it soon enough. My shoulder knocked into the side of the steel bed as Tobias backed up.

He couldn't hear me, so I called him on my cell phone. As much as I hated to admit it, these things did come in handy.

"Pull over once we're out of sight," I said.

"Already on the lookout for a good spot."

He clicked off, and less than a minute later I felt the truck transition from asphalt to dirt. As the scent of pine grew stronger, the truck came to a rest. I heard Tobias's voice. "Nobody's around. You can climb out."

I lifted the tarp. Thick pine trees filled the sky above me. I climbed out and slipped into the passenger seat. If I was sitting on the seat with my legs curled under my chin, there was room for the three of us, with Dorian on the floor in front of the seat, though I doubted it was comfortable for his wings.

"Something's not right," Tobias said.

"I fear you are a bad spy, Monsieur Freeman," Dorian said. "Through no fault of your own, of course, I must add. You are an honest man. This is why you prefer chess to poker. This—"

"Can we focus?" I said.

"Her reaction back there," Tobias said. "I don't understand it. Something really weird is going on."

"Grief takes many forms," I said, thinking of Ambrose's madness after losing his son Percy. "She's either a murderer who's onto you, or she's angry and lashing out because of everything that's going on. Either way, Nicolas is captive at her house."

240

"That place is a castle in more ways than its cosmetic appearance," Tobias said. "Those iron front gates and the high fence that circles the property are no joke."

The painting of Nicolas was so close but beyond reach. It was worse than not knowing where he was.

"There might be a way," Dorian said slowly. "I cannot see outside. Can you tell me, is it safe for me to step out of the truck for a few moments here?"

Tobias nodded.

I opened the door and Dorian climbed out after me. He took a few steps and unfolded his gray wings.

"*Mes amies*," he said, "I have been practicing."

I stared at the gargoyle. I knew it was his biggest disappointment that even though his wings had become feather-like upon his discovery of the Elixir of Life, he'd still been unable to fly. "You've been practicing *flying*?"

He nodded shyly.

"That's why you've been acting secretively and been gone at times when I hadn't expected you to be," I said, thinking back on the gargoyle's unexplained absences. I should have been happy that he was achieving something that meant so much to him, and that it might help us, but I couldn't help feeling hurt. "You could have trusted me."

Dorian flapped his wings, causing a gentle gust of air to float over me. "You would have stopped me."

"I would have stopped you from practicing anywhere dangerous. You were doing it near the river, weren't you? That's how you saw the glittering phoenix charm. Because you were flying above it."

"It was late at night. There are large birds along the water. It should have been a safe place to practice. You would have said *any* location was dangerous. You are too careful for your own good."

"Tobias will back me up," I said.

Tobias was leaning with his elbows on the hood of the truck. He held up his hands. "I'm staying out of this one."

Dorian chuckled. "Monsieur Freeman is a wise man. *Alors*, shall we rescue Nicolas?"

I didn't want to risk it by day, but we really couldn't be sure the police wouldn't confiscate the portrait of Nicolas. We had to act.

"If you're going to do this," I said, "there are some ground rules. Even under these circumstances, our usual safety precautions are in place. *Especially* now, since we don't know what's going on with Isabella. Wear your cape, and turn to stone at the slightest hint of danger."

Once Dorian had agreed, we got back in the car and Tobias drove the three of us to a spot in the hills behind the Castle.

"Remember," I said as Dorian poked his head out of the bag, "if they see you—"

"Yes, yes, I will turn to stone. They will not believe their eyes, and think the true intruder got away and left behind this beautiful statue."

"You're sure you can pick the lock?" Tobias said.

Dorian glared at us. "My father was more skilled at all forms of mechanical tinkering than Houdini, who stole Father's name for himself. Not only was I taught by the best, but I was made for this." He tapped his clawed fingers on the dashboard and narrowed his liquidy black eyes. "Now, shall we rescue Nicolas?"

"You're sure there are no cameras?" I asked Tobias.

"Not unless someone installed them against Isabella's wishes. She's adamant about her family's privacy."

Tobias carried Dorian in the satchel until we were close to the back fence. The gargoyle pushed the starchy hemp fabric down to the ground and stepped onto the soft earth. He tied the cape around his neck and took an object from my outstretched hand: the bag large enough to fit the painting. He gave us a curt nod and unfurled his wings.

In the clearing, Dorian beat his wings a few times. I held my breath, unsure what to expect. For him to take flight, would his wings vibrate quickly like the wings of a hummingbird? Or would he need to take a running start to catch the wind like a hang glider? Neither happened. With a sound in between that of a swoosh and a thump, the underbrush blew away from the spot underneath him. With another grand flap of wings, Dorian's body lifted up from the ground.

A gasp escaped my lips. His wings beat again. My short hair blew upward in the wind. The wings beat faster. Dorian rose higher and disappeared over the fence.

I ran to the fence and searched for a place where I could see through the wooden slats. A few yards away I found a piece of rain-warped wood that allowed us to peek inside the estate. It wasn't a perfect view, but it shielded us from sight as well.

In the space between the slats, I saw Dorian standing on the ground, his wings tucked onto his back and the hooded gray cape covering his body. He scampered away and disappeared from sight.

"It'll be all right," Tobias whispered. "The little guy's got it covered."

"I know he comes across like he can do anything, but his ego—"

"Is probably justified in this case. The son of the father of modern magic? Damn, Zoe. If Dorian can't make himself invisible and pick an intricate lock, nobody can."

In spite of Tobias's words, as the minutes stretched on he grew nervous as well. We paced along the fence, taking turns at the opening where we could see inside.

"This is taking too long," I said. I sat on the soft dirt, but jumped up as something came crashing through trees beyond the fence. The sound of branches snapping filled the air.

Tobias was the one looking through the slats. He swore, then pulled me to the spot in his place. I saw a half-running, half-flying blur of gray bobbing up and down, coming closer to the fence.

"He can't balance with the painting," I said. Because Dorian was so new to flying, I doubted he'd ever practiced while holding anything.

The gargoyle took flight, the bag with the painting gripped tightly in his outstretched arms. The air whoomped as he beat his wings more frenetically than he had earlier.

Whoomp.

"I can't watch," I whispered, backing away.

Whoomp.

"He can do it," Tobias said, taking my place. "He's a smart little guy. I'm sure he'll—"

I jumped as Dorian crashed into the fence. Tobias stumbled backward.

"Are you all right?" I called out.

A string of French curses rang out from the other side of the fence.

"It's too high," Tobias said, jumping in an attempt to reach the top of the fence.

"Give me a boost," I said.

"Even if you can reach the top and get over, you'll never get back out. Especially with your ankle."

"We can't leave him in there," I hissed.

"We'll find another—"

"Will you two please stop arguing so we may go home?"

Tobias and I whipped around.

Dorian stood before us, on the outside of the fence. He clutched the bag containing the painting. His left wing hung at an unnatural angle.

"It is done," he said, wincing in pain. "I have obtained the painting. I have done my part to rescue Nicolas." He handed the bag to me. "The rest is up to you." He faltered.

"Your wing," I said. "Are you all right?"

"*Bien. Je vais très bien ...*"

He proceeded to fall to the ground, unconscious.

FORTY-SIX

I HOPED THE NEIGHBORS were asleep as we supported a limping gargoyle and carried a centuries-old painting into the house in the middle of the night. We draped sheets over both, but I can imagine what we must have looked like.

We were unable to safely carry Dorian up the steep stairs leading to the attic, and Tobias insisted that he not climb the precarious stairs on his own until he was examined.

"You do not wish me to be in comfort in my attic?" Dorian sniffed.

"Soon," Tobias promised. "Let me check out this wing first."

Instead of folding into a natural arc, Dorian's left wing hung at two jagged angles, like a ragged bolt of lightning. We made him as comfortable as possible in the living room.

"Can you move the wing?" Tobias asked.

Dorian's right wing extended fully and knocked a detective novel off the coffee table. The motion was powerful, and the hefty hardback book skidded across the floor. His left wing didn't leave his side. Dorian's black eyes blinked in horror.

"It's okay." Tobias's deep voice was calm and soothing. "We'll get you fixed right up. You'll be good as new in no time at all."

Dorian's nostrils flared and he clenched his gray teeth. "Why, then, does it feel as if a poker of molten lead were being poured over my wing?"

"Let me go get some supplies with Zoe," Tobias said. "We'll be right back."

"Is that true he'll be fine?" I whispered as we hurried down the stairs to the basement.

"I can set a bone. But a gargoyle wing? I doubt there's an anatomy book for that."

"But he's stable?"

"I think so."

"You *think* so?"

"See above: *gargoyle*."

"We can't very well take him to a hospital."

Tobias ran his hand across his face and looked up at the ceiling. "You should go examine the painting. I'll attend to Dorian."

"I can help you with Dorian. The painting is safe. You—"

"It's not for my benefit, Zoe. Why do you think doctors make loved ones leave the room before they get to work? You care too much for the little guy. I'm going to cause him more pain to help him."

I nodded, but reluctantly. "I can give you a relaxing tincture and a salve for aches. That'll help him get more comfortable once you're done."

"Show me where the wine is too."

"Is that a good idea?"

"I'm about to set the badly broken wing of a petulant gargoyle. The wine is for me."

After helping Tobias gather supplies, I removed the painting from the bag and carried it to my basement alchemy lab—but immediately thought better of it. I needed to study the old canvas as I would approach any alchemical problem, which first meant taking it to a space that wasn't infused with my own alchemy.

I carried the painting to the attic and rested the canvas against a wooden shelf as I tore down the web of conspiracy theorist papers that plastered the attic walls. Once that was done, I looked over the warm colors that had been lovingly painted into the portrait of Nicolas, the details in the glass bottles behind him, and the anamorphosis perspective that made the walking stick say *Alchemia* when viewed from the proper angle.

Alchemical transformations can be shifted back and forth through stages—beginning with calcination, the process of heating a substance until it turns to ashes, and ending with coagulation, in which an element that has been reduced to its core is again reconstituted into a solid substance. It's the same process as turning pigments into paint. When Perenelle created her paints, she must have infused her particular energy into the colors she used to paint this image.

What separates true alchemy from modern chemistry is how alchemy requires a connection between the person performing the experiments and the materials they're using—and, of course, intent. In addition to the pure paints Perenelle had created for this masterpiece, she would have had to put her heart and soul into her efforts as she used the rough brush that transformed color into life. How could I undo the alchemy Perenelle had infused into the painting?

I thought about the medicines I'd sold in my apothecary shop, back when artists purchased chunks of earth and powders to create paints, before they forgot their roots and became dependent on colormen. When artists stepped into my shop, they weren't looking to find a color on my shelf. Instead, they anticipated the painstaking process of following a recipe that would turn an element found deep under the earth into a brilliant cobalt to capture the sky, or transform dull lead into a bright white that showed the sparkle in a person's eye.

I drew closer to the painting and lifted my hands within inches of the canvas.

A burst of lightning lit up the sky above us, causing a bright explosion of light to shine through the skylight. The skin on my hands looked nearly translucent in the blinding light, but the painting thrived. Though it didn't physically move, the pigments came alive, their colors intensified.

A reflection in Nicolas's eye caught my attention … I looked closer. It wasn't just an illusion from the lightning. A reflection had been painted into his eye—a mirror image *of the artist*. Perenelle.

Perenelle Flamel was trapped inside the painting with her beloved Nicolas.

Perenelle saw me too. I was sure of it. And it gave me the true purity of intent I needed.

I took a deep breath and reached forward. My fingertips brushed against the rough surface. I didn't hesitate. My hand tingled like a thousand mini lighting bolts as my fingers pierced the surface of the canvas. Instead of breaking the flax fibers, my hand disappeared from view. This was really happening. I didn't think my heart had ever beat so furiously. I felt it pulsing through every inch of me, down to my fingers that were now inside the world of the painting.

A hand gripped mine. A scent overwhelmed my senses. Spicy frankincense, metallic mercury, and sweet honey.

Nicolas.

I pulled with all my might, cajoling the painting to give up her inhabitants. It felt like I was lifting the weight of someone who'd fallen into quicksand.

I held my locket for a moment, then pressed my other hand into the painting. A second hand gripped my arm. My balance shifted. I felt it a moment too late. I was falling into the painting.

I slipped on the hardwood attic floor and fell closer. My heart thudded. My ears rang. My feet cramped as I struggled to grip the floor. What would it be like to live in the world of the painting?

I fell further. My head banged into the frame. I cried out more in astonishment than pain. My arms were still inside the painting, now well past my elbows. The colors of the painting swirled and shifted before my eyes. I heaved with as much strength as my body allowed. The muscles in my arms quivered. My rubber-soled boots screeched as they slid on the hardwood floor.

The hands that gripped mine from inside the painting were warm. Living. The fingers that grasped my right hand were large and calloused. The hand that clutched my left was stronger than its small size would suggest. They both clung to me as if I were a life-boat. I could feel that they didn't mean to pull me into the painting, yet I knew I was losing.

My muscles gave out. I slipped further into the rich sunset colors. *Two of them. Two against my one.* We were out of balance.

"Tobias!" I called out.

Alchemy isn't magic. It doesn't create something out of nothing. Its transformation requires *equal parts* of matter. My solo intent hadn't been enough to transform two people. I needed another alchemist.

"Tobias!"

I was too far inside the painting to turn around when I heard the sound of the floor creaking behind me, but I knew the sound of his footsteps.

Wordlessly, Tobias wrapped his arm around my waist and tugged. I fell backward—along with two people I hadn't seen in centuries. Nicolas and Perenelle. And a pool of blood that was quickly spreading across the attic floor.

FORTY-SEVEN

1597, BOHEMIA

EDWARD KELLEY'S RECOVERY WAS slow and painful. But the gold Perenelle had smuggled to him in her painting had served its purpose, allowing him to bribe his way out of prison to recover with his family.

His servant wasn't so lucky. He insisted on telling stories of his ordeal at taverns. Edward couldn't have that. He convinced the sniveling man, who already knew alchemy was real, that to know the true immortality of alchemy all he had to do was swallow the paints Edward provided him. The stupid man was dead within an hour.

The man was taken care of, but Edward had no money and no prospects. Except one. He was more intelligent than anyone he'd ever met, so he'd learned enough from Perenelle Flamel to find the Elixir of Life.

But at what cost? He had never been able to transform lead into gold in more than minute increments. He had never been able to paint gold into a painting. And as the years and decades passed, he lived on while his family died. It was watching his young daughter grow old and perish that transformed his curiosity into rage.

All he had was his intelligence and his charm. It was enough to get by, but over the years, he grew more and more bitter. He knew what he would do if he ever found the Flamels.

1700s, France

Many years passed, yet Edward Kelley's anger did not abate.

He caught up with them on the first day of winter. The darkest day of the year; how fitting! The coincidence gave him hope that his vengeance would be realized at last.

Edward had followed the directions of a bookseller and found Nicolas in the pub of a small town in southern France. The alchemist had never been painted, nor had Edward ever met him, but Edward knew immediately who he was looking at in the smoky room. Although the man at the bar looked to be in his forties, there was an aura of old age surrounding him, with his wild hair and crystal blue eyes. Or perhaps Edward was simply being fanciful. It was possible the bookseller had simply given him a good description.

The alchemist appeared cautious when the stranger approached, but Edward's charm won him over. Nicolas didn't notice when Edward slipped a powdery substance into his beer.

"Edward Kelley, is it not?" Nicolas asked as he woke up in the barn Edward had taken him to. The snowstorm raged outside, and wisps of wind pushed their way into the barn.

"I'm impressed," Edward said. He didn't like how the alchemist was studying him like a specimen with his crystal-blue eyes. "Our encounter can be brief. I only need you to tell me where I can find Perenelle."

The alchemist refused, even after Edward used his most persuasive techniques. Edward couldn't contain his anger. He hadn't meant to hurt the alchemist as much as he did. He'd only wanted to scare him with the knife. But when Nicolas calmly chuckled at the idea of betraying his wife, Edward brought the hilt of an axe down on Nicolas's head.

The crunch of bone was only satisfying for a fraction of a second before Edward realized the gravity of what he'd done. Nicolas Flamel crumpled to the floor and lay at an unnatural angel. Edward had seen death, and he knew the alchemist would not be moving again in this mortal life.

It took half the night and nearly all of his strength to walk the two kilometers to his home. It was only his need to warn Perenelle that kept him alive, he was sure.

Nicolas stumbled through the door of the house and fell into Perenelle's arms.

"The backward alchemists?" Perenelle asked gently as she peeled off his snow-covered clothing and looked for his wounds. "They found us?" Her voice shook, but her healing hands remained strong.

Nicolas laughed. Blood escaped his lips. "No. They are not clever enough. They never were."

"Then who?"

"Edward Kelley," he said, feeling himself choking on a sulfurous substance. "He has found you. You must flee while there's time. He will find the house in the light of day."

"I'm not leaving you. I'm helping you." But when she saw the knife wound and felt the crack on his skull, Perenelle knew Nicolas needed more help than she could give. She wasn't sure how he was still alive. He needed a doctor. But it was the dead of night with a fierce winter snowstorm. There was no way she could get him help as soon as he needed it. Unless…

She'd seen how a wilting flower's ultimate death was suspended when she painted it into a painting with alchemical paint, and she'd once painted a man into a painting. Would Nicolas's wound hold constant inside a painting while she took the time to escape and travel to summon a doctor?

She found a painting of an alchemy lab she'd been working on. One that she loved, with the dawn rays of the sun showing through the window. It looked like a room where Nicolas would be happy. Perenelle began to paint the love of her life into the foreground.

"What are you writing?" she asked. "Don't use your energy."

"If I don't survive, you'll need help. I want you to find Zoe."

"She's long-dead, Nicolas. She didn't find the Elixir—"

"You weren't watching the experiments she did for Thomas. I believe she did."

In spite of her torment, the idea that Zoe might be alive filled Perenelle with joy. "I'll look for her. I promise."

As she painted, the yellow rays of dawn crept through the windows. She had been concentrating so intensely that she hadn't realized how long it had taken her.

"I'm ready," Perenelle whispered, taking Nicolas's hand. "Once I paint the color into your eyes, you'll be one with the painting."

"I love you more than the heavens above and all the earth below," he said to her. "Whatever happens. Always."

Nicolas disappeared in the same way the guard had—silently yet jarringly, as if the universe had skipped a heartbeat.

But… this time there was also a crashing bang.

No, it wasn't Nicolas entering the realm of the painting that had made the sound. Fists pounded on the door.

Edward. She was too late.

Hastily she hid the painting behind the drapes as Edward burst through the door.

"He's dead, Perenelle. Just as you took my family from me by withholding your secrets, I have taken yours from you. I want you to know that before you die."

She stood to her full height and faced the man whose life she'd saved all those years ago. His once-charming face was contorted with rage. Perenelle didn't fear for her own life, but she couldn't leave Nicolas inside the painting with no means of escape.

Edward gave her the choice of a quick death by stabbing or a slow death by swallowing her toxic pigments. She chose the pigments. That way, there might be time…

She ate the poisons until she vomited, then fell to the floor, unconscious. At least that's what she hoped he'd believe.

Once Edward left, Perenelle pushed herself up and forced herself to vomit once more. Nicolas was already safely inside the painting. She didn't know what it had done to his spirit, but she couldn't leave him alone in there. She knew what she must do.

Before taking the most frightening but certain action of her life, she took the note Nicolas had written to Zoe. A farmer was due to bring them food that week. She would leave him a stack of gold with a request asking him to take the note and her painting to an alchemist friend in Paris, who could help find Zoe. She wasn't sure if she could trust the man, but she had to try. The pile of gold was generous enough that she hoped he would feel no need to betray her.

All she had within her control now was one single thing. She painted her own reflection into Nicolas's sparkling and mischievous blue eyes. The paintbrush clattered to the stone floor as she disappeared.

FORTY-EIGHT

THE FOUR OF US sprawled across the attic floor, limbs entwined. It took a minute to realize that the dark red blood was coming from Nicolas.

My relief that he and Perenelle were alive after being extracted from the painting was tempered by the gravity of the scene before me. *What had I done?*

There was no escaping the reality that they were gravely wounded. Nicolas was bleeding profusely from both his head and stomach. Perenelle clutched her stomach in agony, but I saw no blood. Had I misunderstood the alchemy it would take to safely pull them from the painting?

Tobias and I helped them up. It became immediately clear that Nicolas was incapable of standing on his own, but Perenelle rushed to his side and helped me support him.

Nicolas draped one arm over my shoulder and the other around Perenelle. He breathed a shallow breath and whispered, "Zoe, I knew it was you. I knew you'd done it." A weak smile formed on his lips and his light blue eyes sparkled in the midst of the wrinkles surrounding them. "Before I entered the world of the painting, I'd heard rumors of a woman I thought might be you. I knew … I knew you would be the one to save us."

I looked from his cracked lips to the blood on my hands. "But I haven't … Look what I've done to you."

"Don't try to speak, my love," Perenelle said to Nicolas, then turned to me. "This wasn't your doing, Zoe. Our injuries are from long ago."

Looking at their clothing, I could tell just how long ago. I hadn't seen them since 1704, and their clothes looked much the same as I remembered, from Nicolas's layers of starchy shirts to the yards of fabric in Perenelle's dull-colored house dress.

Aside from their wounds, the two of them looked so much like I remembered them. Nicolas's untamable gray-streaked hair, the deep lines on his face that were most prominent around his kind eyes, and his dexterous hands, like those of a magician. Perenelle's auburn hair, firmly set jaw, and tiny frame that belied her strength.

That strength made it difficult for Tobias to push her aside to see Nicolas's wounds.

"Please," Tobias said, "let me help him."

"You're a doctor?" she asked.

"Close."

"It feels like only yesterday," Nicolas murmured, his thoughts reflecting my own, before his energy gave out. His grasp caught Perenelle's voluminous skirts, and we were dragged down with him. I winced in pain as my ankle twisted.

"The backward alchemists … " Nicolas mumbled, struggling to sit up but finding himself more and more tangled in the soft fabric.

"Calm yourself," Perenelle whispered. "There will be time to deal with them once you're well."

Nicolas had always warned me away from backward alchemy. Pieces clicked into place—they must be speaking of the backward alchemists that Dorian and I had dealt with in Paris and Portland that summer.

"We must stop them." Nicolas's voice rattled. His bright blue eyes flickered and closed. I felt stillness overtake his body.

"I can't lose you again," I whispered as Tobias helped untangle Perenelle's brown skirts so we could get up. "Not like this."

"He's still with us," Tobias said, feeling his pulse.

"He's been stabbed and hit," Perenelle whispered, folding him into her arms, "and I've been poisoned."

"Do you know what the poison was?" Tobias asked. He spoke in the peaceful, steady voice of someone who wished to impart a sense of calm to those around him, even though I knew it was far from what he was feeling inside.

"Pigments," she rasped.

My throat clenched. She'd been poisoned by paint?

"Let's get you some activated charcoal," Tobias said.

"No." Perenelle's voice was resolute. It was the same tone I remembered her using when advising Nicolas not to try a risky experiment. "I pray you, attend to Nicolas first."

"I'll go," I said. "Tobias is the one who can best help Nicolas right now."

Tobias gently lifted Nicolas's slashed shirts as I left for my alchemy lab to gather supplies.

Returning to the attic, I gave Tobias an anxious look as Perenelle swallowed the temporary antidote.

"The abdominal stab wound isn't deep," he reported, "but this wound on the back of his head ... " He examined Nicolas for a few minutes in silence as I sat with Perenelle. I couldn't tell if she was feeling better or if her interest in watching Tobias's care of Nicolas superseded her own pain.

"I really can't tell what's going on with this head wound," Tobias said finally. He forced a laugh. "Even my cayenne can't cut it." He pulled me aside. "They need a hospital. Only … "

"I know. They're not supposed to exist. They have no ID—"

"That's not what I meant. Though you're right, that's a problem too. It's the nature of his wounds. Their bodies aren't behaving as I'd expect. I don't think standard medical care will be able to help them."

But I knew someone who'd been brought up with an inquisitive, open mind, and who practiced integrative medicine—the type of medicine that combined standard Western medical care with a more holistic approach. I took a deep breath and made a phone call.

"Max, I know I'm the last person you want to hear from right now, but it's an emergency."

"What's wrong?" The immediate concern in his voice gave me the courage to carry on.

"For what I'm going to say, I need you to trust me."

"I do trust you, Zoe. Sometimes I don't know why, and I don't know where you're leading me, but God help me, I love you and trust you."

The words meant so much to me, but this wasn't the time to touch on our relationship.

"I need your sister's help." I looked at my injured friends. I had to take the risk. "Old friends of mine … They're in desperate need of medical attention. Mina can help them. But neither of you can tell anyone."

The silence couldn't have lasted more than a second or two, but it felt like an eternity. "Are you at your house?" Max asked. "I'll call 9-1-1 and tell them—"

"No!" I shrieked.

"Where are you, then?"

"No. No ambulance. That's why I'm calling you—I can't call 9-1-1. And I can't go to the ER. You said you trusted me."

"I do. But if your friends need medical attention, that's something completely different."

"A hospital can't help them. I need Mina. Please."

Max swore. "You're asking her to risk her license? She'd still need to report—hell, *I* should report—"

"That's not why I need her. It's nothing illegal, I promise. I need her mind. Will you help us?"

FORTY-NINE

Max swore creatively again, but didn't hang up on me to call 9-1-1.

"It's Mina's decision," he said, and gave me her number. "If you can't reach her, please, Zoe. Go to the ER."

It was already evening, so Mina's medical clinic was closed for the day. That was the only reason she even entertained the idea of seeing us.

"No promises," Mina said. "But if it's a choice between your EMT friend treating them in an unsanitary attic or me at my clinic, here's the address."

A shriek rang out as I jotted down the location. I nearly dropped my cell phone at the sound of Perenelle's cry. She jumped protectively in front of Nicolas, who remained unconscious.

"What's going on?" Mina asked. "I heard that scream. You need an ambulance—"

"That wasn't the patient," I said, following Perenelle's wide-eyed stare.

"Zoe," Mina snapped, "what on God's green earth is—"

"We'll see you soon." I clicked off.

"*Je suis désolé*," the newcomer said from the doorway. "I am so sorry to have disturbed you. Zoe has spoken so much of you both. I wished to meet you."

Dorian bowed awkwardly. His left wing was bound so thoroughly that he nearly toppled over. I rushed to his side and steadied him. His arm was warm. Could a gargoyle run a fever?

"Perenelle Flamel," I said, "may I present fellow alchemist Dorian Robert-Houdin."

Perenelle nodded and pursed her lips. "Something went wrong with the transformation?" She stepped forward cautiously but remained in front of her husband.

Dorian sniffed indignantly and Tobias stifled a laugh.

"You can explain everything after we get Nick stabilized at Mina's," Tobias said. "We've gotta go."

Though Tobias had rigged a sling for Dorian, the gargoyle wasn't especially mobile. He wished to accompany us but understood it would be unwise. Tobias carried Nicolas to the built-in couch of the Airstream, and Perenelle leaned into my shoulder as I helped her into the trailer.

"A gargoyle ... " she murmured. Repeatedly. "He turned into a gargoyle? I must speak with him to discover how this was possible ... "

"Try to keep Nick still," Tobias said, "and if he wakes up, make sure he doesn't move the bandages."

"My foot is well enough for me to drive," I said. "You should stay in the back to take care of him."

Tobias shook his head. "He's as stable as I can get him. If he wakes up, it's your face he's going to want to see. At this point, the faces of loved ones will do more than any medical care I can give him."

"You're a good man," Perenelle said, clasping his hands in hers. "Thank you. Yet," she continued, "do people here think nothing of blood?" She tipped her head toward Tobias's white T-shirt, which was now dotted with the dark reddish brown of blood and its accompanying sulfurous smell.

"Let me get something to fix that," I said, and hurried to the house. My ankle protested as I rushed up the squeaking porch steps, but I didn't slow down until I reached the second floor. Tobias had taken his bag of clothes when he moved out, and he was twice my size, so I proceeded to the attic and my Elixir inventory. A man's starchy dress shirt that had been tailored over a century ago would do. Clothing back then was made to last.

I was back in the trailer in less than two minutes. I found Tobias and Perenelle huddled together in conversation and handed him the clean shirt. He pulled his bloodied T-shirt over his head, revealing long, deep scars that covered his entire back. The cruel markings crisscrossed his back and shoulders. I'd seen those patterns before, when the wounds were fresh.

"Let's get the trailer hooked up to the truck," I said. We worked quickly in silence, and pulled out of the driveway within a few minutes.

The Airstream shook as Tobias navigated down the slope and onto the street. Perenelle stood and took my hands in hers, gasping as the trailer shook. "What's happening?"

"We're driving. This is a conveyance."

"Ah." She smiled with embarrassment. "I expect we have much to learn."

I blinked back tears. "I never thought I'd see you both again. I'm so sorry it took me so long to find you."

"We didn't feel pain as strongly within the painting," she said. "I'm thankful for that. This is hella painful."

Hella? "Your English," I said, realizing they'd been speaking English instead of French this whole time. "It's, um, interesting."

She smiled the mischievous smile of hers I remembered. "As is your choice of clothing. Trousers?"

"How do you speak modern English but not know that women wear trousers?"

Perenelle squeezed Nicolas's hand and wiped his brow. "I'm attempting to think how best to explain it. We were *semi*-awake inside the painting. It was like a vivid dream, both real and imagined, and with no sense of time. I don't know how many years went by—many, by the looks of this rounded silver box." She looked around the Airstream and clenched her stomach again.

"You don't have to talk. The poison—"

"Your doctor's ministrations helped." She waved away the concern but clenched her jaw as another wave of pain overwhelmed her. "And I want to tell you. There's so much I want to tell you, dear Zoe ... Since it was like a dream, I don't know how long I have until the memories fade. We heard the words spoken around us, and learned to speak as they did. Naturally, like a child learns a language. It was easier to hear than see, because even when it was night, or when we were enclosed in a crate, we could hear people, and we came to learn their ways of speaking. But usually we had a prominent placement high on a wall. We lived with a family in England for generations. Then there were the sounds of war, followed by darkness. When the light returned, we found ourselves in a strange land called *California*, where people brought invisible musicians into their homes, enjoyed standing on planks on the ocean, and drank wine while discussing books ... "

I couldn't help laughing at that. It explained "hella" as well.

"How many years has it been?" she asked.

"It's the twenty-first century."

She stared at me with wonder. "But that is far too long for us to have been away from our quest! The backward alchemists—have they escaped France? Stopping them is more important than our own problems." Her face paled. "Your face betrays you. They have, haven't they? What havoc have they wrought?" She gripped Nicolas's unmoving hand more tightly. "I should have listened to him about what they were capable of." She swept Nicolas's hair off his forehead again. It refused to stay put. "I always believed them to be stupid, lazy men. I didn't believe they were a threat."

"You and Nicolas were both right," I said. "They *were* lazy"— which was why they'd found an alchemical loophole to allow themselves to feed on the life forces of others instead of putting in the work themselves—"so they did nothing threatening until their life forces began to fade. That didn't happen until recently. But Dorian and I stopped them. You don't have to worry about them."

"The two of you defeated them? You and the Frenchman in your attic whose alchemy experiment went terribly wrong?"

"Dorian . . . Yes, and he can tell you about his alchemical history himself."

She nodded. "You did what Nicolas couldn't. I always knew you'd go on to do great things. Though I regret that you've led a difficult life. I can see it in your eyes and the scars on your skin."

I looked into her eyes. They couldn't be described as kind eyes, yet there was compassion and love behind the strength and wariness. "You didn't want me to discover the Elixir of Life."

"I didn't want this life for you. I wanted you to be happy. Not to do merely what you were *capable* of, but what you truly wanted. That's why I was so hard on you."

"You could have told me."

"Would you have listened?"

She was right, of course. I wouldn't have. As a young woman in my twenties, I'd misunderstood so much.

"And what about you?" I asked. "Not only a female alchemist, but having to paint under an assumed name as Philippe Hayden in order to be considered a real artist."

A gleefully proud smile flashed across her face as she clasped her hands together. "You figured that out. Is that how you found us?"

"Partly."

Perenelle held Nicolas's hand as she told me about the sacrifices she'd made to bring true alchemy out of the realm of secrecy through her art, and then her discovery of alchemical painting, a technique that combined alchemy and art by using alchemical processes to turn natural substances into pigments and then paint, which allowed an artist to transfer living objects into the world of a canvas.

"I wish I'd known how ill Thomas was," Perenelle said. "I could have done this for him." She reached for my hand and squeezed it. Her palm was clammy but the heartfelt gesture comforting.

"The portrait of me and Thomas," I said. "I never knew you'd done such a thing."

She blinked at me in surprise. "You've seen it?"

"Only in a book."

"A book?"

"An art history book. It's not attributed to Hayden—er, to you— but your work is so magnificent that it's taken its place in history."

I expected her to tell me how honored she felt that her work had survived, but instead Perenelle asked shyly, "Did you like the painting? I painted it from memory right after Thomas died. I always wanted you to have it…"

"But I left before you could stop me. I was young and foolish."

"We were all young and foolish once. But you grew up. You grew up and rescued us." She clutched her stomach and closed her eyes.

"We'll be there soon. Mina will be able to properly pump your stomach and take care of Nicolas."

"Pump my stomach?"

I supposed she hadn't seen modern medical treatments from the walls of wealthy households. "I wish I could have stopped the backward alchemists before they did this to you."

"Our injuries?" She shook her head so emphatically that locks of her auburn hair fell loose. "No. None of those imbeciles did this to us."

I stared at her. "It wasn't a backward alchemist who attacked you?"

"Edward Kelley," Perenelle said. "He's the one who did this to us."

"*The* Edward Kelley? I didn't think he was a true alchemist." I thought about what I knew of the historical figure. It wasn't much. Given that I didn't think he was a real alchemist, Edward Kelley hadn't especially interested me. History books recorded him as a charming charlatan who'd died at age forty-two in the late 1500s. He was smart and had used multiple surnames to cover up his various crimes. "I thought he was a fraud."

"He was—at first. He—" Perenelle broke off as the trailer lurched, and gripped the Masonite wall with her free hand.

"It's okay," I said. "Tobias knows what he's doing." Tobias was driving the trailer like it was an ambulance. I hoped he didn't draw so much attention to us that we got pulled over. But as the one to examine Nicolas, he knew how quickly we had to get to Mina.

But I wondered... was there a bigger danger lurking? A suspicion was forming in my mind. "Edward Kelley... Didn't he die long before I was born?"

"We don't need to worry about Edward now. He discovered the Elixir of Life, but he believes us to be dead."

"I don't believe he does."

FIFTY

HEAVY RAIN CRASHED ONTO the sides of the Airstream. The familiar clatter of rain outside while I was warm and safe in my trailer was normally a comforting sound, but now it did nothing to alleviate my worry. A dark suspicion was swirling in my mind.

I didn't have time to think about what it all meant. We pulled into the parking lot of Mina's medical practice, and a few seconds later Tobias opened the door of the trailer. The rain was now torrential, but when I stepped onto the asphalt, I saw Mina waiting outside under a forest-green awning. With Max. There was a veiled darkness in his eyes. He didn't let his feelings affect his actions. Ignoring me, he and Mina rushed into the trailer. Max lifted Nicolas from the narrow bed into his arms and carried him inside. Mina helped Perenelle across the lot, following behind them.

"These don't look like gunshot wounds," Mina said as Max eased Nicolas onto a gurney. "So I don't have to report these injuries. Why can't you take them to a proper ER?"

"It's a long story," Tobias said. "But they need your help."

"Who *are* these people?" Max asked. He blinked at Nicolas in his torn and bloodied clothes not of this century or even the last one, as if not quite sure whether or not he should believe his eyes.

"I hope," Perenelle said, "that Zoe thinks of us as her surrogate mother and father."

"I do," I said, feeling tears again welling in my eyes.

"I'm not treating them here so you can have a family reunion," Mina snapped.

"I'll explain everything," I said. "After."

Mina looked as though she was going to protest, but Tobias stepped in.

"I've dealt with a lot of injured folks over the years. These two … their injuries aren't responding to standard care. I know this is the best place for them."

After a brief hesitation, Mina nodded. "You're the EMT? Get washed up. I need to know what happened, to best treat them."

"The back of his head is the most serious injury. Abdomen is superficial. The knife didn't clip any organs."

"My husband was both stabbed and bludgeoned," Perenelle added. "I didn't see with what. And I was forced to swallow poisonous paints."

Max gave me a strange look. "Luciana was right … Miss, what exactly happened? Who did this—"

"Not now, Max," I said. I couldn't very well have them tell him Edward Kelley was the culprit.

"This is important, Zoe."

"It can wait," Mina and I said at the same time.

"Actually," Max snapped, "it can't. Detective Vega is missing."

I stared at Max as Mina shouted, "Leave. Both of you. Now. You can talk elsewhere. I need to focus on my patients."

"Don't argue," Max said, steering me out of the room. "There's no point when she sounds like that."

"What do you mean Detective Vega is missing?" I said once we reached the waiting room. I'd been worried when she hadn't returned Tobias's call, but hadn't wanted to read more into it.

A lock of Max's hair had fallen onto his forehead but he didn't seem to notice. "The pendant you found is made of multiple pieces of metal. Luciana found a fingerprint on the inside. But … the print was from a guy who died several decades ago, by the name of Eddie O'Kells."

I gasped. I knew that name.

"Which makes no sense," Max said, beginning to pace, "because Isabella crafted that damn charm. Theoretically she *could have* done it when she was a kid, and fingerprint analysis isn't perfect—"

"Oh no … " My mind screamed at me. Could the connection really be this simple? A few letters …

"What is it?" Max stopped pacing and cocked his head anxiously.

"Eddie." My hand shook as I picked up my cell phone and typed a name into a search.

"You know him?"

"What did Detective Vega do with the information?" I asked.

"That's the thing—what could she do with the fingerprints of a dead man? Nothing that I know of. But she's MIA. No signs of foul play, so we're not calling in the cavalry yet. But it's not like her."

"They should call in the cavalry," I said. "I know who killed Logan Magnus. It's Eddie O'Kells."

"The guy is long dead, Zoe."

"No, he's not. He faked a death certificate."

"He'd be well over a hundred now."

"And his real name is Edward Kelley."

A man as intelligent at Edward Kelley would have known that the best way to keep up an illusion is to make it close to the truth. He'd want to continue to use the same first name: Edward. One of the few facts I knew about the famous Edward Kelley was the alias he most commonly used: *Talbot.*

"Here in Portland," I continued, "he goes by a different name. But a related one. Ward. The art dealer married to Logan Magnus's daughter."

FIFTY-ONE

"Ward Talbot," I continued, "is the person who did this to Nicolas and Perenelle."

"They told you that?" Max's expression and voice were skeptical.

"They knew him by another name, but yes, Perenelle told me it was him."

The name Ward wasn't the most common diminutive of Edward, but I should have seen the similarity sooner and become suspicious when a person named Eddie O'Kells had purchased a large rush order of real antiques from me earlier in the week. After I'd shown up asking questions about the painting, Ward must have been trying to figure out if I was a true alchemist. I'd dismissed him as a possible alchemist because Dorian's research had uncovered Ward's family lineage. He'd cleverly covered his tracks by inventing a respectable and plausible identity, just as Tobias and I had done for ourselves. It was fake.

"You're sure about this?" Max asked. "This isn't like that ... other stuff you were telling me?"

"I'm right about this."

Max called in the information about Ward Talbot. When he did so, he learned that Detective Vega still hadn't been heard from.

"I've gotta go," Max said.

"Max, I—"

"I can't, Zoe. I really have to go." He pushed past me and out the doors.

"Be careful," I called after him, but he was already gone.

Tobias was right. I shouldn't have confided in Max about myself. I thought after the time we'd spent in Astoria that he'd be ready, but I was wrong.

I sank into one of the cushioned orange seats in the waiting room, underneath a weeping fig tree that reminded me of the one in Blue Sky Teas except that it was contained in a cherry red planter. A row of lilies lined the empty reception desk, and a mural showing people picnicking in a tulip field lined one wall. It was meant to be a comforting space, and succeeded. At least as much as it could.

I listened for sounds coming from the other room, but heard none. I closed my eyes.

I was so close to piecing it all together, but there were still too many unanswered questions. Edward, AKA Ward, could be the killer, or the person who'd given Isabella the method to kill her husband. Since he'd convinced Perenelle to swallow toxic paint, it stood to reason that he'd been able to convince Logan to do the same. But how? And why? Perenelle had chosen to try her luck at being poisoned instead of the more certain death from being stabbed, hoping that she would survive long enough to make it back to Nicolas. Had Logan Magnus made a similar choice? Why hadn't he tried to fight Ward? Was Ward also involved in the Portland art forgery ring? And what of Isabella, a forger who also possessed ergot, a deadly poison.

Why would she keep something like that in her studio if she didn't intend to use it?

I opened my eyes and looked around the cozy waiting room again. Lilies didn't bloom at this time of year. I walked to the reception desk and squeezed one of the pristine blossoms. Fake. I walked back to the weeping fig tree and felt a leaf. Also fake. Normally I wouldn't have been fooled by fake plants, but I'd wanted to be comforted by nature. *We see what we want to see …*

I silently cursed myself. This wasn't the only instance this week where I'd seen what I wanted to see. I had assumed that Isabella used ergot to subdue her husband so he'd swallow the toxic paint. Ergot could also explain why Isabella was acting so erratically. She could have been poisoned herself. Like the people I'd known in Salem Village, she could have been an innocent victim. Could it have affected her mind enough to make her turn to forgery?

I had seen that she had a stack of antique books. A danger of working with antique books is that funguses and molds can take hold in the old leather and paper, poisoning not only the book itself but the people in its presence.

Tobias burst through the door. He was now wearing light blue scrubs that Mina must have given him.

"Man, those two are fighters." He wrapped his arms around me. "They're stable."

"But they're still in danger," Mina said from the doorway. "There are some unexplained behaviors. That's why you brought them to me, isn't it?"

I lifted my head and looked up at Tobias. He gave a subtle shake of his head.

"Their bodies are behaving like they've come out of a coma," Mina said. "But not like any coma I've ever seen. And their clothing … it's old. *Seriously* old. Those aren't costume pieces."

"No," I said.

"Zoe," Tobias snapped.

"Which of you wants to explain?" Mina asked.

"You deserve an explanation after saving their lives," I said, "but I have to ask … Do you really want to know?"

Mina considered the question seriously. "It's not only those two, is it? Both you and Tobias. The scars on your bodies… They don't look like any scars I'd expect to see on a woman in her twenties and a guy in his forties."

"Surely you jest!" a deep voice shouted from the other room.

Tobias gave me a smile. "Sounds like Nick is awake."

"The twenty-first century?" Nicolas's French-accented voice carried through the doorway. "The new millennium? Help me up, my love. This is something I must see."

FIFTY-TWO

MINA SCOWLED, BUT SHE followed us into the room where Perenelle was watching over Nicolas. The top of his head was swathed in gauze, but even the bandages couldn't get his wayward hair under control. The gray and brown strands stood on end in every direction. His eyes were as intelligent and alive as ever. I think that was what pushed me over the edge. The tears I'd been holding back flowed down my cheeks.

"Don't cry, my dear," Nicolas said, beckoning me to his bedside. "I will stay in bed. For now."

I laughed through the tears. Nicolas was his old self. "I'm sorry I never knew you were trapped in the painting."

"The wonders I have seen from walls, my dear Zoe," Nicolas said.

"Walls?" Mina said, checking Nicolas's temperature.

"Perhaps you should have your family reunion later," Tobias suggested with a sharp glance.

"You wish us not to speak freely in front of the doctor?" Perenelle asked.

"Let's focus on getting you well," I said.

"I assumed alchemical paint was now used widely in the world," Perenelle said, "and in ways that far exceeded my own methods."

"Why would you think that?" I asked, "since you didn't have a chance to pass along your knowledge."

"From our confines inside the painting, I saw very clearly that people spent many hours looking at paintings that moved."

Tobias laughed. "Television. They were watching TV, not alchemical paintings."

"I don't believe you're all suffering from a mass delusion," Mina said. "You told me you'd explain everything once they were stable. They're stable. Start explaining."

Tobias caught my eye and shrugged. "Your call."

"You saved their lives," I said to Mina. "I still need to ask for your discretion."

Mina nodded. "You're all patients, as far as I'm concerned. I'll treat you with the same confidentiality I give all my patients."

"What do you know of alchemy?"

Mina stared at me in silence for a few moments. At first I thought she was going to laugh or accuse me of putting her on to avoid telling her the truth.

"Your hair and scars," she murmured. "Their clothing. When were you all born?"

"Speaking for myself," Nicolas said, "1340."

"Do you need to sit down?" Perenelle asked.

"Grandmother spoke of people like you," Mina whispered. "When I grew older, I thought it was a fairy tale."

Tobias handed Mina a flask. "I thought it might come in handy."

Mina took a hearty swig.

"I don't mean to be rude," Perenelle said, "and I can't speak for Nicolas, but now that I'm feeling more myself... I'm famished. I feel as though I haven't eaten in weeks."

"Centuries, my dear," Nicolas said. "You didn't paint any bread or wine into the painting."

Mina took another long swig from Tobias's flask. "You can't take them to a restaurant," she said. "I'll go get food. Um … What do you like to eat?"

"No, I'll go," Tobias said, snatching the flask back.

"How will you know where to go around here? It's the middle of the night."

"You can come too, but I'm driving," Tobias said.

While we waited for Tobias and Mina, Perenelle explained to me what Edward had done to her in Prague, and how the painting known as *The Alchemist* that had unknowingly hidden Nicolas and Perenelle for centuries had a circuitous route to Portland.

"But what of my letter?" Nicolas asked. "How did it find its way to you after so long?"

"He left it at your old house in Paris," I said, "hidden behind a brick with an alchemical carving that wasn't part of the original design. I hadn't visited Paris in decades, and that house in centuries."

"He meant well after all," Perenelle whispered.

Perenelle also told us of her memories of a charming Edward Kelley, a brilliant man who could have been a great scholar if he hadn't cared more about pride and money. He wished to impress great leaders, and went to great lengths to do it, even though as a genius he could have used much easier schemes to gain wealth for himself and his family.

"It's terrible," Perenelle said, "that as he grew older with the years alchemy allowed him, instead of growing wiser, he became filled with hatred and vengeance."

"Do you wish you hadn't saved Edward all those years ago?" I asked.

She shook her head and gave me a motherly look—a combination of admonishment and love. "Everyone deserves that chance.

You were rather reckless in your youth as well. Though I'm sorry for what he became, I would be no better than Edward if I'd left him to die when I could have prevented it. My own humanity would have left me. Speaking of humanity … I smell food."

Tobias and Mina strode through the door with an armful of takeout containers.

"Slim pickings at this time of night," Mina said, "but there's a twenty-four-hour supermarket nearby."

"And fresh bread for the new day had just been dropped off." Tobias opened a paper bag and I caught the scents of sour yeast and earthy walnuts. I hadn't realized how hungry and tired I was until that moment.

We ate in silence for a few minutes. I thought of Ward, driven by greed, pride, and also a quest for vengeance because he'd been forced to watch his own child die. But since Ward wasn't an artist, he couldn't be our forger. Even if he had taught himself to paint while Perenelle and Nicolas were trapped in the painting, his hands remained too crippled for him to pull off even a forgery. And why would he have killed Logan Magnus?

I checked my phone. There was no word from Max. Where was he? What was happening with Ward and Detective Vega? I shoved the phone back into my bag.

"I've never seen you look at your phone so much," Tobias said. "The police have got it covered now. Max has got better things to do than give you updates."

"What did you think of Ward?" I asked.

"He's a charmer," Tobias said. "One of those people who draws out all of your own secrets but doesn't tell you a damn thing about themselves, and you don't realize it until it's too late."

Were we too late now?

FIFTY-THREE

As the sun rose, we prepared to drive home. Mina had declared the Flamels stable enough to be moved, and Tobias and I could care for them just as well from my house.

Tobias offered to drive, but I could see the tiredness in his eyes. I took the keys from his hands.

"You sure that's a good idea?" he asked. "You've been up all night. The planetary cycles affect you more than me. You're in no shape to drive."

I pointed at the rising sun, breathing in the crisp air of the new day. "I am now. I'm tired, but the sun is waking me up. Get some sleep in the trailer."

He nodded, but paused as he stepped in. "Hey Zoe, when we get to the house, call me before you get out of the truck."

"Why would I—oh. Ward."

"We don't know where he is. If he knows you're the one who discovered his identity, he'll be angry, and he might come for you like he did for Nicolas."

Before I started the engine, I called Dorian from the trailer to let him know we were on our way.

"Will Max be with you, or only the alchemists?" he asked.

"Max is away looking for Ward Talbot. No need for you to hide."

"The art dealer Ward? He is the murderous forger?"

"He's the alchemist Edward Kelley."

I heard the sound of claws tapping on a keyboard. "*Bof!* But of course. Talbot … He is a smart one. I believed the false trail of family lineage I uncovered. *Très stupide!* Kelley … Did you know some people believe him to have created the Voynich manuscript? Before it was called by that name, of course, but—"

"We can talk when I get home. I'll be there soon." I hoped. It seemed that rush hour traffic began earlier and earlier each year in all the cities I'd visited in the twenty-first century. I needed to get on the road. But I had one more call to make first. I tried Max, but only got his voicemail.

Just as I'd thought, we hit the beginning of rush hour, with drivers from outlying areas commuting into Portland. As I sat behind a line of cars on the paved I-5 freeway in my 1942 Chevy, with tech workers on either side of me and three centuries-old alchemists in the trailer behind me, I began to laugh.

Tobias would have said I was slap-happy, but it wasn't lack of sleep making me laugh. As if my life wasn't strange enough, I needed to prepare Nicolas to meet Dorian.

I eased into my driveway half an hour later. Tobias opened the trailer door before I could call him.

"You weren't sleeping," I said as he met me at the door of the truck.

"That Nick is a talker," he muttered. "C'mon, let's go."

Tobias and I circled the house together, checking for any signs of Ward. We stopped at the side gate after doing a full loop.

"I don't think he's here," I said. "He's probably fled the city by now. I wonder if he convinced Cleo to leave everything behind and go with him."

"More foolish decisions have been made by people with far fewer resources."

"Speaking of which," Tobias said as we hurried back to the trailer, "the Flamels gave me the best gossip. Two centuries' worth about the rich folks who owned the painting they were trapped inside. I only wish I knew which parts of their half-awake interpretations were true."

I paused at the door. "Did you happen to prepare Nicolas to meet Dorian?"

"Perenelle did. She told him not to stare at their fellow Frenchman whose alchemical transformation went awry."

Moments after I opened the front door, Dorian hobbled down the stairs.

"Where's your sling?" Tobias asked.

"I could not bake with it on. And I wished to fulfill my duties for Blue Sky Teas as well as cook breakfast for our esteemed guests."

"We have already broken our fast, good man," Nicolas said after I introduced him to Dorian.

"We would be honored to partake in a meal with you, sir," Perenelle added. "I, for one, am hungry enough to eat a hundred meals."

Dorian beamed at her. "*Bon!* I will not disappoint you, mademoiselle."

We came together for a most welcome second breakfast. Due to Mina and Tobias's care, Nicolas was doing better than anyone had expected, so he joined us at the table, still dressed in the purple scrubs Mina had given him. Perenelle remained in her brown dress. She'd declined my offer to loan her some of my clothes. She refused to wear slacks, and didn't think my one dress of green silk included nearly enough fabric.

"Where did you learn to cook such exquisite food?" Perenelle asked Dorian.

"It is a long story," Dorian said.

Nicolas grinned at him. "We are alchemists. We have time."

"You are both from the 1300s," Dorian said. "Many centuries before Viollet-le-Duc reimagined Notre Dame de Paris, but I believe gargoyles and grotesques had begun being carved a century before your births. You are familiar with such creatures?"

Perenelle gasped. "You are not a man whose alchemical experiments went awry?"

Dorian shook his head. "I am a proud gargoyle."

I was glad to have Perenelle and Nicolas pepper Dorian with questions about his life. It was a welcome distraction from thinking about what had become of Ward and the detective.

"The iron sculpture in front of your hearth," Perenelle said, rising from the table after finishing a second plate of food. "It's exquisite."

"Isabella Magnus," I said.

Perenelle stopped with her hand partly outstretched toward the metal sculpture of intertwined birds. "A relative of the man you believe Edward murdered?"

"His wife," Tobias said. "She's a talented artist."

"That she is … " Perenelle stifled a yawn. "I can't quite believe I'm saying this after half-sleeping for all these years, but I feel like I need to rest."

I was exhausted myself, but I needed time to figure out what to do next. Being in the presence of Nicolas and Perenelle was all-consuming.

I was preparing a bed for them when my phone rang.

"Max." I let out a breath of relief, but the feeling only lasted a moment.

"It's Isabella Magnus," he said. "She's in the hospital. It's bad, Zoe."

FIFTY-FOUR

"Is she all right?" I asked. "What happened?"

"You were right about the ergot poisoning," Max said. "It looks like she's been breathing in bad fumes from the moldy old books she was using as inspiration. She's not in good shape, but it's too soon to tell what'll happen."

"Ergot is extremely toxic," I said. "And hallucinogenic."

So Isabella had been *accidentally* poisoning herself. I tried to think about what herbal remedies might help ergot poisoning. Modern medicine was best to treat it in its acute state, and I would bring something to help her recuperate. If she made it.

"So I hear," Max said. "That's probably what got her talking. She admitted she was the artist behind Logan Magnus's success. He made his own paint and did the final technical execution of the pieces, but she gave him the subjects and composition, and set up the lighting with shadows that gave the work its unique qualities. She's our forger, Zoe. She—"

"That's collaboration, not forgery."

"I know that." Max's voice was harsh. "I wasn't finished. That's not why she's going to be arrested. She's going to be arrested because the team found forgeries hidden in her secret art studio."

They had? What was going on? And it wasn't only Max's words. Snapping at me wasn't like him. Not the Max I knew. Neither was the fact that he was telling me so much about an active case.

"Why are you confiding in me now?" I asked. It wasn't even his case, after all.

"Because Detective Vega is officially missing now. Something isn't right. It's all hands on deck."

"I wish I could do more to help."

"Your friends … or step-parents, whoever they are … Mina told me they're all right. I'm glad."

"Me too."

"Someone needs to interview Perenelle. She said Ward poisoned her, and he's still missing."

"She doesn't have any information." I could only imagine what the police would think of Perenelle if she shared the information she actually had. I expected I'd only ever see her again in a room with padded walls.

"We'll be the judge of that."

"She's not well enough to talk."

"You and Mina have both confirmed she's okay. She can talk."

My hand gripped the phone. That was why Max had told me so much. Because he needed something from me. "Is this an interrogation?"

"Of course not," he snapped. "But we need to find Luciana."

"So you're going to bust down my door?"

For a few moments I heard only the faint sound of Max's breathing. The time stretched on until I wondered if I'd lost the signal or if he'd hung up on me. I also wondered if he had indeed sent someone to the house. Dorian could escape through the attic skylight, but Nicolas and Perenelle...

"This is serious," he said finally.

"I was serious about what I told you in my lab too."

"I can't have this conversation right now, Zoe."

"We're talking about the same thing. I can swear to you that Perenelle is telling the truth, that it's Ward who did this to them—and I know with equal certainty that whoever questions Perenelle won't believe her story."

"Because she entertains the same delusion as you do, that she's hundreds of years old?"

I clenched my jaw shut and resisted the temptation to scream at him. "Questioning Perenelle won't tell you where Ward is. Max? Are you there?"

The phone was dead.

I rushed downstairs. "Change of plans. Nicolas and Perenelle are sleeping in the trailer."

"What's going on?" Tobias asked.

"Detectives are going to be showing up to question Perenelle."

She gasped. "Inquisitors?"

"They won't hurt you," Tobias said, squeezing her hand. "But you don't want to talk to them."

"I suppose alchemists are no more welcome in this century, eh?" Nicolas asked as he struggled to stand up. His body faltered and he gripped the side of his head. "*Merde*."

Perenelle and Tobias rushed to his side and helped him.

I scanned the room. "Where's Dorian?"

"Cleaning up in the kitchen," Tobias said. "He's slower than usual with only one good shoulder, but he wouldn't let us help."

"So thoughtful," Perenelle said. She didn't know it was more likely due to selfishness. Dorian didn't like anyone to disturb his kitchen.

I tossed my keys to Tobias. "Get them comfortable in the trailer. I'll meet you in the truck in a minute."

I found Dorian scrubbing the counters and told him it was time for him to hide in the attic. "You'll be my eyes and ears," I said. "You can let me know if the police show up."

He frowned. "Where will you be?"

"I don't know yet."

"What if Edward Kelley finds you?"

"I don't think he's after us."

Dorian clicked his gray tongue. "He searched for the Flamels for years, *mon amie*. He is a dangerous man."

"And there are four of us against one of him."

Dorian's scowl deepened. "Yet Ward is the only one of you who possesses evil in his heart. He is only one person, but he will not pause before striking."

I grabbed Ashwagandha tinctures that might come in handy for energy on the run, then met the others outside.

"Where to?" Tobias asked as I hopped into the truck.

"We do what we've always done," I said. "Hide in plain sight." I directed him to a trailer park along the Columbia River.

"We can't hide out forever," he said.

"I know. And I wish we could ask for more help from the police, but if even Max won't believe me about this ... "

"He'll come around."

I studied Tobias's profile as he drove north on Highway 5. His broad hands rested on the large steering wheel, and he hadn't glanced my way when he spoke.

"You don't believe that," I said.

He shrugged. "I'd like to believe it."

The sun was at its zenith when we reached an RV park where we could rent space. We were all exhausted and no good to anyone in our current fatigued state. I cleared space in the trailer for the three of them to nap. But in the middle of the day, with a sun I hadn't seen in days high overhead, there was no way I'd be able to sleep. As Nicolas began to snore, I slipped out of the trailer and went for a walk.

I walked past towering oak and Douglas fir trees that lined the river. A few yellow and brown leaves were beginning to appear on the oaks as autumn approached. A blue heron swooped through the sky overhead. With its elegant long neck, it reminded me of a phoenix.

I walked for what felt like both minutes and hours. Leaves gave a satisfying crunch under my feet, energizing me with every step.

When I got back to the spot where we'd parked, I didn't see the Airstream or my Chevy. I rubbed my eyes. I was suffering from exhaustion. I must have misremembered where we'd parked.

But I hadn't. Imprinted in the dirt were tire tracks from the truck and trailer. They were gone. And they'd left in a hurry.

FIFTY-FIVE

I FRANTICALLY SEARCHED MY bag for my phone to call Tobias. When I found it, I also found I'd missed several text messages from him.

GET BACK HERE.

WHERE ARE YOU? ALL OK, BUT WE NEED TO GO.

ZOE, WHERE ARE YOU??? WHY DON'T YOU EVER CHECK YOUR PHONE? NICK WOKE UP, LEFT THE TRAILER. ATTRACTED UNWANTED ATTENTION.

WILL CALL TO LET YOU KNOW WHERE WE ARE.

I called him back, but the phone went straight to voicemail. I tried Dorian next, using our coded ring system, and he picked up the phone.

"*Les flics* have not arrived," he said. "You may return home. It is safe."

"I've lost them."

"The police were chasing you?"

"Not *them* them. Tobias, Nicolas, and Perenelle."

"*Pardon?*"

I told Dorian what had happened.

"And you say *I* am the reckless one because I practiced flying at the river?"

I gasped. "The waterfront where the warehouses are. That's where you found the phoenix pendant. Which we now know that Ward dropped..."

"Though I cannot see you, I can tell you are thinking more than you are saying."

"When I first met Ward at the art gallery, he told Cleo *he was glad she used this space* for the gallery. That means she owns more warehouse spaces, many of which are still empty—"

"You believe Ward could safely use these spaces, and this is where he has gone."

"I don't know," I said. "But I know one way to find out."

The cab driver dropped me as close as I could get to the spot where Dorian told me he'd found the phoenix pendant.

What had Ward been doing by the river? Why had he been here with Logan Magnus's pendant? And what had led him to abandon it? I walked north along the path and realized it wasn't as far from the Logan Magnus memorial gallery as I'd imagined. How many of these warehouses did Cleo own?

It was now nearly sunset. My energy would be fading with the sun, so I had to act quickly. A dim street lamp clicked on overhead as I circled a cracked asphalt parking lot. I walked from building to building as the sunlight faded. Most were empty spaces, so I was alone. I kept my senses on alert, but there was no sign of Ward or anyone else. It wasn't the presence of a person that made me stop walking—it was a scent. The acidic aroma of paint.

Given that there were warehouses around me, it could have been paint used for some legitimate purpose. But I was in the lot of an abandoned-looking building. A stone-and-metal exterior, wooden boards over two windows, and a padlocked door. Yet the scent came from inside. Along with my connection to plants, my sense of smell has always been acute.

I tried the padlock. It didn't budge. I wished I had Dorian's claws, or at least his lock-picking skills. He'd told me it was a skill that could be taught...

When I pulled my phone from my bag to call him, I saw I'd missed a message from Tobias with the location of the RV park where they'd moved to. He assured me he'd keep the Flamels inside until they were better acclimated to this century.

"Dorian," I said when he answered my call, "can you walk me through picking a lock?"

"The first step is the most important."

"I'm listening."

"Try the handle."

"What?"

"The door. It has a handle, no? It is amazing how many times a door is unlocked to begin with."

"There's a large padlock. I already tried it. It was properly locked, as I expected."

But I didn't expect the footsteps behind me, or the searing pain that crashed down on my head.

FIFTY-SIX

I woke up with the room spinning and my head vibrating. I couldn't see. My mouth felt like cotton and hay, and with my bruised body and spinning head I felt like I was trapped in a washing machine.

"Can you hear me?" The voice of a woman. Did I recognize it?

I tried to answer, but found that the cotton in my mouth was more than a feeling. A musty cloth had been wrapped around my jaw. "Mm-hmm," I grunted.

"There's a chair," the voice said. "I kicked it over, and now I'm going to push it over toward you. If you're bound like me, your hands are behind you, but if you can move your head to the metal legs, you might be able to pull your gag off like I did. Hurry. He's gone for now, but he'll be back."

I was lying on my side, and while something was preventing me from moving my feet, I could move my upper body enough to back up until I hit the chair. I freed my mouth and took a few deep breaths of acidic air.

"Where am I?" I asked.

"Zoe?"

"Detective Vega?"

"Yes. You've been unconscious for a long time. Are you all right?"

My head throbbed and I felt panic rising as I blinked. My eyes weren't adjusting. "I can't see—"

"That's not your vision. There's not a drop of light in here. But did he hurt you? Are you injured?"

I tried moving. Nothing was broken, but I couldn't move. Rope cut into my wrists and ankles. "I'm tied tightly, but aside from a headache I don't think I'm hurt. But this isn't how I intended my entrance to be. I'm here to rescue you." I tugged as hard as I could at my bindings. My only reward was scratched wrists and pain shooting through my ankle.

"Please tell me you called for backup."

"Sort of … " I said, thinking of my conversation with Dorian. What had he heard? Would he send the police? He had a deep skepticism of them, but he couldn't very well fly across town to help. Even if he'd been willing to do it, his wing was broken.

"Why does your answer sound so uncertain?"

"The call was cut short." I closed my eyes. The scent of paint was stronger in here. And also something else … "I think I'm going to be sick."

"It's not just the smell in here. Judging by how long you were out, he must have knocked you out pretty good."

"I didn't see him. Was it Ward Talbot?"

"He was here when I checked inside the warehouse." I heard her squirm. "Listen, he took my gun and keys, but he missed the Leatherman in my back pocket. I can't reach it, but maybe you can. We need to move quickly. Tell me how you're bound."

"Both hands and feet." I tugged on both. My feet swung wide, but not my hands. "The ropes on my hands are tied to something. I can't move."

She stifled a groan.

"Doesn't your team know you're here?" I asked. "Don't you have a partner or something?"

This time she didn't bother covering up a string of curses. "They didn't believe me that this was a murder in the first place. Poisonings are always tricky, even without the factors that complicated this case. The guys on the force thought my interest in criminal justice history made me imagine a connection that wasn't real. No way was I going to tell them I was following up on a long-shot lead of looking at all the properties Cleo Magnus owned."

"But you were right."

"Not completely. I didn't think Ward would be here. Cleo owns a lot of property on the waterfront. In addition to the memorial gallery for her late father, she had a failed gallery of her own in one of the buildings a while back, and she rents to other artists—" Vega broke off and swore. "Point being, nobody's coming. It's up to us to get ourselves out of here."

"The fact that we're alive," I said, testing out my own tight bindings again. "That's a good sign." I couldn't figure out what I was tied to. The ropes around my wrists were tied to something metal. A copper pipe?

"Not always. Ward is smarter than I gave him credit for. He wouldn't want to kill us here. Not a place he can be linked to."

"Oh!"

"Did you hurt yourself?"

"No. If Cleo owns this place, Max and the police will find us. I told Max it was Ward who tried to kill Perenelle." I tugged again at the ropes. The rough weaving bit into my skin.

"Who's Perenelle?"

"Long story. But the point is, he believed me. They'll look into Cleo and find—"

"I expect they already did." Detective Vega sighed. "I thought I heard footsteps above a while ago. I hadn't gotten my gag off yet to yell effectively. If you hadn't noticed, we're not exactly *in* the warehouse. I was in and out of consciousness when he carried me down a set of stairs."

"Down?"

"This city has a history of smuggling and Shanghaiing. There's a whole network of tunnels."

"I know," I grumbled into the darkness.

"As far as I can tell, this basement isn't connected to a tunnel, but it's meant to hide things. And it's well hidden."

"But if it's not tied to a tunnel," I said, "he won't be able to come back until the police are gone from the area."

"We don't have infinite resources like they do on television. The police don't know where Ward is, and they can't stake out every location he has a minor connection to."

"But Ward is careful," I said, thinking out loud. "He won't take risks."

"You're talking like you know him well."

"Someone I'm close to does."

"This Perenelle person?"

"He forced her to swallow poisonous paints, just like he did with Logan Magnus."

"He tried that on me. I spit it back up in his face."

"Odd. He could have forced you."

"I know," she said. "It was as if once he couldn't *convince me* to do it, he had no interest in forcing me himself."

"So he left you here to die?"

"He'll be back. He won't leave it to chance."

"What about our phones?"

"Smashed. Along with my radio. No way to trace us."

"Your car?"

"He took my keys, so it'll be far away by now. Get back to work on your ropes. He'll return before sunrise. He won't want any witnesses for whatever he has in store for—" She broke off, and when she continued, her voice was a whisper. "What was that noise?"

"Me. I was moving to sit up."

Her breath caught. "You can sit up?"

"Barely. I think I'm tied to a pipe running along the wall."

"Can you move closer to me?"

I slide my body toward her voice. My head felt dizzy, but it worked. I shuffled across the floor until I bumped into her shoulder.

"My back right pocket," she said. "Can you reach it? He took the tools in my jacket, but he missed this one."

"My hands don't reach," I said, "but … " With a twinge of pain, I kicked off one shoe. My ankles were still bound, but I could move my feet.

Detective Vega grunted as I accidentally kicked her stomach.

"Sorry."

"No," she said. "That's good. You're a few inches away. Just move to your left. That's it."

I wriggled my toes until I felt the small metal tool. She moved a little bit, and a moment later I felt the tool slide out and heard it hit the floor. My hands didn't reach the floor, but I gripped it between my feet and placed it in her hands.

The detective worked in near-silence for the next several minutes. I heard her labored breathing and cursing as she sliced through the rope binding her wrists. In the pitch black and air that was becoming increasingly stifling, I imagined I was deep under water. I thought back to Logan Magnus's painting *The Underwater Underground*—the modern, man-made junk deep in the ocean with the ghostly figures of people from medieval times. If circumstances had been different, I would have laughed at the parallels as a female detective used a multifaceted metal tool to free us from the centuries-old alchemist who'd tied us to modern metal pipes.

"I got it!"

I heard the sounds of Vega shuffling on the ground, and a moment later I felt her hands in mine.

"Be still," she said. "The knife is sharp."

It took her several minutes to cut through the thick rope, and as she worked I felt a wet substance dripping onto my palms. My first thought was that she'd nicked the water pipe—until I realized the wetness was sticky.

"You're hurt," I said.

"I'm fine."

"You cut yourself. Badly."

"Be still."

The ropes gave way from my wrists, and as I carefully felt the area around me she cut through the ropes on our ankles. I had to find something to wrap around her injuries. Her hands had been slick with blood.

"Stay here," she said, her voice above me.

"I'm not—"

"I need to find our way out. It could be dangerous."

"You need to bandage your hands—"

"What I need to do is get you out of here." Her voice was further away.

I stood and followed the path along the wall toward her voice. A blinding light filled the room.

Detective Vega stood at the top of rickety wooden steps, her hand on a light switch and a grin on her face. The narrow wooden steps were built against one wall and led to a wooden door. "Door's locked as expected," she said, "but I think I can pick it."

My gaze dropped from her face to her hand, my happiness of being freed replaced by dread. Dark red blood dripped down her forearm. She saw the fright in my eyes, and her expression turned to horror as she followed my gaze.

"I didn't think it was this bad. Adrenaline…" She trailed off and sat down on the step. Hard. The silver pocketknife clattered down the steps as she clamped her right hand around the deep cut across her left wrist. We were locked underground and she was losing blood quickly.

FIFTY-SEVEN

I scanned the room, looking for anything I could use to staunch the blood. It was a storage room, with boxes and narrow crates stacked on metal shelves. A lumpy six-foot rug was rolled up in one corner. There was also an easel with a cloth draped over it. I pulled the cloth off and ran up the stairs to the detective. The easel crashed to the floor behind me.

The detective winced as I stopped the flow of blood by tying the cloth around her wrist.

"We have to get you out of here," she said. Her voice was weak. "Where did...?" Her eyes seemed unfocused as she looked around.

"I've got it," I said, picking up the knife, which I saw now contained a whole set of tools. "Sit tight."

I stepped past her and tried the door handle. As she'd said, it was locked. I looked down at her. Detective Vega was in no shape to pick a lock, and I didn't have my phone for Dorian to talk me through it. I looked to the hinges, remembering the way I'd opened another locked door the previous year. There were no hinges here. They were on the other side. That meant the door swung outward ...

I was willing to bet this room hadn't been built with the purpose of locking people inside. At least I hoped so. If it was meant to hide illicit goods, its creator would want it to be hidden on the outside, but not necessarily secure on the inside. Which was why Ward had tied us up so tightly.

"I have an idea," I said, rushing down the stairs. I pushed my way through the various boxes on the shelves until I found something that was both heavy and maneuverable. A heavy, flat crate sat on a high shelf. Inside was a canvas painting, but that's not what interested me. It was the ornate iron frame. Perfect.

I hauled the framed canvas up the stairs and helped Detective Vega scoot down a few steps until she was out of the way. She didn't object, which told me how much blood she'd lost.

I swung the iron frame through the air a few times, getting a feel for the arc it made. I braced myself against the wall and heaved. The iron crashed against the door. I heard the wood crack, but it didn't give.

"Good," Vega whispered. "Go for the frame of the door, not the door handle."

I swung again, this time aiming for the spot where the wall met the door. The wall didn't appear to give, but I tried the door one more time. It swung open a few inches.

Detective Vega smiled weakly. "We make a pretty good team. Now let's get out of here."

I helped her up and we stepped out of the underground storage room. Or rather, we took half a step, and then the door stopped. The door was behind a file cabinet. I slammed my shoulder into the door three times before it was open far enough for us to slip through.

We stepped into a dimly lit space, and I realized it wasn't lit at all. It was the first rays of daylight coming through a narrow, high window. We were inside a sprawling warehouse—and we weren't alone.

"I thought I heard a commotion." Ward approached, a knife in his hand.

Detective Vega stepped in front of me. "Don't make this worse for yourself. Help is on the way. Make it easy by turning yourself in." Her voice was the perfect balance of calm and commanding. But she had better control of her voice than her body. She began to sway.

Ward noticed it too. He and I both stepped toward her. Me to support her before she collapsed, Ward with the knife clenched in his gloved fist.

I reached her and pushed her out of the way. We landed in a tangle on the hard floor, and I slammed into the side of the cabinet that had blocked the hidden door. The crash echoed through the warehouse. No, it wasn't an echo. It was the sound of chains spinning as a wide metal door swung open.

"Hey, you guys!" a young voice called. Veronica. "I told you I heard something in this one."

Sunlight streamed over us and three teenagers rode their bikes into the warehouse.

"That's him!" Ethan cried.

Brixton hurdled his bike straight toward a shocked Ward. The knife flew from his hand as the bicycle collided with him. Brixton flew over the handlebars, but something soft broke his fall. Ward.

Veronica and Ethan stopped their bikes in front of the mess and helped Brixton up. He'd scraped his palm but otherwise looked all right.

Veronica jumped off her bike and gave Brixton a hug. "That was the bad guy, right, Ms. Faust?"

"It was." I looked at Ward. He wasn't moving. Neither was Detective Vega. "I need one of your phones. The detective needs medical attention. I need to call 9-1-1."

"On it," Ethan said.

"Thank you all," I said, "but how—"

"Your French friend called Brix," Veronica said. "He said the police didn't take his anonymous tip seriously. He had to try Brix like half a dozen times before the phone finally woke him up. Sorry we're late. There were a bunch of warehouses to try."

"But it was pretty cool we got here at sunrise, just like in Max's favorite movie."

"I don't know which warehouse," Ethan was saying to the 9-1-1 operator. "How am I supposed to know that? Can't you use GPS or something?"

The sound of brakes screeching sounded from nearby. I knew modern emergency services were quick, but Ethan had called only a few seconds before. And the sound was familiar … especially after the door opened.

"Mr. Freeman?" Veronica said as Tobias rushed inside with a duffel bag over his shoulder.

He scanned the scene, his eyes widening at the sight of Ward lying unconscious on the floor, then jogged to Detective Vega's prone form. "Anyone else hurt?"

"No," I said. "She's lost a lot of blood. A knife sliced her wrist while she was cutting off the ropes. Ward hit his head when Brixton crashed into him to save us."

Tobias knelt at the detective's side, took her pulse, and ripped open the bag.

"I called 9-1-1," Ethan said. "Paramedics should be here soon."

"We got here in time, didn't we?" Brixton asked.

"You did." I couldn't resist pulling him into a hug. His dark wavy hair was windswept from the waterfront bike ride to find us, and his body shook from adrenaline. I would have kissed the top of his head if he hadn't sprouted several inches in the past year. "But I still can't believe Dorian dragged you into this."

Tobias's head snapped up. "They know Dorian?"

"He's too shy to meet them in person," I said. "They email. So he called you too?"

Tobias shook his head as he continued to monitor the detective. "I don't think he has my number. It was a cold night. Too cold for someone sick to be in the trailer. Nick needed more heat to recuperate, so I drove us back to your house, and—"

"Um, you guys?" Veronica said, "I think that man on the floor is starting to wake up."

"Should I kick him in the head?" Ethan asked.

"No!" I said. "Get away from him. I'll be back in a few seconds. Tobias—watch Ward."

I ran down the steps of the room where I'd been held captive and grabbed the longest intact pieces of rope I could find. Just as he'd done to me, I bound Ward's hands behind his back, and his ankles.

The sound of a siren sounded in the distance. The ambulance was nearly here.

I looked down at Ward. After mumbling for a few seconds while I tied him up, he'd fallen unconscious again. We couldn't let the police get hold of him. I couldn't let him go, either. Nor could I harm him…

Tobias must have had a similar thought. "This was really heroic of you all," he said to the kids, "but I'm guessing your parents won't think of it that way. If you want to slip away to get to school before the authorities show up and question you, we won't say anything."

The boys began to protest until Veronica said, "My dad will *so* kill me if he learns I'm here. I won't be allowed to see either of you for the rest of the school year."

The handlebars of Brixton's bike were bent but the bike was functional, so the three of them rode off, with only Brixton casting a glance back at us before they disappeared from sight.

"You thinking what I'm thinking?" Tobias asked.

"We can't hand over Ward to the police for him to end up in jail," I said. "He doesn't age. We need time to figure out what to do with him."

"Take his feet. Hurry. I don't think the ambulance knows exactly where we are, but the sirens are getting closer."

We carried Ward to the floor of the passenger side of my truck and tossed the blanket over him that was there to cover Dorian. We were back at the door of the warehouse when the ambulance pulled into the parking lot.

"She's inside," Tobias said, jogging alongside them as he took them to the detective.

"Caller mentioned a second person who needed help," the medics said.

"He's long gone," I said. "The man who attacked me and the detective got away."

Tobias went with Detective Vega in the ambulance, and I hurried home with my captive. Only I didn't make it nearly that far.

As I pulled out of the parking lot, Ward stirred. Slowly at first, but by the time I'd gotten a few blocks he must have been conscious enough to feel his confined surroundings on the floor of the passenger seat of the Chevy. He grunted and began kicking wildly. Though his arms and legs were tied and he couldn't move far, he wasn't affixed to anything. Using his head, he knocked into the gearshift and hit my elbow, sending the steering wheel spinning.

I grasped the steering wheel, trying to gain control as we pitched forward—toward the river.

FIFTY-EIGHT

I SLAMMED MY FOOT down on the brakes. The truck's tires bumped over the vegetation at the side of the river.

"What's happening?" Ward cried. Curled in front of the passenger seat, he was still covered by Dorian's blanket.

"You should have asked that"—I regained control of the stiff steering wheel and veered away from a fir tree—"before you head-butted me."

The brakes groaned and the truck stalled. We came to an abrupt stop before we hit the water. I wasn't sorry to hear Ward's head knock into the glove box. He groaned and swore.

"I misjudged you." His voice was muffled under the blanket. "I didn't take you for a killer."

"You could say I'm returning the favor." I ripped the blanket off. Ward's hair was out of place, revealing his clipped ears.

"I'm sorry you misunderstood my actions back there," he said. His voice was outwardly calm, but his eyes were afraid. "I wasn't going to kill you and the detective. I needed to keep you out of the way until I could finish making my plans to get away. I was never going to—"

"Don't bother lying," I said. "I know about what you did to Nicolas and Perenelle."

"Me?" Ward gasped. "It didn't—"

"I'm going to give you a choice," I said, an idea forming as I spoke. My heart rate was returning to normal, and I assessed our surroundings. Hulking chunks of steel surrounded us. We'd come to a stop underneath one of Portland's many bridges. Morning traffic was beginning to hum high overhead, but with our position next to the solid underpinnings of the bridge, none of the cars above could see us.

"A choice," Ward repeated.

"Give me my cell phone."

"Sorry, dear, that's been smashed to bits."

I reached my hands into his pockets.

"What are you doing?" he protested. "I'm a married man—and that tickles—damn."

My hand emerged with a cell phone that wasn't mine.

"You'll never get it unlocked," he said.

I studied his face, a mask of smugness between his clipped ears. My gaze fell to his gloved hands that I'd thought caused him pain from arthritis. Before he had time to realize what I was doing, I lunged toward him, pulled the glove off his right hand, and pressed the phone screen to his thumb. He tried to struggle, but he was wedged snugly in between the front seat and dashboard. When I lifted the phone again, the screen was unlocked.

"Don't go anywhere," I said as I slipped out the driver's-side door to make a quick call to Dorian.

Ward glared at me with unconcealed rage when I pulled the truck door shut behind me a few minutes later.

"You're going to tell me everything," I said, "or I'm going to turn you in to the police."

Ward had the audacity to laugh. "I'm the one who's being held prisoner. Do you really think they'll—"

"Detective Vega is recovering in the hospital. She has some interesting facts to tell her colleagues, doesn't she? It's up to you to convince me not to turn you in. I want to understand what happened, and I want the evidence to clear my friend Tobias from any remaining suspicion in Logan Magnus's death."

Ward's lips turned to a snarl. "It's Perenelle's fault, you know. All of it."

"Tell me."

"These bonds—" He tugged at his arms behind his back, but he was wedged too tightly into the space in front of the seat to be a threat now that we weren't moving. "This space isn't large enough for a grown man."

"Talk."

Ward seemed to hover at the edge of indecision for a few seconds, then closed his eyes before speaking. "She killed my daughter," he said softly. "You have to understand, it's because of Perenelle that I watched my own daughter die."

When he opened his eyes, a tear slipped out. "Everything I've ever done, I've done out of love."

I resisted the urge to comfort him. It was the terrible curse of immortality to watch children grow old and die. The death of my beloved Ambrose's son had driven him to madness.

"I know that's not entirely true," I said. "I rescued the Flamels from the painting. I've spoken to them."

Ward laughed mirthlessly and a few more tears rolled down his cheek. "It's the truth, but I suppose as they say these days, it's not the whole truth and nothing but the truth. When you become an alchemist, nobody ever tells you the truth about it, do they? I've been watching you. You're one of us. And you're not as happy as you pretend to be. How long have you been alive?"

I looked from the lapping water to the earth we'd disturbed, following the arc of my gaze up the steel bars and bolts to the gray sky above. It was the same water I'd known over three hundred years ago, but industrially forged metal was something I could never have imagined as a child coaxing life from plants. "This isn't about me."

"Suit yourself. I can see you're old enough to understand, even if you haven't lived enough to understand *the anger* ... The Elixir of Life doesn't cure ailments. My hands are still deformed from being broken, my ears remain misshapen, and my daughter will always be dead."

He let the words hang in the air for a few moments. "And gold. Nobody tells you how damnably difficult it is to make."

"No," I agreed. "They certainly don't."

That broke the ice, at least as much as was possible under our strange circumstances. Ward laughed, and the rest of his story spilled out of him without much prompting. And without much humility either.

He was a genius, he explained, so he thought he should have been able to master transmuting impure metals into gold much more easily once Perenelle showed him it was possible. But he didn't realize how much purity of intent mattered in alchemy. He became wealthy through other means. Because he'd known Philippe Hayden, he'd been able to become a successful art dealer, both because he'd purchased some of Hayden's artwork for a pittance and because he'd learned so much about art that he was able to identify talent before artists became famous.

"But people didn't respect me as they did when I'd been a court alchemist and scryer," he said. "Claiming to talk to angels has a cachet that knowing about art can't match."

"You did much more than understand the art market," I said. "You manipulated it by finding struggling artists and encouraging them to become forgers."

He gazed at me with the respect he said he'd been lacking. "Very good, Zoe Faust. Very good indeed. Like you with the trinkets you sell at Elixir, I played the long game."

"You didn't have to faux-age paintings that were in the style of Old Masters. You simply had to wait for them to truly age. Though the con was rather unfortunate for the artists you promised wealth to."

Ward shrugged. At least that's what I think he was trying to do in his bonds. "It wasn't quite as simple as waiting. I had to insert false provenances into historical archives that could be 'found' in the future. Long after my artists had died, of course."

"But they could never sue you for breach of contract during their lifetimes, since they knew they were participating in an illegal activity."

"It worked surprisingly well as a means to becoming a well-known art dealer. I had to reinvent myself in a new city every couple of decades, of course. Then eight months ago … " His face transformed from pride back to anger. "I saw a painting in an auction house simply titled *The Alchemist*. But I knew what it was. *Who* it was. It was Nicolas Flamel. It unnerved me more than words can adequately explain. I looked into the eyes of the man in the painting and had the strongest suspicion that it was Nicolas himself in there. I knew Perenelle was capable of painting people into portraits, but I thought Nicolas had already died."

I didn't point out that I knew from Perenelle that Nicolas had nearly been killed by Ward himself. I wanted him to keep talking.

"I had to know what happened," Ward continued. "I bid on the painting, but lost. I didn't have enough funds because I'd recently had a financial setback. One of the real Philippe Hayden paintings I'd acquired was declared to be fake because the modern methods of dating artwork showed it was painted long after Hayden was thought dead." He scoffed. "I couldn't tell them Hayden was an alchemist, and a woman at that. I had to bow down to the so-called experts' opinion, leaving me in financial ruin."

"Why did you bid on the painting if you knew you'd never be able to prove it was a Hayden portrait?" I asked. I couldn't imagine him wanting to rescue the man he'd tried to kill.

"If Nicolas was really in the painting, I wanted to get him out and ask him to teach me the secrets of transmuting lead into gold properly. I knew there must be a secret I was missing that would make it easier … and I couldn't have anyone else recognizing him. That's why I arranged for an old associate to steal the auction house's records of the painting."

Foolish man, I thought to myself. If he hadn't been so intelligent, he would have fit in with the backward alchemists.

"But you lost the bid at auction to Cleo Magnus," I said, "who wanted the painting for her famous artist father, Logan Magnus. Logan had become interested in the art of alchemy after seeing a painting that intrigued him earlier in the year. Cleo—"

"I love her," Ward said. "Whatever you do to me, leave Cleo out of this."

"I believe you," a voice said from the rocky sand in front of the truck. The person I'd asked Dorian to summon had arrived.

FIFTY-NINE

AUBURN TRESSES SWIRLED AROUND her head, carried by the wind underneath the bridge. She was still in her old clothing, and the fire in her eyes was otherworldly. On the gray morning along the edge of the water, I could have sworn she was a selkie from Scottish mythology. But this was no mythical creature. Perenelle Flamel had arrived.

Perenelle stepped to the side of the car, carrying a satchel under her arm. I thought at first it was Dorian in stone form, but it was the wrong shape.

"For all your faults," Perenelle said to Ward, "which are legion, you've always been a romantic." She reached out for my hand. "Thank you for calling me here. Your friend called a conveyance that delivered me."

"Perenelle," Ward said, "you're as beautiful as ever. I always thought it was a tragedy you couldn't reveal your true self. The years have been good to you."

"After you tried to kill me, you mean."

"I was young and foolish."

"And now you are old and foolish. I'll be putting an end to that." She reached her hand into the satchel.

"What are you doing?" he cried. "You're not a killer. You saved me once, long ago. Zoe—" He turned to me, his eyes pleading. "Tell her I'm cooperating!"

"Ward was telling me everything he's done," I said. "In exchange for me not turning him in to the police."

"And not killing me," Ward added.

Perenelle nodded. She set the bag at her feet.

Ward looked between us and nodded slowly. "Keep Cleo out of this and you have a deal."

"Why would we need to keep Cleo out of it?" I said, but as I spoke the words, the realization dawned on me. It wasn't only that Ward loved her and didn't want her dragged down by association with him.

I thought back to what Perenelle had said about both me and Ward being reckless in our youths. And how Tobias had found a hidden art studio at the Castle. If I assumed Cleo was working with Ward as an art forger, everything about Logan Magnus's death made sense.

Cleo wasn't responsible for her father's murder, but her actions had set in motion his inevitable death. Her father didn't know Ward had convinced Cleo to become an art forger. But as Isabella had said, Logan suspected what was going on with an art forgery ring in Portland.

"Logan Magnus found out about you," I said. "He found proof that not only were you running an art forgery ring, but you'd enlisted his own daughter."

Ward's chest rose and fell, but he remained silent.

"Silence is the same thing as a lie," Perenelle said, her voice calm but so cold I shivered.

"How did you convince her to become a forger?" I prompted. "Was it because she's a failed artist?"

"She wasn't a failure," Ward snapped.

"But she wasn't successful. Not like her father. You convinced her she could get back at the art experts who had shunned her."

"Experts." He spat out the word.

"Isabella had built a secret art studio at the Castle, when she was helping Logan establish himself and they needed a space where she could do the first drafts of the pieces he'd finish. She was telling the truth that she hadn't used it in years. But someone else had. Her daughter. That's whose paintings the police discovered."

Ward swore. "They found them?"

"They think they're Isabella's right now, but they'll put it together."

"I wouldn't bet on it," Ward said.

"All these years," Perenelle said, "and you haven't changed. Your arrogance…"

"I'm only being honest."

"Then continue," Perenelle said.

Ward nodded and resumed his story. He'd decided to seduce Cleo to get *The Alchemist* painting. But then he discovered Cleo's artistic endeavors. Her work was technically competent, but it had no originality; she was like her father and needed a guiding hand. Ward would be that hand, and he convinced her she could get revenge on the art world that had ignored her by becoming his next forger. He wooed her, and even moved to Portland to be near her.

"I had to do something to pay for my relocation," he said, "so I did what I was good at. I found a young, aspiring artist who called himself Neo. He was almost homeless, finding little respect and even less money. He was all too happy to paint a few copies I suggested, to pull one over on the critics. I set up a small studio for him. We didn't leave a paper trail—I never do—but Cleo's ex-boyfriend Archer saw us and figured out what was going on. Archer wanted to ruin me without Cleo knowing it was him, but he underestimated the care I took to make sure I wasn't connected to Neo. After Archer gave an anonymous tip to the police about the studio, Neo fled and the police seized the artwork, but they never put it together with me. All it did was anger Cleo that Archer had made the accusation. It brought us closer together."

"And brought you closer to the painting of Nicolas," Perenelle said.

"I tried to rescue him," Ward said. "I tried to pull him out of the painting when I visited Logan at the Castle with Cleo, but it didn't work. What was the secret I missed?"

"The same one you always did," Perenelle said. "You wanted it for all the wrong reasons. Your *intent* was lacking. After all these centuries, you still haven't learned."

Ward groaned. "You'll appreciate the irony, Perenelle. Do you know the thing that made me stop trying to get the painting and get Nicolas out? I fell in love with the girl. I didn't marry Cleo as a con. She's the best thing that's happened to me in centuries. She's innocent, you know. Whatever you think I've done, it's only me."

"Chivalrous of you to lie," Perenelle said.

"I tried to corrupt her at first," he said, "but she always resisted."

"How did you convince Logan Magnus to swallow toxic paints?" I asked.

"You gave me a choice," Perenelle said, looking up at the rumbling cars on the bridge above and the clouds rolling in. "It's so strange, remembering that day as if it were only a few days ago, but awaking in this new world…"

314

"I gave him a choice as well," Ward said. "I appealed to his interest in alchemy—and his ego. I convinced Logan of the connection between art and alchemy, which he was already open to after receiving *The Alchemist* from Cleo. I told him he'd achieve immortality if he swallowed his pigments. The pain he felt was the path to immortality. I didn't kill him. He did it to himself."

"Always rationalizing," Perenelle said. Wind pushed its way through the open car window, but Perenelle seemed impervious to its chill.

"It's the truth," Ward said. "Do you want details to convince you? Logan began raving about how he would rise from the ashes just like the phoenix. When the fool realized he was going to die rather than become immortal, he started babbling about how the phoenix pendant would prove what I had done. He was hardly lucid, but I thought it couldn't hurt to take the damn charm. I took it with me to the warehouse where I'd been working away from the Castle, thinking I'd dispose of it later with … Well, let's not talk about that. But the point is that I was attacked."

"Attacked," Perenelle repeated.

"Perhaps the word 'attack' is a bit strong. But a huge vulture circled overhead. It was unlike anything I'd ever seen before outside of Prague Castle centuries ago. I fell, and lost the pendant."

The sound of police sirens sounded in the distance.

"That sound," Perenelle said. "I know it from the moving paintings. Police?"

"They won't see us right away," I said, "but they will eventually."

"It's time, Edward," Perenelle said.

"Time for what?" Ward asked, shrinking back. "You promised—"

"Then keep talking," I said. "Quickly. I need to know, why did you suspect I was an alchemist?"

"Archer put that damned painting of Nicolas in the window of the gallery, again trying to mess with me. Your interest in the painting made me wonder if you could be a real alchemist who had known Nicolas. How would you know otherwise what he looked like? Rare for a woman, but not impossible, as Perenelle proves. So I ordered some items from your store, assuming they would be modern reproductions. They weren't. I suspected you were an alchemist, but I still didn't know what you were up to. I wanted to test you, to see if you'd lost your humanity as so many do. So I paid a visit to your friend who paints alchemical artwork."

"Heather."

"I didn't try to kill her. I was only trying to figure out who on earth you were. You see, I haven't killed anyone, ever. Led people astray, perhaps … but—"

"We saw Neo's body," I said. It was a long shot, but one I thought was right. That lumpy rug near the easel, in the room where Detective Vega and I had been found … I'd been focused on saving her life at the time, but when I thought of the shape of the lumps the rug had been rolled around, I hoped I was wrong, but I didn't think I was.

Ward's eyes flashed with anger.

The sirens grew louder. And there were more of them. They must have discovered the body while searching the warehouse. I was right. Ward had killed another one of his art forgers.

"If you lie one more time," Perenelle said, "it will be the last thing you ever do in this world."

"Neo knew too much," Ward snarled. "He wanted to cut a deal and save himself. It was his own fault. I'm not a bad man. Don't let her kill me."

"I'm not going to kill you, Edward," Perenelle said. "I'm going to save you one more time. Safe, but in a place where you'll never hurt anyone again."

Her auburn hair bellowing in the wind, Perenelle lifted a familiar canvas out of the satchel, followed by alchemical ingredients I recognized from my basement lab and a paintbrush from a hidden pocket of her dress.

With quick, assured strokes, she painted Ward into the painting in which she and Nicolas had lived for centuries.

SIXTY

THE FOLLOWING DAY, I opened the front door of my house to someone I wasn't sure was going to forgive me.

Max hesitated after stepping inside, but I took his hand in mine,
smelling the scent of jasmine that lingered on his fingertips, and
pulled him through the swinging kitchen door.

The kitchen was officially packed to capacity. Tobias and Brixton leaned against the counter, laughing with Nicolas and Perenelle.
I'd had a chance to buy the Flamels proper clothing. Perenelle
couldn't stop grinning at the soft fabric of her purple maxi dress,
and Nicolas was as giddy as a young boy at the multitude of helpful
pockets in a jacket designed for camping.

"Yo Max," Brixton said, giving him a fist bump.

"Nicolas and Perenelle," I said, "there's someone special I want
you to meet. Perenelle sort of met him already when her injuries
were being treated … "

"It's wonderful to meet you properly," Max said, shaking their
hands.

"The pleasure is all ours, my good man," Nicolas said. Even modern hair-care products couldn't tame his unkempt hair.

"You've all gotta try these cookies," Brixton said. "They don't taste at all like they're full of vegetables."

"This is your French friend?" Max whispered to me, watching as Nicolas and Perenelle accepted carrot cake cookies fresh from the oven. "He's short, but hardly disfigured."

"This kitchen isn't big enough for a party," Tobias said. "I'll bring these to the dining table."

Max held me back from following. "And why does he insist on hiding behind you as the chef of Blue Sky Teas? And going so far as to insist on treating his life-threatening injury at Mina's clinic? What were you *thinking*? Is it an immigration issue?"

"This isn't the French chef," I said, laughing as I remembered how little Nicolas cared for food. Perenelle, on the other hand, was a connoisseur.

"He's not?"

"You remember when you spoke on the phone to another French friend of mine?"

Tobias poked his head back into the kitchen, holding out his cell phone for me. He handed it to me with a wink. "Dorian is on the line. He wants to talk to Max."

I covered my grin as Max took the phone. Tobias must have gotten Dorian to call from my land line in the attic.

"Dorian?" Max said. "Yes, I'm with Zoe now. Uh-huh … Yes, she already confided in me that she's not the chef for Blue Sky Teas … I really think you're underestimating people if you think they'll judge you for your appearance. This is Portland … Yes, of course I'll respect your wishes … Zoe, he wants to talk to you."

I took the phone.

"How long is *le flic* staying?" Dorian asked. "I wish to join the party."

"I'm not sure," I said, looking hesitantly at Max. "We'll save you some food."

"Since I cooked it," he huffed.

"I'll talk to you later." I hung up before he could say more.

Max and I were alone in the kitchen. The voices of laughter and glasses clinking from the other room made my heart swell. Was it too much to hope that I could have Max in my life as well?

"So … " Max said.

"So … "

"I've gotta hand it to you." He ran a hand through his dark hair and smiled nervously. "You've got the most interesting friends, Zoe Faust."

"Family," I corrected. "Though they're not blood, they're family."

He nodded. "I talked to my sister this morning."

"Oh?"

"She wanted to talk about the things our grandmother had shown us when we were kids."

"Did you let her?"

"I did. I'm not saying I understand … but I want to. I really do. For you."

Max wasn't ready to believe. Not fully. But now that I had Mina on my side, I had hope. And Max had taken the first step. He was here with me and my eccentric family. I pulled him toward me and kissed him.

"Get a room, you guys."

We broke apart and saw Brixton smiling in the doorway.

"I'm just here to get more blackberry compote," he said. "Your step-mom has a wicked appetite." He grabbed a mason jar from the fridge and went back to the others. Max and I followed.

Perenelle patted the empty seat next to her. "Join us," she said to Max.

I stood watching the group for a few moments before joining them myself, wondering how the past had brought me to this moment.

I'd been at the police station earlier that day, explaining what had happened with Ward Talbot. Detective Vega was concerned that he'd gotten away but glad to have closure on what had happened, and validated by her coworkers that she was right about a copycat killer. She assured me the police wouldn't be digging into Tobias's past. He'd taken such good care of her after she'd been attacked by Ward, which I suspected was part of the reason.

Cleo had admitted to painting copies of Old Masters found at the Castle's hidden studio, but she insisted she hadn't broken the law. It's not a crime to just paint copies or to keep your art studio a secret. She hadn't defrauded anyone.

Isabella was recuperating from ergot poisoning in the hospital, and the press revealed that she was half of the genius behind Logan Magnus's art. She and her daughter would now be working jointly on art projects with their complementary skills.

The following week was a blur that bound my past to the present.

I participated in the Autumn Equinox Fair, at which I sold tinctures and Heather sold her paintings. Isabella redesigned the memorial art gallery (which was now renamed for both Isabella and Logan) so that it could also display other artists' works—and offered Heather the first guest artist showing.

At home, I had a full house. Dorian was living in the attic and I'd given Nicolas and Perenelle my master bedroom. I'd taken the smallest bedroom, in which hung a framed reproduction of the portrait Perenelle had painted of me and my brother. Tobias was staying in the other extra bedroom for the time being, so that Nicolas would have a doctor at hand. I was glad it gave him purpose in the aftermath of Rosa's death.

Dorian was so pleased that he had more people to cook real meals for (not simply pastries at the teashop) that he didn't complain too much about wearing the sling Tobias had fixed for his broken wing, and he seemed to have forgotten about tracking down the now-harmless backward alchemy book that had caused us so much trouble earlier in the year.

We lingered over meals together, but tried not to stay up too late because Nicolas needed his rest. Perenelle and I went on many long walks together, and she loved visiting local art galleries. Inspired by Isabella and Cleo, I had an idea.

"You deserve the recognition for Hayden's art," I said to Perenelle one morning, as we sat in the living room drinking tea and watching the shadows of Isabella's iron crows dance across the floor.

Perenelle smiled and shook her head. "Even if we could convince people Philippe Hayden was a woman, I painted the art hundreds of years ago."

"But there's nothing wrong with a descendant of Perenelle Flamel digging into history to prove the true identity of Philippe Hayden ... "

As for Alchemical Paint and Perenelle's knowledge of how to paint objects and people into a canvas, we thought it was best to keep that to ourselves.

The police never did catch up with Ward Talbot, but I had a portrait tucked into the darkest corner of my attic that looked a lot like him. What a funny coincidence, that.

THE END

RECIPES

Carrot Cake Breakfast Cookies (vegan)

Total cooking time: 30 minutes (plus 1 hour for baking the sweet potato, if not using canned pumpkin)
Makes approx. 16 cookies

Ingredients:

- 1 cup baked sweet potato (or substitute 1 cup canned pumpkin puree, unsweetened)
- 2 cups rolled oats
- 1 cup finely chopped and pitted Medjool dates (around 10–12)
- 1 cup shredded carrots
- ⅓ cup melted coconut oil
- 1 tsp cinnamon
- ½ tsp ground ginger
- ½ tsp ground nutmeg

- 1 tsp baking powder
- ¼ tsp salt
- dash cayenne (optional)
- ½ cup chopped pecans
- ¼ cup raisins (or substitute dried cranberries)
- ¼ cup almond flour (optional, but good to use if you want the cookies to be more durable to transport them)

Directions:

Advance prep: Bake a large sweet potato ahead of time (1 hour at 400°F), if you want to use fresh sweet potato instead of canned pumpkin. If your dates are too hard to work with, place in a shallow bowl and soak them in hot water for 10 minutes.

Preheat oven to 350°F and prepare a large baking pan with parchment paper. In a large bowl, mix the oats, sweet potato (or pumpkin), carrots, coconut oil, and spices. Combine well, using a fork or your fingers. Stir in the pecans and raisins. Using a ⅓ cup measuring cup, scoop mixture onto the parchment paper. Bake for approximately 22 minutes.

Variation: If you prefer a smoother cookie, mix the first batch of ingredients (everything except nuts and raisins/cranberries) in small batches in a food processor.

Variation: There's no added sugar to the recipe above. If you'd like to turn this into a sweeter dessert treat, add ¼ cup date syrup or maple syrup, make the cookies slightly smaller with a ¼ cup measuring cup, and reduce the cooking time to 20 minutes.

Summer Fruit Compote (vegan)

Total cooking time: 10 minutes
Makes 8 servings

Ingredients:

- 1 ½ cup frozen summer berries, such as blackberries, blueberries, and strawberries
- 1 tsp maple syrup
- 1 tsp fresh squeezed lemon juice
- ¼ tsp ground ginger
- ¼ tsp ground cardamom

Directions:

Combine all the ingredients in a small saucepan on medium-low, stirring periodically, for approximately 10 minutes, until syrupy.

Use to top oatmeal, toast, or scones.

Variation: If it's summer and you have fresh berries, you can use fresh berries instead, but add 1 Tbsp of water or more, to make sure the mixture doesn't burn.

Fire Tea, Four Ways

All of the teas below are a mix of healing spices, acids, and optional sweeteners. For each, pour near-boiling water over the ingredients in your favorite mug, stir, and enjoy.

The Flamels' Fire Tea

- ¼ tsp cayenne
- ¼ tsp turmeric
- ¼ tsp ginger powder

- ¼ tsp cinnamon
- dash of salt and pepper
- lemon juice
- optional ½ tsp coconut oil

For easier prep, mix a larger batch of the dry ingredients in a glass jar with a lid. Scoop 1 tsp when ready to drink.

Tobias's Cayenne Fire Tea

- 1 tsp cayenne
- 1 tsp freshly sliced ginger
- 1 tsp freshly squeezed lemon juice
- 1 tsp honey

Zoe's Simple Fire Tea

- 1 tsp cayenne
- dash salt
- 1 tsp freshly squeezed lemon juice

Blue's Added-Kick Fire Tea

- ½ tsp cayenne
- ½ tsp cinnamon
- 1 tsp freshly squeezed lemon juice
- 1 tsp Apple Cider Vinegar (raw with the "mother")
- 1 tsp honey

Author's Note

Historical research is one of the most enjoyable parts of writing the Accidental Alchemist mysteries. Although alchemy as described in the book is fictional, the ideas behind alchemy, and its historical precedence when early chemists were figuring out scientific transformations, are real. Nicolas Flamel, Perenelle Flamel, and Edward Kelley were real people, although whether or not they were alchemists is another question. However ... Kelley claimed to be an alchemist and sought the patronage of Rudolf II, and after the Flamels spent their life together giving large amounts of money to charity, their graves were indeed discovered to be empty.

Jean Eugène Robert-Houdin and Eugène Viollet-le-Duc are real historical figures, who you can read much more about in the earlier books in the Accidental Alchemist series, especially *The Masquerading Magician*.

Ergot poisoning is one of the many theories to explain the Salem Witch Trials. A fungus that can grow in rye (a staple crop the people of Salem Village ate), ergot poisoning can cause delusions and hallucinations.

A few research materials of note: The Getty Museum in Los Angeles held an exhibit, *The Art of Alchemy*, while I was researching this novel. I was fortunate to visit in person, and though the exhibit is over, much of it has been catalogued as an online exhibit, which I highly recommend. My bookshelves are overflowing with research books, and a few that were especially helpful include Noah Charney's *The Art of Forgery*, Victoria Finlay's *The Brilliant History of Color in Art*, Cennino Cennini's *The Craftsman's Handbook* (originally *Il Libro dell' Arte*, a fifteenth-century text translated by Daniel V. Thompson, Jr.), Rosemary Gladstar's *Medicinal Herbs*, and Guy Ogilvy's *The Alchemist's Kitchen*.

Why a vegan gargoyle chef? As many readers know, I wrote a draft of *The Accidental Alchemist*, the first book in this series, while undergoing chemotherapy for an aggressive breast cancer. I was thirty-six years old. At the time, I didn't cook. My husband bought cookbooks to make nourishing meals for me, which I quickly snatched from his hands. It was the beginning of heading down the wonderful rabbit hole of learning to cook. Through cooking classes, cookbooks, and kitchen experimentation, I learned that healing foods can taste more amazing than anything I used to eat, and helped me feel healthier than ever. While battling cancer, I was going to write the book I wanted to write, which meant that after a lifetime of being fascinated by mysterious gargoyles, I was going to write a fun gargoyle character, even though I doubted anyone besides me would enjoy it. I was thrilled to discover I was wrong, and that readers love Dorian the gargoyle as much as I do. He learned to cook plant-based meals at the same time I did. The process transformed me into an accidental almost-vegan, now six years cancer-free.

Acknowledgments

Thanks go to critique readers Nancy Adams, Ritter Ames, Alexia Gordon, Sybil Johnson, Sue Parman, Brian Selfon, and Diane Vallere, each of whom bring their unique talents to show me things I never would have seen without them. Special thanks to former homicide detective and mystery writer Lissa Marie Redmond for advising me on police procedure and brainstorming the possibilities in fiction. And to Amanda Midkiff of Locust Light Farm for herbal tips.

I'm grateful for the team at Midnight Ink, especially Terri Bischoff for taking a chance on my misfit alchemist and gargoyle, Amy Glaser for the keen editorial insights, and the team that creates the amazing book cover art. My agent Jill Marsal, for her ongoing support and words of wisdom. The writing community I've met through Malice Domestic, Sisters in Crime, and Mystery Writers of America, for more support than I ever dreamed possible. My family, for always believing in me and understanding when I disappear for hours at a time. And my amazing readers, who make those long hours worth it. This book wouldn't have happened without all of you.

© Michael B. Woolsey

ABOUT THE AUTHOR

USA Today bestselling and Agatha Award-winning author Gigi Pandian is the child of cultural anthropologists from New Mexico and the southern tip of India. She spent her childhood being dragged around the world on their research trips, and now lives outside San Francisco with her husband and a gargoyle who watches over the garden. Gigi writes the Jaya Jones Treasure Hunt mysteries, the Accidental Alchemist mysteries, and locked-room mystery short stories. Find her online at www.gigipandian.com.